SECOND
TIME
SWEETER

SECOND TIME SWEETER

A BLESSINGS NOVEL

Beverly Jenkins

wm

WILLIAM MORROW
An Imprint of HarperCollins*Publishers*

HarperCollins books may be purchased for educational, business, or sales promotional use. For information, please email the Special Markets Department at SPsales@harpercollins.com.

FIRST EDITION

Designed by Diahann Sturge

Map of Henry Adams by Valerie Miller

Library of Congress Cataloging-in-Publication Data has been applied for.

ISBN 978-0-06-269926-8 (paperback)
ISBN 978-0-06-284617-4 (library edition)

18 19 20 21 22   LSC   10 9 8 7 6 5 4 3 2 1

To all seeking a second chance at life and love

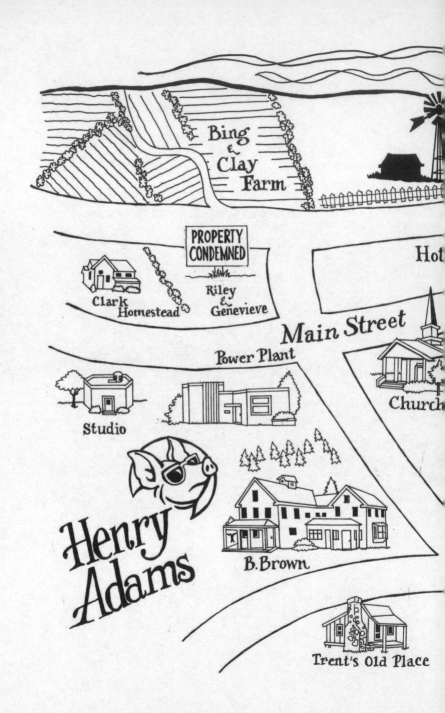

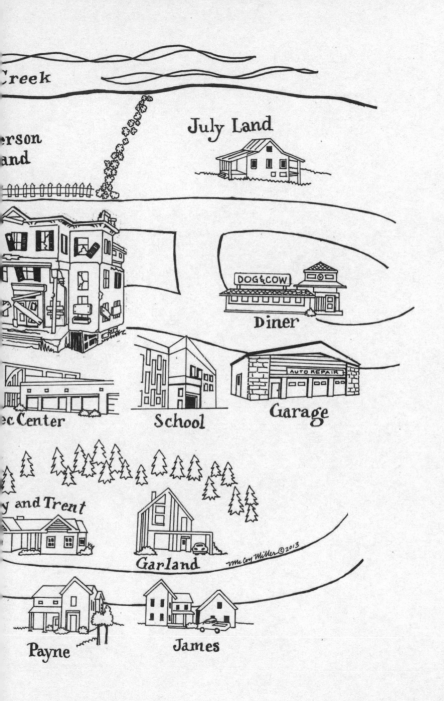

Creek

erson
and

July Land

DOG&COW
Diner

ec Center

School

Garage

AUTO REPAIR

y and Trent

Garland

McCoy Miller © 2013

Payne

James

SECOND
TIME
SWEETER

PROLOGUE

The hired gun eyed the photo of her new targets. "Big guy."

"Not too big for a bullet, though," her client noted in his Russian-accented English.

The second person in the photo was a woman. "His wife?" she asked.

"Yes. Government changed their faces. This is what they look like now."

She compared the before and after. The wife was heavier; hair shorter. Even though the husband had a new face, there was no disguising his height or girth. "How'd you find them?"

"Everyone has a price, especially if you work for the Bureau and have enough gambling debts to fill the White House."

"Where are they?"

"Little town in Kansas called Henry Adams."

She'd never heard of the place but a Google search would remedy that. "I'll check out the lay of the land, and if I can do it quickly I will. If it will take more than a few days, I'll let you know."

"Don't make it too long."

"Don't tell me how to do my job."

He inclined his head. "You're the expert."

"You deposited the first half of my payment?"

"Of course."

She pulled out her phone to check the balance. The increase showed. "Anything else I should know before I go?"

"No."

"I'll alert you when the job is done. I expect the second half of my payment within twenty-four hours, as agreed."

"It will be there."

She walked out into LA's smoggy heat, fired up the engine of her black Ferrari, and roared away.

Across the street, in a building with windows of one-way glass, a Bureau agent lowered her binoculars and spoke into her earbud mic. "Let the Kansas field office know she's on the move."

CHAPTER
1

Malachi July viewed himself in the mirror and stared back at his ebony face and eyes. He stood just over six feet tall, had a mustache, a full head of hair, both peppered with gray. For a guy in his midsixties, he thought he looked pretty good. He was also dumb as dirt. How else to explain his embezzling? The stupid stunt cost him the respect of everyone in his hometown of Henry Adams, Kansas, and broke the heart of Bernadine Brown, the woman he loved. They'd been a couple for almost three years, and he thought he had no problem with her being rich as the Queen of England until they went to Key West on vacation last Christmas. Having to stand by while she paid for everything had been embarrassing. He was a product of his times; men were supposed to foot the bills, not the ladies. Granted, on his small pension and Social Security check, doing so would've been akin to breathing underwater, but reality took a backseat to his bruised male pride.

Upon returning home, in a misguided attempt to boost his

ego, he'd logged into the bank accounts tied to the diner he co-owned and helped himself to over $70,000; money that belonged to the town, the diner, and to Bernadine. His plan had been to invest it with a condo developer, make enough to cover what he took, put the initial seventy grand back, and come out of the deal with his own small fortune so he could pay for his and Bernadine's next vacation.

It didn't work out that way. The developer disappeared, along with the cash, leaving him flat broke, and everyone in Henry Adams wanting a piece of his hide when word got out about what he'd done. He then made the situation worse by showing up at the wedding of his goddaughter, Rocky, with another woman, further shattering what he and Bernadine once had. It was a mess. He'd tried to minimize the damage by taking a job in the Oklahoma oil fields, but working straight shifts as he needed to do in order to quickly earn enough money to make restitution was difficult at his age. Over the past month, he'd managed to replace some of the money, and would keep at it until he paid back the full amount.

In the meantime, he had to find a way to make things right with Bernadine. He just had no idea how. She was the best thing to ever happen to him, even though his pride temporarily blinded him to that truth. When they first met, he'd been a player, known as the Gigolo of Graham County, Kansas, sporting women young enough to be mistaken for his granddaughters. After meeting Bernadine, he found her sharp mind and curvy figure so intriguing he dropped all the young girls. She'd heard about his reputation, though, and shooed him away like a swarm of flies. He kept up the pursuit, found the courage to open up about his struggles with alcohol, his hard-fought sobriety, and in the end, she relented. He taught her kite flying and treated her to picnics in the bed of his truck. One Christmas, he even dressed up as Santa Claus and took her for a sleigh ride in the snow. Bernadine wasn't keen on marrying again, having escaped one bad marriage. And he'd never married and couldn't see tying the knot at his age. What he was seeking was a relationship with a fabulous, levelheaded woman who made him a better person, enjoyed his company, and was willing to let his easygoing, laid-back personality balance her hard-charging existence as the hand turning Henry Adams's world. So, when she accepted his promise necklace he'd felt blessed. Knowing she was officially his lady filled him with pride. Then he blew it. To hell and beyond. If he could go back and change things, he would. Seeing as how that wasn't possible, all he had left was shame and the invisible sign around his neck that read "THIEF."

He turned away from the mirror and picked up his keys. He was having dinner with his son, Trent, and Trent's family. He hadn't seen them since his ill-fated appearance at Rocky and Jack's wedding two weeks ago. Facing Trent was going to be difficult, but having to do the same with his grandsons, Amari and Devon, made Mal want to call and beg off.

Leaving his apartment above the diner, he walked to his truck in the parking lot. It was mid-September, and the evening air was chilly. Seeing people he knew heading inside for dinner, he acknowledged them with a halfhearted wave but kept walking to avoid viewing their disapproval. Getting into his old Ford, he started the V-8 engine and drove away.

In spite of his mood, it was impossible to ignore the physical changes his hometown had undergone courtesy of Bernadine's vision and investments: the rec center, the church, the paved streets and sidewalks. In his youth, the roads had been dirt and the only entertainment the dilapidated movie house that had been a nineteenth-century showplace called the Sutton Hotel. Now, thanks to a recent remodel, the hotel stood like a jewel, boasting apartments, a new coffee shop, offices for town doctor Reggie Garland, and other small businesses. He was proud of the resurgence. Too bad that pride didn't extend to himself.

Trent and his family lived a short drive away in the new subdivision also built thanks to Bernadine. In fact, her house was next door to Mal's, and as he pulled into Trent's driveway and killed the engine, he sat a moment remembering how it used to be when he could run over, knock on her door, and see her smile. Now? He could be on fire and she wouldn't even look up. Not that he blamed her. Extracting his key from the ignition, he exited the truck and climbed the steps to Trent's door.

Trent answered the doorbell. "Hey, Dad."

"Hey."

Like his father, Trent was tall, lean, and dark-skinned. During Mal's drinking days, he'd rescued his father time and time again. Mal thought Trent'd always been a better son than he'd ever deserved. "Let me take your jacket."

Mal passed it to him and followed his son into the living room that held the faint fragrant scent of tomato sauce simmering.

Trent's wife, Lily, appeared, apron tied around her trim waist. She and Trent had been in love since high school. She was also one of Bernadine's best friends. "Hey, Mal."

"Lily."

The embezzlement was the elephant in the room and they

all knew it, so Mal jumped in. "Look. I know what I did was stupid and uncalled for, and that I hurt a lot of people."

"Yeah, you did," Trent quietly agreed.

Mal's lips tightened. A part of him chafed at being told the obvious, but he was in no position to argue. Trent could've just as easily not extended the dinner invite and left him to stew alone in the consequences of his actions. "I assume the boys know what's going on?"

Lily nodded tersely. "You might want to talk to them at some point."

"I will." Even though he had no idea how he'd explain himself. He then asked the question he knew he hadn't earned the right to ask, at least not yet. "How's Bernadine?"

To prove his point, Lily turned away. "I need to check on dinner." And she left the room.

Stung, he lowered his head.

"Not sure what you expected her to say?" Trent asked. "Long road ahead, Dad. Long road. For a lot of people."

"I understand that."

"I hope so. People are angry, disappointed. Bernadine's handling her business, as always, but underneath she's hurting. How could you bring another woman to the wedding?" Seeming to think better of it, Trent waved his question off. "Never mind. Let's just move on. I'm pretty upset, too. Just so you know."

"I know. Trying to make amends, however I can. Thought I'd start here. Amari have anything to say?"

"Not that he's shared with us."

Mal wondered if his grandson had talked with his best friend, Brain, or the other kids. He had so much cleaning up to do. So much.

Dinner was an awkward, nearly silent affair. The boys, sixteen-year-old Amari and thirteen-year-old Devon, loved him the way a man hoped his grandsons would, and they filled his world with laughter and joy. This evening, however, they sat at the table seemingly as uncomfortable as he felt. Neither met his gaze full on, or spoke to him directly unless prompted. Mal tried to get them to open up. "Amari, who's teaching your class while Jack and Rocky are on their honeymoon?"

"A new guy named Mr. Abbott."

"You all getting along?"

Amari nodded.

Devon said over his plate of spaghetti, "OG, I think you should paint Ms. Marie's fence for stealing the money."

Everyone froze. Trent shot a quelling look at their sometimes smart-mouthed, thoughtless youngest. "Devon, how about we talk about that another time?"

Devon pushed back. "I had to paint when I stole money."

Lily weighed in. "Yes, you did, but as your dad said. Another time."

Devon's face soured.

Lily added, "Or you can go to your room."

"Yes, ma'am," and to everyone's surprise, he picked up his plate and left.

Amari stole a quick look Mal's way before asking his parents, "Okay if I go, too?"

Trent and Lily viewed each other and sighed. Trent grudgingly nodded permission. Amari picked up his plate and followed his brother upstairs.

Lily, eyes brittle, asked, "Can I get you anything else, Mal?"

Chest tight with hurt, he shook his head. "No." Not wanting to stay any longer, he said, "I should probably go. I have to drive back to Oklahoma tonight."

"Okay," Trent replied. "But so you'll know, all the Dog's passwords have been changed." The Dog, formally known as the Dog and Cow, was the town's diner.

Guilt and embarrassment filled Mal because he co-owned the place. At the time of the theft, he'd thought himself quite the mastermind for duping the kids into changing the passwords. In reality, it was just another dumb move.

Trent added, "We changed the locks, too."

That surprised him. "Why?"

"Security."

"Half the town has keys to the front door," Lily explained. "We made everyone turn them in."

Mal nodded. "I'll give you mine before I go. Do you have a new one for me to use when I come back?"

Trent replied quietly, "No."

"Then I'll pick it up next time I visit."

Trent shook his head. "You aren't getting one."

Mal was confused. "Why not?"

"You're no longer trusted, Dad."

"That diner is mine," he gritted out.

"But the seventy thousand dollars you stole wasn't."

Tight-lipped, he looked away. "Whose idea was this? Bernadine's?"

"No. Mine," Trent replied. "And Barrett agreed." Retired Marine colonel Barrett Payne headed up town security.

"I own that building."

"The town's trust owns it. That was the deal you made with Bernadine when she agreed to pay for the remodel, remember?"

Mal's life was shattering like a dropped pane of glass. "So, what now? You want me to tuck my tail between my legs and slink out of town and never come back?"

"Of course not."

"You banning me from my own business?"

"No. If you want to come back to work there, you can. You just won't have a key or access to the cash register, the books, or the computers."

Mal turned away in disgust.

"What did you expect?" Trent asked tersely. "Had you pulled this stunt somewhere else, you'd be in jail."

Mal knew Trent was right, and he should be grateful he hadn't been arrested, but it didn't mean he had to like it. That diner had been his life for the past twenty years, and now? He stood. "I'll see myself out."

"Dad."

He stopped with his back to Trent.

"This isn't fun for me, either."

Mal turned and in his son's eyes saw a familiar pain. Back when Trent was a teen, instead of hanging out with his friends on Friday and Saturday nights, he'd spent his time tracking down Mal so he could take his keys to keep him from killing himself or someone else while driving drunk. Humbled, Mal left.

NEXT DOOR, BERNADINE Brown was having dinner with her eighteen-year-old adopted daughter, Crystal Chambers Brown. Crystal had become quite the chef in the past few years thanks to all the TV cooking shows she consumed and her job as a waitress and hostess at the Dog. The evening's menu consisted of baked salmon brushed with a honey pepper butter, sautéed brussels sprouts, and tasty little baby carrots. "This is very good, Crys."

"Thanks. I try."

Her modesty knew no bounds, one of the many reasons Bernadine loved her so. This was their first meal together since Crystal's move to her new loft apartment at the refurbished Sutton Hotel. Bernadine was happy about the visit because she still missed Crys's presence in the house they'd shared since her adoption. Back then she'd been a foster child, one of the five Bernadine relocated from distressed situations to the pastoral, drama-free plains of northwest Kansas. Having graduated from high school this past spring, she was now attending the community college. "How are classes coming?"

Crystal took a sip of her water. "Not bad. Not sure I'm liking my math professor, though."

"Why not?"

"Real serious. Never smiles. Math's not my best subject, and if I have trouble with an assignment, I don't know if I want to go to him for help."

"It's still early in the term. You might change your mind about him."

"Maybe, but if not, I already talked to Leah. She said she'd help." Leah Clark was the daughter of grocery store manager Gary Clark, and an astrophysics wunderkind. She and her boyfriend, Preston "Brain" Payne, were high school students also taking online college-level physics classes at KU and Stanford. According to their professors, they were among the smartest kids in the country.

Crystal asked, "So, have you talked to Reverend Paula?"

"About what?"

Crystal eyed her with the seriousness she'd always had, even as a young teen. "Mal."

"I don't need to talk to Paula about him."

"Come on, Mom. Holding stuff in is what makes people go postal."

"I'm fine, Crys."

"Nope. You're not. You're hurting. I know it and so does everyone else, which is why you need to be talking to Reverend Paula."

Reverend Paula Grant was an ordained priest and the town's resident therapist. She specialized in children but always had wise words for everyone, regardless of age. "Paula has enough on her plate with all the mess going on at home in Oklahoma. Besides, I'm fine." Bernadine didn't want to talk about Mal. She appreciated Crystal's concern, but she was done with him and had moved on.

"You sure?"

"Absolutely."

"Okay, I just don't want to see you up on the Dog's roof pelting folks with bricks."

Bernadine smiled. "Don't worry. No bricks. Promise."

The worry in her daughter's eyes was plain, so she added, "I survived my divorce from Leo. I'll survive Mal. I'm done with relationships, though. Not putting myself through this again."

"You two were good together—before he lost his mind."

"I agree, but I'm too old for crazy. He should be the one talking to Paula."

Crystal's concern remained visible, so Bernadine pushed away her now empty plate and changed the subject. "What's for dessert?"

Later that evening, as she prepared for bed, Bernadine paused before the full-length mirror in her walk-in closet and assessed herself. She saw a fiftysomething, dark-skinned woman who was okay with her curvy weight, wore her hair in twists, and was known for her glam. She was worth millions, owned the town of Henry Adams, Kansas, and wanted to smack Mal July into next week. He'd broken her heart with the embezzlement, then stomped on the shards by showing up at Rocky's wedding with another woman. In the two weeks since, Bernadine'd kept a low profile. Everyone knew she was hurting but allowed her to grieve privately, and she loved them for that.

She turned away from the mirror and got into bed. Tomorrow was Monday, the start of a new week. She was done crying over Mal's betrayal; she had a town to run.

CHAPTER
2

Store manager Gary Clark arrived at Clark's grocery store at five o'clock Monday morning. The doors wouldn't open to the public for another two hours, but he and his employees were preparing to begin the day. On the way to his office, he greeted the staff with smiles, calls of "good morning," and waves. He enjoyed his job, something he hadn't expected when he began running the place two years ago. Back then, he'd just come off a nasty divorce, gotten custody of his teen daughters, Leah and Tiffany, and relocated their family from Franklin to his hometown of Henry Adams. Bernadine Brown's proposal that he manage the town's new grocery store took him by surprise. He'd spent his life selling cars. He knew nothing about selling produce or canned goods, yet he'd agreed. Learning the ins and outs of the business while raising his daughters as a single parent had been difficult. Seeing to their everyday needs of homework, chores, and meals had him burning the candle at both ends.

Then life changed for the better last spring when his uncle Terence came from Oakland to visit. Quickly assessing what Gary needed, he volunteered to take on some of the household duties. The help had allowed Gary to breathe again, and now for the first time in what felt like decades, he was happy. He had a good job and his girls were thriving. For some men, finding a lady to share their newfound happiness might be icing on the cake, but he was gun-shy after his disastrous marriage and was content to remain single.

"Morning, Gary."

"Morning, Gem."

Gemma Dahl was his assistant manager. The Chicago native was raising her grandson, Wyatt, as a single parent after the death of her daughter in Afghanistan. Over the summer she'd taken two orphaned kids into her home with an eye to adopting them as soon as the state gave her the go-ahead. Everyone in town thought she was amazing, and Gary was no exception. After working as a cashier for the past two years, she'd applied for the vacant position of assistant manager, and hiring her was another decision he felt good about.

In his office he turned on the coffeemaker. Once the coffee was ready, he got himself a cup and sat at his desk to go over the reports left for him by the store's night manager. He also checked in with the security staff, headed up by Barrett Payne, and with no pressing issues on either front, left his desk to check the store. He and Gemma usually split the duty. They talked to the heads of the departments, inspected the specials stacked at the ends of the aisles, and kept an eye out for any problems with the store's physical operation. Burned-out lights or nonworking hand dryers in the restrooms were usually taken care of by maintenance, but Gary and Gemma made sure nothing had been overlooked.

The doors opened at seven and at seven fifteen he was back in his office when he received a call on his headset from security that Mrs. Beadle was on the premises. He sighed. She was one of the store's recurring problems. When she wasn't opening a bottle of wine, drinking it, and stashing the empty before getting in line to check out, she was trying to return things that she'd either worn, partially eaten, or purchased elsewhere. Gary wished she'd find another store to share her eccentricities with.

"Thanks. Keep an eye on her," he replied into his wireless mic, and turned on the camera bank on his office wall. "Hey, Gem," he called.

She appeared in the doorway. "Yes?"

"Mrs. Beadle is in the store."

Gem sighed and walked over to view the camera screens. She and Gary spotted the little old lady in her stylish gray coat and red, high-top Chucks pushing her buggy down the baking aisle. As she passed the shelves of sugar and flour, the woman quickly glanced around, reached into the cart, and unscrewed the top of a bottle of red wine. Taking a good-sized swallow, she hastily redid the top, put the bottle back in her cart, and began making her way down the aisle again.

"Why doesn't she just buy the wine?" Gemma asked.

"Who knows? I talked to her son in DC. He says she has plenty of money. He thinks she likes the attention when she's caught."

"She needs a good therapist."

"She needs something." Gary peered at the screen more closely and asked, "Is her bag moving, or is it just my eyes?"

Gemma stared. Mrs. Beadle had a large flower-patterned tote in the buggy's well, and yes, it appeared to be moving. "Do we want to know what's in it?"

"No, but—" and as he said that, a brown Chihuahua stuck its pointed nose out of the bag, looked around, and leaped to the floor.

In Gary's ear, the security supervisor let out a loud curse.

Gemma was already flying out the door and Gary was right behind her.

It only took a few minutes for them to get to the floor, but by then, the store was in full chaos mode. Customers were jumping out of the way, some screaming, others laughing as the snapping, growling dog ran through legs and around buggies in its effort to stay ahead of the store employees hot on its tail. Mrs. Beadle was among the chasers, screaming shrilly, "Don't hurt him!" And "Lorenzo! Lorenzo!" Which Gary guessed to be the little terror's name. And of course, people had their phones out filming the madness. Because the store was a good size and little dogs were not only fast but could turn on a dime, they lost Lorenzo in the produce section.

Gary turned to Barrett. "Well, now what?"

"Probably send everybody outside so we can do a thorough search."

Mrs. Beadle was nearby peering around, clapping her hands and shouting, "Lorenzo! Get over here!"

Gary asked, "Who names a dog Lorenzo?"

Gemma walked up. "Someone in the store called the health department. I just got off the phone with them. We're to find the dog and close the store. They have to do an inspection before we can open again."

Gary looked at his watch. It was only 8:00 a.m. He needed a drink.

BERNADINE ARRIVED AT her office in the building the town affectionately called the Power Plant and turned on the lights. As always, she was the first to arrive. Stashing her handbag in her desk, she booted up her laptop, turned on the coffeemaker, and sat down to begin her day. Henry Adams had come a long way since she purchased it on eBay five years ago. Back then, there'd been no tax base or infrastructure, and the small core of residents, many of whom were descendants of the town's nineteenth-century founders, were mostly senior citizens. Now, thanks to her business acumen and generosity, it was a twenty-first-century jewel fueled by growth in both people and modern technology. The freed slaves who founded Henry Adams after the Great Exodus of 1879 certainly wouldn't recognize the place.

"Morning."

She looked up to see her good friend and administrative assistant Lily Fontaine July. "Morning, Lil."

Lily had gone to high school in Henry Adams, but moved away after college. She'd returned the year Bernadine purchased the town and was now married to Mayor Trent July, her high school sweetheart.

"Mal had dinner with us last night."

Bernadine paused. "And . . . ?"

"Devon told him he should paint Marie's fence."

Bernadine's smile peeped out. "Is it wrong that I love him for saying that, because I agree." Painting the Jefferson fence was a long-standing Henry Adams tradition used to punish kids who screwed up.

"I do too, but Trent told him to save it for another time. Devon didn't like that and ended up leaving the table. Amari, too."

She'd worried about the kids' responses to the theft by their OG—as they affectionately called Mal. "Mal have a rebuttal?"

"No, but their leaving the table hurt him a lot."

"I'll be petty and say 'good.' It's what he deserves. Those boys worshipped the ground he walked on."

"I'm not sure if Devon's hurt is sincere, though. Knowing him, he was just being a smart-ass. But Amari's pretty torn up. He hasn't talked to us about it yet, but we can tell."

Bernadine's heart went out to him. He took being a July seriously and to have his idol crash and burn in such a stupid way was undoubtedly devastating.

Lily then relayed the conversation about the keys.

"How'd Mal respond to that?" Bernadine asked.

"Not well. Wanted to know if it was your idea."

Bernadine blew out a breath. "Of course. Blame me because all of this is my fault."

"I know. I just want to shake Mal because this is breaking Trent's heart, too. He hasn't shared much of his feelings, either."

Bernadine imagined Trent's pain to be like her own. From the stories shared with her about Mal's years as an alcoholic, she'd learned that the then-teenage Trent had been thrust into the role of parent. Rather than let her sadness rise further, she changed the subject. "How're the class reunion plans going?"

"Pretty well. I've gotten most RSVPs back. We're going to

have quite a crowd. I'm hoping the weekend will put a smile back on my honey's face. He could use some fun." Lily was organizing a reunion of the people she and Trent had gone to high school with. It would be held in two weeks.

Lily continued, "We have a committee meeting this evening, so I have a few things to work on. Do you need my help with anything?"

"I don't. Going to go over to the Sutton place and check on the Millers in a few. Their appliances are scheduled to arrive today." Pastry chef Sam Miller and his accountant wife, Brenda, had recently relocated to Henry Adams from Vegas. They were opening the town's first combo coffee shop and bakery. Bernadine liked the couple and looked forward to their integration into the community.

Lily said, "Okay, tag me if anything comes up."

"Lil?"

Lily stopped.

Bernadine said, "Thanks for being such a good friend."

"Not a problem. You know how much I love you. Just trying to help."

"Doing a great job."

Lily nodded thanks and left Bernadine alone.

Seeing the Millers was at the top of her to-do list, but as always, there was more. BFF Tina Craig intended to open the town's first bed-and-breakfast and would be flying in later to show the blueprint for the structure drawn up by her architect. Bernadine was eager to see what Tina had in mind. If everything worked out, being able to enjoy their decades-long friendship daily was a joy to contemplate. She also had to stop by the Dog and make sure the diner's kitchen was running smoothly. With Mal in the role of *persona non grata*, and the co-owner, Rochelle "Rocky" Dancer James, away on her honeymoon, Rocky's trusted assistant, Matt "Sizzle" Burke, was in charge. Although only in his twenties, Siz was competent, trustworthy, and one of the best young chefs around.

She also wondered if she needed to check on Kyrie Abbott, the new teacher hired as a substitute while Jack was on his honeymoon with Rocky. Bernadine usually left school matters to Superintendent Marie Jefferson, but Marie and her best friend, Genevieve Barbour, along with Gen's husband, TC, were in Alaska visiting his son. Abbott was twenty-seven and hailed from Baton Rouge. His degree from LSU was in elementary ed and American history. Marie said his résumé, filled with the community organizations he'd been involved with at home, placed him head and shoulders above everyone else she'd interviewed. Upon Jack's return, Abbott would be given his own classroom and teach the younger kids.

Checking her email one more time and finding nothing needing her immediate attention, she gathered her belongings and left the office.

Bernadine loved fall. The cool crisp weather and bright sunshine were always a balm after the hot and humid stickiness of summer. But on the plains of Kansas, autumn could be a step or two away from the cold and snow of winter, so she did her best to enjoy it for as long as it lasted. She parked her blue Ford F-150, lovingly called Baby, at the curb and got out to walk to the doors of the newly refurbished Sutton Hotel. The Italian artisans Lily found to restore the historic stone façade had done a magnificent job and the structure sparkled in the sunlight. Inside, as she crossed the small atrium with its gorgeous plants and large skylight, her heels echoed softly on the beautiful tiled floor.

The building had two levels. Loft apartments were upstairs, while business offices occupied the first floor. To her left were glass doors leading to the Liberian Ladies and Gents Salon, the beauty shop managed by hairdresser Kelly Douglas. Kelly's assistant, former mayor and resident pest Riley Curry, served as barber. The shop didn't open until ten, so the place was closed. Next door was the office of private investigator Sandy Langster. Bernadine hadn't seen Sandy since Rocky and Jack's wedding, so she assumed she was somewhere covering a case. Down a hallway in the back of the building was the practice of pediatrician Dr. Reg Garland. Until now, he'd been working out of a clinic over at the school. He was glad to finally have a dedicated spot, and Bernadine was, too. The Millers' coffee shop was on her right. It was the largest business in the front of the building. As she pulled open the doors and walked in, she was pleased to see the shop starting to take shape. The tables and chairs were in. The ceiling with its pot lighting was finished, and the long, polished wood-topped counter had been installed. The large window facing the street gleamed in the sunshine.

Sam Miller came out of the back. "Hey, Ms. Brown. Good morning." He was tall, bald, and the size of an NFL linebacker.

"Morning, and please, for the fiftieth time, call me Bernadine."

He grinned. "Just trying to put some respect on your name, as the young kids say."

His wife, the diminutive Brenda, joined them. "Morning, Bernadine. How are you?"

Bernadine smiled. "Morning. I'm fine. Still trying to convince your hubby to call me by my given name. But I appreciate the respect."

Brenda turned loving eyes on her big bear of a mate. "We'll work on him."

Bernadine remembered viewing Mal with the same mushy sentiment, but immediately squashed the memory. "The shop looks to be coming along nicely. How about giving me a tour?"

"We'd love to."

So, she was shown the new ovens, mixers, and the other industrial appliances, along with cases of flour, sugar, and yeast. There were pots and pans, cast-iron skillets, and boxes of raisins, nuts, and spices. In addition to coffee, the shop would be offering a variety of Sam's made-from-scratch breakfast pastries and breads.

"The refrigerators and coffeemakers are coming this afternoon," Brenda informed her.

Bernadine asked, "When will you be ready for customers?"

"If the deliveries come through, we should be ready Friday morning. We're interviewing employees online now, too."

"Music to my ears," she said. "Hours of operation?"

"Six a.m. to five," Sam replied proudly.

"Folks in town are going to love you."

"I hope so. We'd like to stay in business for a while, you know."

Brenda said, "I like the peacefulness here. You don't get much crime, do you?"

Bernadine thought about the fire set by Odessa Stillwell and the mess a few weeks back with former social worker Aretha Krebbs. "Every now and then we have to call the authorities, but every inch of town is covered by cameras. If anything does jump off, we can often view it in real time."

The couple shared a pleased look.

"Any other questions or concerns?"

They had none.

Impressed that everything seemed to be in order, she said, "Thanks for the tour. I'm off to my next stop. Keep me updated on the deliveries."

Brenda promised. "Will do."

Bernadine got back in Baby and drove the short distance to the Dog. Breakfast was still being served, so she planned to sit and eat. She wondered if Mal was still around or if he'd gone back to Oklahoma. If she crossed paths with him, she was determined to be pleasant. Not that he deserved it. The parts of herself that still loved him were saddened by the consequences playing out in his life. The Dog was his baby and one of the anchors he'd used to ground him as he conquered his alcohol addiction. No longer having a say in the operations probably saddened him, but he should've taken that into consideration when he stuck his hand in the cookie jar. Harsh? Maybe. But it was the truth.

Pulling into the parking lot coincided with a text from Gary Clark that read: *Dog loose in store. Health dept. on way. Shut down for now. Keep you posted.*

Her first instinct was to drive there but she decided not to. Had Gary needed her on-site, he would've said so. Wondering why her town was never calm and uneventful, she got out and walked to the entrance of the Dog.

As always, the diner was crowded. The chatter of myriad conversations rose over the jukebox playing Grover Washington's iconic "Black Frost."

At the hostess stand stood Kim, one of the college students who made up most of the waitstaff. "Morning, Kim."

"Morning, Ms. Brown."

Bernadine took a quick glance around the dining room. "Has Mr. July been in?"

"Not that I know of. Siz may, though."

"Okay. I'll go talk to him, then come back and have something to eat."

"Yes, ma'am. He's in the kitchen."

"Thanks."

In the kitchen, rap music blared on the CD player. Siz and his assistant chef, Randy Emerson, were flipping and frying and dicing and chopping while the waitstaff grabbed plates and platters and moved in and out of the double doors with choreographed precision. "Morning, Siz!"

"Morning, Ms. Bernadine," he called back, breaking eggs onto the hot flattop and immediately using a spatula to scramble them. His current hair color was jade green with deep purple highlights.

"Has Mal been in today?"

Siz paused and glanced at her over his shoulder. "No. Is he back?"

She nodded. "Can we talk in the office?"

He looked to his assistant. "Hey, Randy, take over a minute, will you?"

"Sure."

The office interior was as quiet as the kitchen was loud.

Siz asked, "Does Mal know he's basically banned from having any say on what goes down here, now?"

"Yes. Trent informed him last night."

"That's rough. In a way I feel sorry for him."

Bernadine did too, even as she didn't. "He won't have a key to the doors, either."

"Even rougher. Okay. But he's welcome to eat here, right?"

"Of course. I'm not sure what his plans are, though. Last I heard he was working in Oklahoma, so I don't know how long he'll be around." She also didn't know if he was still seeing Ruth, the woman who'd been his date at the wedding.

"I got a text from Rock late last night. She and Jack will be back on Wednesday. She's been checking in every couple of days, making sure we haven't burned down the place."

"You've done a great job being in charge."

"Thanks. Can't wait for her to get back so I can just cook. All this other stuff—scheduling and ordering—not my thing."

"Good practice for when you open your own place in the future after your apprenticeship."

"I suppose."

"Have you heard anything new from the chef who offered you the apprenticeship?"

"Only that he's still traveling around Asia."

Even though no one in town wanted Siz to leave, they were all rooting for him and this opportunity to take his career to the next level. In the meantime, she could tell by the way he kept eyeing the door that he was anxious to get back to the kitchen, so she asked, "Any concerns before you go?"

"Mal isn't going to be trouble, is he?"

She shrugged. "Hope not. Let me know if anything jumps off, though, okay?"

"Got you on speed dial."

"Good. Love the new hair color."

His laughing reply of "thank you" accompanied him out the door.

UPSTAIRS ABOVE THE diner, Mal had slept in. Were he working in the oil fields or still riding point at the Dog, he would've reported for duty hours ago. Instead he was lying in bed angry that the consequences of his theft had reduced his life to a steaming pile of manure. As if last night's dinner with Trent and family hadn't been disastrous enough, he returned to his apartment to find a message on his landline from the oil company. He'd been laid off. No explanation or reassurances to rehire him sometime in the future. Simply: *we no longer need you*. He'd been crushed. Still felt that way. With no job, how was he supposed to make restitution? Granted, he could probably find employment somewhere else, but the likelihood of an employer offering a senior citizen like himself the hourly rate he'd earned with the oil company was slim to none. Times like these could play havoc with a former alcoholic's commitment to sobriety, but he had no urge to be both the town pariah and the town drunk. Been there. Done that. He didn't see himself ditching his sobriety, but losing his mind was an option. The smells from the kitchen downstairs were scenting the air, driving home the realization that on a normal pre-embezzlement morning, he would've already had breakfast as well. Sitting up, he perched on the edge of the mattress and ran his hands wearily down his unshaven face. He was hungry but wasn't in the mood for the censorious eyes of his neighbors. Breakfast with BFF Clay Dobbs would be a better bet, so he washed up, dressed, and went to his truck.

Clay lived west of town on a hog farm he'd inherited from his parents. He'd also inherited WW2 vet Bing Shepard, the town patriarch, whom he'd taken in after the death of Bing's wife. Like Mal's mother, Tamar, Bing would probably live until the year 2525.

As he parked his truck and got out, he could honestly say he and Clay had known each other since they could walk.

They'd been inseparable growing up: school, parties, hunting trips. Then came the draft and Vietnam. Placed in different platoons, they were forced to deal with the horror separately. Once home again, they renewed their friendship, but the war took its toll. Mal began drinking to rid himself of the nightmares that plagued him like parasites in his brain, and Clay, who'd once been the biggest jokester in Kansas, returned home closed off and joyless. Now, forty-plus years later, they still had each other's back. In fact, Clay was the one who'd recommended the condo developer that ran off with Mal's stolen money. The only reason their relationship hadn't crashed and burned was that the man disappeared with Clay's life savings, too.

Mal knocked on the screen door. "Dobbs, you home?"

Inside, Bing called back, "He's in the barn."

"Thanks!"

He found Clay tossing fresh hay into the pens. It was a yearly task. If winter decided to come early, as it did sometimes, he needed them ready to house his stock.

"Hey, man," Mal said.

"Hey. When'd you get back?"

"Yesterday afternoon. Had dinner with Trent last night so I could find out the lay of the land."

Clay paused his work. "How'd it go?"

He shook his head.

"That bad?"

"Yeah." Mal told him about the keys, his standing at the Dog, and being laid off.

Clay said, "Yeah, that's rough. What're you going to do?"

"Try and find another job."

"Have you talked to the Lady yet?"

Knowing he was referring to Bernadine, Mal replied, "No. Not yet. Maybe this evening. Maybe tomorrow, sometime. I don't know, man. Everything's so screwed up."

"Tell me about it."

"She probably doesn't want to see me anyway."

Clay went back to tossing hay with the pitchfork he held. "You never know."

"I do know. Coming to the wedding with Ruth was one of the dumbest things I've ever done." And it was. Adding to the mess was trying to extricate himself from Ruth, who wanted a relationship he had no plans to cement.

"Almost as dumb as me letting Genevieve get away. Now that she's married to TC, I can't be mad at how happy she is, but she could've been mine. Why can't women be as simple as they were back in the day?"

"They've never been simple. We men were just delusional in thinking they were."

"I suppose. So, you planning on hanging here all day?"

"If you'll have me. Could use some breakfast, too."

"It's almost eleven o clock."

"Does that mean I can't eat?"

"No. It means what have you been doing all morning?"

"Wallowing in a tub of self-pity. How about you?"

"Trying not to think about having to get by with no savings."

"We need a plan."

"A plan is what got us in this mess."

Mal grudgingly agreed. Clay touting the big profit they'd make investing in the condos was what suckered Mal into stealing the money from the Dog, but instead of profits, they'd reaped the whirlwind.

Clay spread more hay. "You go on in and find something to eat. I'll be there soon as I finish this."

Mal nodded and left him to his chore.

Inside, Mal was just sitting down to a plate of bacon and eggs when Clay entered.

"Bing left with Orville," Mal told him. Orville Caster was a young vet who'd served in Afghanistan. He was also a farmer and a member of the local Black Farmers Association. "Said to tell you bye."

Clay walked to the kitchen sink and washed his hands. "They're going to Lawrence for a WW2 event at the Buffalo Soldier Monument. Bing asked if I wanted to ride over. Told him no."

Mal eyed his friend. As close as they were, Clay had never shared his experiences in Vietnam, and Mal had never pressed him about it. His own nightmares nearly stole his life, but he'd talked about them to anyone who'd listen in the hopes of finding peace. Mal sensed Clay still struggled with the darkness he brought back from the jungles of Southeast Asia, thus his reluctance to participate in anything tied to the military. He also sensed his friend might exorcise the demons by talking to one of the shrinks at the VA, but Clay would never agree. In his mind, he was fine.

"Any news on Dresden?" Mal asked, starting in on his plate. David Dresden was the condo guy.

Clay sat down. "No. I talked to Jimmy last night. He's heard nothing. Said he's thinking about going to the police, but he doesn't want his wife to know he lost the money." Jimmy Green was Clay's cousin.

"Hasn't told her, I take it?"

"No."

Jimmy and Dresden were fraternity brothers, a tie that went back to their college years at KU. Because they'd done business deals in the past, it never occurred to Jimmy that Dresden couldn't be trusted.

Clay said, "Jimmy's thinking about hiring a private eye."

Mal didn't know how he felt about that. "What do you think?"

Clay shrugged. "I don't know. Might be throwing more money down a hole."

"Money we don't have. At least I don't."

"Me, either."

Mal picked up his cup of coffee and took a sip. "Be nice if we could find him and get our dough back, though. The town could've had me thrown in jail." He set the cup down.

"We both know Trent wouldn't have stood for that."

"I'm not so sure. He's pretty mad." The hurt in Trent's eyes last night continued to weigh on Mal's heart. "Devon thinks I should paint Marie's fence."

"That's punishment for the kids, not grown folks."

"I know." He'd find some other way to atone for his sins.

Clay continued, "Devon needs to worry about Devon. He's way too sanctimonious for a boy his age."

Mal didn't like hearing his grandson described that way, especially by someone who had sanctimonious issues of his own. "Dev's okay. He can be a little high-and-mighty at times, but that's just part of his charm."

That earned him an eye roll from Clay, but Mal let it go. Bigger fish to fry. "But getting back to the private eye thing. Sandy Langster has an office in town. She did a good job busting Astrid Wiggins. I wonder what she'd charge if we hired her for, say, a week?"

"No idea. I can run it by Jimmy and see what he says."

"Okay. In the meantime, how about me whipping your butt in some dominoes?"

"Penny a point?"

"I think I can afford that. Not that I'm going to need it playing you."

A smiling Clay left to get the dominoes.

CHAPTER
3

Standing outside the Marie Jefferson Academy, the hired gun, now calling herself Lisa Stockton, shook the hand of Mayor Trent July. "Thanks for the job. You won't regret hiring me."

"We hope you enjoy being here."

Where some women would've been smiling seductively in response to July's handsomeness, Lisa kept herself in character. She'd just been hired as the school's second-shift custodian. She and July just finished a tour of the school. The building was impressive, but she wasn't there to be wowed by it. Her real interest lay in a building a block or so down the street. "When do I start?"

"Tomorrow is good."

"Can I start this afternoon? I really need the pay."

He hesitated for a moment, then finally said, "Sure. I don't see a problem. All your paperwork is in and processed. Just make sure everything's locked up tight when you leave."

He'd given her a small ring of keys earlier. "Will do. Thanks again for the job, I'll be back in time to begin my shift."

"Call my office if you need anything or run into problems."

She nodded. He walked to his shiny silver truck and she to the old green Fiesta she was driving to fit the role she was playing: a down-on-her-luck lady custodian. She decided to drive down Main Street before heading back to her motel room. The building housing her prey, a place called the Sutton Hotel, was easy to find. In fact, everything in Henry Adams was easy to find: the school, the church, the recreation center, a diner called the Dog and Cow, were all located within feet of each other on both sides of the street. Surrounding the buildings were acres and acres of flat, wide-open, undeveloped Kansas countryside, and that was a problem. Often after a job, escaping depended upon melting into dense traffic, crowded buildings, hordes on the sidewalks. There was none of those things in Henry Adams, so a night plan might have to be used. Another issue. There were no tall building to hide an armed sniper. But the most surprising complication lay with the security setup. The surveillance-equipment detection software on her phone was beeping like mad. The place seemed blanketed with it. Why would such a small town be outfitted with sophisticated electronic bling? She'd done a Google search of the town and its website and chuckled upon finding a job opening at the school. Piece of cake, she'd said to herself, but now, knowing that Big Brother had eyes in the sky, the cake wasn't as tasty. She'd been in this business for almost a decade and the challenge of it was still a rush. Taking out the targets was going to be a task requiring thoughtful planning, and possibly a bit of luck. But she always got the job done.

THE STUDENTS OF Marie Jefferson gathered outside at the picnic tables for lunch. "So, what do you think?" Amari asked, removing his pastrami sandwich from his backpack.

Preston withdrew his own sandwich and a small ziplock bag of carrot sticks. "About what?"

"Mr. Abbott."

Leah sipped her juice. "He's cute."

Preston's jaw dropped in disbelief.

She tossed back, "Hey, if you can drool over Beyoncé, I can do the same over Mr. Abbott."

Amari smiled and wondered what Brain and Leah would be like as a couple when they were old and gray. To bring the conversation back to the issue at hand, he said, "Other than his cuteness, what do you think?"

Leah replied, "Too soon to tell. I like him, though."

Zoey said, "I like his accent."

Devon countered, "He sounds like that skunk on those old Bugs Bunny cartoons. You know the one always trying to kiss the cat."

Zoey rolled her eyes. "No, he doesn't. You've got an accent too, you know, and so do I."

Leah's sister, Tiffany, said, "He seems nice. He hasn't yelled at anybody."

"Looked a little lost," Wyatt added.

"He's new," Lucas sagely pointed out. "Just like me and my sister, Jaz."

Amari thought the new kid had a point. Lucas and his

little sister, Jasmine, came to live in Henry Adams this summer and were being fostered by Wyatt's grandmother, Ms.
Gemma. Amari was still trying to figure Lucas out. He rarely
spoke, which led Amari to believe there was some deep thinking going on inside.

Devon boasted, "Last night, I told OG he should have to
paint the fence for stealing."

Preston said, "Quit lying."

"I'm not lying. Ask Amari."

Skeptical eyes turned his way and Amari grudgingly nodded.
The skepticism morphed into surprised amazement.

"What did he say?" Leah asked.

"Nothing," Devon said. "My dad told me to let it go. When
I made a face, Mom said if I couldn't let it go, I should leave
the table, so I picked up my plate and left. Didn't I, Amari?"

Jaws dropped, and every eye turned Amari's way again.
He knew agreeing would only make Devon that much more
of a jerk, but he couldn't lie. "Yeah, he did."

Devon added proudly, "And Amari backed me up. He got
up, too."

"I didn't do it to back you up. I got up for my own reasons."

Devon asked, "What reasons?"

"None of your business." Sullen, Amari bit into his sandwich. He was still processing his feelings about what OG had
done, but he wasn't sharing any of it with Devon's pain-in-
the-butt behind. He might with Brain, but Devon? Not a
chance.

Everyone continued to stare, so he asked coolly, "Do I look
like I'm in a cage at the zoo?"

Eyes quickly dropped.

"Thank you."

A few minutes of silence passed before Preston said, "The adults aren't going to make him paint the fence."

Zoey agreed. "Nope. Not going to happen. That's just for us kids."

Devon said self-importantly, "I'm going to talk to Tamar about it."

That drew another Zoey eye roll. "Yeah, right."

"Bet you five dollars I will."

"Bet you don't even have five dollars."

Snickering followed that.

Having been smacked down by Zoey more than once, Devon shut up, which suited Amari just fine. Truthfully, he thought maybe OG should be painting the fence too, but he didn't want to say that out loud. Knowing his grandfather was a thief had him torn between disappointment and anger. Not to mention the embarrassment of knowing everyone in town was whispering about it. Amari felt the OG'd dirtied the July name. Granted, the family did rob trains back in the day, but they never stole from the people they cared about, and certainly never helped themselves to money owned by the town. And even he hadn't stolen a car since the disastrous night he tried to help Crystal find her birth mom. Talking to Tamar might be a good idea, but without Devon.

Upon returning to the classroom, they took their seats. On Monday afternoons, Mr. James usually let the rest of the day be Montessori time, which meant you could do anything you wanted if it was education related. You could free-read, or head to the art room, work on homework, use the computers to check out approved sites like National Geographic, museums like the Smithsonian, and the new National Museum of African American Heritage and Culture, or sites such as

NASA—where Preston's birth mom worked as an astrophysicist. Mr. James said it fostered independent learning, a skill they'd need as they grew into adults. Since doing a project a few years ago on the Jacob Lawrence paintings of the Haitian revolution, Amari had a growing interest in other cultures, and he spent his Montessori time reading up on people who lived in faraway countries like China, Botswana, and Brazil, and in places he knew nothing about like Iceland and Paraguay. He enjoyed checking out what the people looked like, how they dressed, and stuff like their churches, religions, and what they ate.

He was on the computer checking out the island of Madagascar when Mr. Abbott appeared beside him. "Hey, Mr. Abbott."

"Hey, Amari. What're you doing?"

"Learning about Madagascar."

Abbott paused to check out the screen before asking, "Why there?"

Amari shrugged and clicked on a picture of the country's cloud forests. "I just like learning about other people."

"So, you want to study anthropology?"

"No. I want to drive NASCAR."

Abbott stared. "Really?"

"Yes."

"Mr. James didn't tell me much about you all. He said it would be best to find out on my own."

Amari understood. "He's big on self-discovery, as he calls it."

Mr. Abbott looked around the classroom at what the other kids were doing. "I've never taught in a school where students are allowed this kind of freedom. Little kids, yes, but not older ones."

"It's only one afternoon a week, but Mr. James is a great teacher." Realizing he wasn't going to get anything done, Amari turned away from the screen. "So, what do you want to know?'

Abbott grinned. "You're pretty up front, aren't you?"

"I think we all are. Comes from being in foster care and then living here. Tell you what, we know you've been trying real hard to be a good sub, and since you'll be getting your own class when Mr. James and Rocky come back, how about you get to know us all, now?"

He seemed surprised. "Okay. How do you propose we do that?"

Amari stood. "Hey, guys?"

Everyone looked up.

"Mr. Abbott wants to get to know us better, so can we give him like an hour to ask us questions and stuff?"

Brain looked to Leah. Amari saw her nod. A few minutes later, they pulled their chairs in a circle and began to talk.

Later, Amari walked into his dad's garage and found him working under the hood of the car they were restoring. The 1969 Chevy Camaro belonged to Ms. Marie, but had been sitting under tarps in her barn since the mideighties. When he and his dad pulled the tarps off, the tires were flat, mice had eaten all the upholstery and wiring, and the front end was crushed from the tree Ms. Marie crashed into one night while driving in a snowstorm. She wanted to maybe sell it after it was drivable again.

"Hey, Dad."

"Hey, Amari. I got your brother's text about band practice."

"Yeah, he and Zoey and Wyatt are at the rec."

"How was school?"

Amari dropped his backpack onto the old sofa and headed to the refrigerator and grabbed a soda. "I was a facilitator today."

His dad straightened. "A facilitator?"

"Yeah. Mr. Abbott wanted to know about us, so I made it happen. He's an okay dude. He asked us a bunch of questions about who we were before we came to Kansas, and how we liked living here. We learned about him, too. He has six brothers and a sister."

"Wow."

"He's the baby and his parents are from New Orleans."

"Interesting."

"Ms. Bernadine stopped by, too. I think she wanted to make sure we didn't have him gagged and tied in the storage room."

His dad chuckled. Amari set his soda bottle down and walked to the car. "What are you doing?"

"Trying to figure out why this carburetor doesn't fit."

"Did we order the wrong one?" Amari asked, watching his dad try to maneuver the piece into place. One edge wouldn't lie flush.

"Maybe," Trent replied, adding, "More like probably, though." There was disappointment in his voice.

"Do you want me to go online and order another one?"

"Yes, but later. I want to talk to you about something for a few minutes first, if that's okay?"

Amari took in his serious face. "Am I in trouble because I left the table last night?"

"No. But I am wondering how you feel about the whole thing with Mal."

Amari remained wary. "How do you feel?"

"Mad. Disappointed. Upset."

"Me, too. Devon was at school bragging about leaving the table, but I didn't leave it because he did."

"Your mom and I wondered about that."

"I left because . . ." Amari paused, trying to find the right words to explain his mixed-up feelings. "Is it wrong that I don't want to be around OG right now?"

His dad placed a light hand on his shoulder. "No, son, it isn't. Honestly, I feel you."

"I just don't understand how he could do something so messed up."

"I know."

"Thought maybe I'd talk to Tamar about it. Is that okay? Not trying to hurt your feelings or anything by not talking to you about it."

That earned him a soft smile. "My feelings aren't hurt. I may do that, too. She's good at helping people sort through things."

Relieved, Amari continued, "Devon said he's going to talk to her about making OG paint Ms. Marie's fence."

"Even if Tamar thinks he should do it, she's not going to *make* him do anything."

"Why not?"

"Because he's a grown man and should be able to figure out a fix for himself. Even though it's been only done by kids, your mom and I think him painting the fence would probably go a long way in making amends."

Amari asked a question that had been bothering him a lot, and he hoped his dad didn't think it was inappropriate. "Why did he take the money? Do you know?"

"Male pride."

"What's that mean?"

"Your grandfather grew up in a time when men paid for everything. Women were mostly moms and housewives. Only in the last forty years have they moved into the workforce and begun making their own way. So when he and Bernadine went to Key West for Christmas last year, she paid for everything."

Amari was confused. "But that's what she does."

His dad smiled. "I know, and he knew that, too. However, knowing and having to stand aside while she took care of the bills are two different things. And it made him feel less."

"Less than what?"

"A man."

"That's dumb, Dad."

"Yes and no. Remember what I said about the times he grew up in. Men were the providers, and now times have changed."

"So he took the money to make himself feel better?"

"No. He wanted to be able to treat her, take her on vacation, take her to dinner."

"With money that he stole?" Amari asked skeptically.

"According to him, his plan was to invest it, make a killing, repay the stolen money, and have enough left over to do the vacation and dinner and the rest. And he'd pay for everything."

"So how come he hasn't paid the money back yet if he invested it?"

"Because the guy he and Clay invested with was a crook. He disappeared with the money and they don't know where he is."

"This is like a bad television show."

"Tell me about it."

"Do you think Ms. Bernadine will forgive him?"

"That, I don't know. Him bringing his new lady to the wedding was one of the dumbest moves I've seen in my life, but stealing the money shows he wasn't thinking straight to begin with."

Amari agreed. OG and Ms. Bernadine had been so tight everybody thought they'd be hooked up forever. Now she just looked sad all the time even though she thought nobody could see it.

Amari and his dad spent the next hour working on the brakes and replacing the lining in the trunk. They didn't talk much, which was okay. Just being with Trent and doing something they both enjoyed always made him feel special. Once they rolled out from beneath the car, Amari told him, "Thanks, Dad."

"For what?"

"Just for being my dad."

"Thanks for being my son."

That made him feel even more special. "Growing up back in Detroit, I used to see kids at stores and in cars with their dads, and I wanted to be them. Having a dad, you know."

"I always wanted a son, too. And you fit the bill perfectly."

Amari smiled.

"You ready to head home?" Trent asked. "We can go on the Camaro website after dinner and look up that carburetor."

"Yes. Who's cooking tonight? You or Mom?"

"I am. I took some chops out of the freezer this morning."

"Can we have mashed potatoes, too? Maybe some broccoli and cheese sauce? I'll help."

"You got it. Do you want to drive home?"

Amari's eyes lit up. "Yeah!" He'd gotten his permit last week. State law mandated he put in fifty hours of supervised driving with an adult before he could move up to the phase that led to driving alone. He'd been driving since the age of ten, but waiting to be legal was killing him.

His dad tossed him the keys. Amari caught them deftly.

"Lead the way."

Amari picked up his backpack. His dad locked up and they walked out to the truck.

LATER THAT EVENING, Gary left Leah and Tiffany at home doing homework and drove to Trent and Lily's for the homecoming meeting. Lily, being Lily, put him on the committee unbeknownst to him, but he didn't mind. The gathering would be in two weeks and he was looking forward to renewing old friendships. The only thing giving him pause was the possibility of seeing Eleanor Price again. Affectionately known as Nori back in the day, she'd been one of the smartest girls around. She'd also been the girl he'd been in love with and hoped to marry, until Colleen lied about being pregnant with his child. His lips tightened at the memory. In the blink of an eye, he'd gone from preparing to attend Notre Dame on an academic scholarship to being married and selling cars at the dealership owned by Colleen's overbearing father, Milton. For her part, Nori left Henry Adams after graduation to attend school out east, and then her parents moved away. He heard she'd become a math teacher. In the years since, he thought about her off and on and wondered what life might have been had circumstances been different.

Gary pushed the doorbell button. Trent answered and stepped back so Gary could enter. "Hey. Bernadine said the health department gave you a tentative okay to open tomorrow."

Gary sighed thinking about the crazy morning at the store. "Yeah. All the floors have to be mopped and sanitized."

"Who knew an eighty-two-year-old lady could be such a menace?"

"If I never see Mrs. Beadle or Lorenzo again, it'll be too soon."

"Come on, we're meeting in the den."

Lily looked up at Gary's entrance. "Hey there. Rough day, I hear."

"Yeah. I wound up sending the staff home. Maintenance crew is dealing with the health department's requirements. We should be good to go tomorrow."

They then got down to business and Lily passed them each a blue folder. They were the only people from their class still in the area, so they were a committee of three.

"In your packet, the first page is our tentative agenda for the weekend. We'll open Friday evening with a meet and greet. I sent Rocky a text and she's okay with closing the Dog so we can use it. She's going to put a sign on the front door a few days in advance so folks will know it'll be closed to the public."

Gary liked that idea.

Lily continued, "On Saturday morning, I can't see closing the Dog again without folks complaining, so we'll have breakfast at the rec. Tamar and her crew have volunteered to handle the skillets and waffle irons. Gary, I'll get you a food order in a day or two, so we'll have enough on hand without having to raid Rocky's fridge."

"Okay. Just let me know."

"Then, after breakfast, I thought we'd have a walking tour of the town. None of them have seen the new Henry Adams, so I want to show it off. Especially the school."

Gary thought back on the former Henry Adams High School. It had been almost sixty years old in those days, and just big enough to hold the seventy students in grades nine through twelve. Compared to the other schools in the area, it had been wholly inadequate in terms of science labs, athletic facilities, and what passed for technology back then, but it had been theirs.

Lily's voice cut into his thoughts. "After the tour, we'll go back to the rec and have a cookout, weather permitting. And Saturday night will be the dance, complete with DJ."

Gary asked, "So how many people are coming?"

"The list is in your packet."

Gary found the list and, as he scanned it, froze at the sight of two names: Eleanor Price and Colleen Ewing Baker, his ex-wife. "Colleen's coming?"

Lily nodded, looking unhappy. "I sent her a flyer, just being polite. I never thought she'd actually RSVP, but she did."

He blew out a breath. She was the last person he wanted to see.

"I'm sorry, Gary."

He waved it off. "No apologies needed. It's just a weekend. I'll deal with it." He hoped Colleen and her husband had a hotel room because staying with him and the girls would not be an option.

Lily still wore a concerned look, so he said, "I'm okay, Lil. Promise." He reread the list, this time taking in the names of some of the guys who'd been on the basketball team he and Trent co-captained. Thinking about them made him smile and remember the good times they'd shared, but his eyes kept straying back to Nori's name. She was listed as "Price," the surname she'd had back in the day. Had she not married?

Would she speak to him? Would she remember him? When he glanced up again, he saw Lily still watching him. She and Nori had been on the track team together. Did Lily know what he was thinking? Had she and Nori continued their friendship? After the way his relationship with her crashed and burned, did he even have a right to question Lily about her?

Trent asked his wife, "Is there anything else we need?"

"I would like any old pictures you may have. I asked our classmates to bring theirs. We'll set them out so everyone can see them."

"Tamar has all mine," Trent said. "I'll grab them from her next time I'm out there. We might also want to break out the video Amari and Preston surprised us with at our wedding reception."

"I'd forgotten about that. I'll make myself a note to dig it out."

Gary said, "I have my old albums at the house. I'll look through them. I'm sure I have some photos we can use."

Lily nodded. "Good. The hotel in Franklin is where most of the people will be staying, so the three of us may have to play taxi drivers that weekend. We may also need to make a few runs to the airport."

"I'm in," Gary said, wondering where Nori lived now and if she'd be flying in or driving. "I plan to take those days off. I've already told Gemma."

They spent a few more minutes talking over some minor details. He did his best to not let the prospect of having to deal with Colleen dampen his enthusiasm, but it was difficult.

Arriving home, he turned out the porch light and climbed the stairs to the second floor to check on his girls. This was the house he'd grown up in. He was an only child, so all the love his parents had was poured onto him. They'd been strict but fair and he tried to apply that same love and standard to his own parenting. Colleen hadn't let him participate much in the girls' early raising, but he liked to think he was making up for that now.

He stuck his head in Leah's open door. "Hey, Leah."

She was seated on the bed with her laptop. "Hey, Dad. How'd the meeting go?"

"It went well. It's going to be fun. Found out your mother's coming."

Distaste flashed over her face for a second, then vanished before she asked flatly, "Is she staying with us?"

"No."

He thought he saw her tension drain.

"You didn't talk much about how things went in Atlanta this summer."

Still focused on the screen, she replied, "Not much to talk about. We went, we stayed, we came home."

Gary studied her silently. She finally looked up again. "Honestly? When I'm eighteen, I won't be going back."

She and her mother had never meshed the way Colleen and Tiffany had. Colleen seemed intimidated by Leah's intelligence, and instead of taking pride in all that Leah was, she did her best to undermine it by insisting being smart wasn't as important as being stylish and pretty. When Leah was in middle school and wanted to attend Space Camp, he and Colleen had a huge argument over whether she'd be allowed to go. Colleen felt it was a waste of money, but he took Leah's side and refused to back down. Colleen eventually relented, but it was the first of many battles he waged on behalf of Leah's right to become who she wanted to be. "Lee, do you want to talk about it?"

"Not really, Dad. I . . . maybe one day, but not now. Is that okay?"

"Yes, but one more question, and I need you to be truthful." Leah waited.

"She didn't hurt you physically, did she? Nothing happened with her new husband?"

Leah shook her head. "No, Brad's nice. She just hurt my feelings, as always, but we'll talk about that too, when I'm old enough to process it better."

Her stoicism broke his heart. "I'm here for you, Lee. No matter what."

"I know."

"Do you need to talk to Reverend Paula?"

"No, I'm good. Promise. Now, let me get back to this. Okay?" She smiled.

"Okay. But, Lee—"

"Daddy. Bye."

He grinned and dropped his head. Their smiles met, and he left her and walked across the hall to check on Tiffany.

She was painting her nails. "Hey, Tiff."

"Hey, Daddy. How'd it go?"

"Went okay. Your homework done?"

"Yep."

"Just want to let you know your mom's coming to the reunion."

Tiff paused, looked him in the face for a moment, then refocused on her task. "She staying with us?"

"No." Tiff and her mother had always been close. In fact,

right after the divorce, she'd been so distraught he'd worried about her daily. Colleen initiated the divorce, but Tiff believed that all he had to do was apologize and things would go back to the way they were. Now she seemed to have accepted the reality of the situation. Either that or she was hiding it well.

"Did you tell Leah?"

"I did, and she asked the same question about whether your mother would be staying here."

Tiff didn't respond, and he wondered about her silence. He knew Leah's moves better than he did his youngest's because during the marriage she'd spent most of her time at Colleen's side. "Do you want her to stay here?"

"Doesn't matter. I'm okay either way."

He couldn't decide if she was being truthful. "I was just saying to Leah that you two never really talked about being in Atlanta this summer. Did you have a good time?"

She looked up, met his eyes, and went back to her nails. "It was okay. Can we talk about something else?"

That threw him a bit. "Sure. Do you have a particular subject in mind?"

"Yes. I have a question."

"And it is?"

"Are you ever going to get married again?"

That threw him too, because the question was so unexpected. In the three years since the divorce, the subject had never come up. The earnestness on her face as she waited for his reply let him know how important his answer was. "I'm not planning on it. Why?"

"I don't want you to be lonely when Lee and I go away to school."

"Ah. That's real thoughtful of you, Tiff. Do you have some-one in mind for me?" he asked, keeping his tone light.

"Not really, but will you think about it?"

"I will."

She smiled for the first time. "Good."

"I'll let you finish your nails."

"Okay. Thanks."

He left her and went back downstairs to watch *Monday Night Football* wondering how the trip to Atlanta had really gone.

BERNADINE SPENT ALL afternoon waiting for Tina to fly in from New York, but bad weather kept delaying her flight. It was now 7:00 p.m. and Tina had just called to say she'd made it to Chicago. However, due to a fall thunderstorm, Midway was under a ground stop. She and her pilot wouldn't be flying out until morning. The news was disappointing. Bernadine wanted her friend to be safe, though, so she shut down her laptop and prepared to leave the office for the day. She'd just put on her coat when she saw Mal standing in the doorway. Flooded by conflicting emotions she refused to acknowledge, she asked coolly, "Yes?"

"Just stopped by to say hello."

She waited. He looked uncomfortable and she thought he ought to be on his knees crawling over glass and begging for mercy, but she kept that to herself. "Do you need something?"

He looked away for a moment as if gathering his words, then responded with, "Your forgiveness, but I know it's too early for that because I haven't earned it."

She didn't respond because if she opened her mouth all kinds of ugly anger would spill out and she was too old to be screaming at him. Instead, she rummaged around in her purse and took out the small blue velvet box she'd been carrying around for the past two weeks. Pain rose as her mind replayed the words he'd said to her when she received it. *I promise to be there when you need me . . . up front, honest, dependable.* Box in hand, she closed the distance between them and handed it to him. "You can have this back."

He took it but didn't open it. He knew what it held. "Bernadine, if I could undo what I did, I would. I know I hurt you. What we had was special. I'm so sorry I screwed it up. If I had just talked to you after we got back from Key West . . ."

"Did you sleep with her?"

The abrupt question caught him flat-footed. She saw it in his face but didn't care. She wanted the answer.

He shook his head and offered a quiet "no."

She supposed that meant something, even if she wasn't sure what. "I'm locking up and heading home. Anything else?"

"No, baby."

Eyes narrowed at the endearment, she almost told him what he could do with it, but kept that to herself, too. Instead she said, "I have to go."

He offered a terse nod and departed.

She stood there fighting the urge to run after him and curse, yell, and run him down with a combine. She acknowledged the pangs seeing him again gave rise to. Accompanying them was Reverend Paula's mantra of choosing kindness over rightness. But in this instance, she chose being right. After what he put her and the town through, that he hadn't been arrested and thrown in jail was the extent of the kindness he'd be receiving. And unless things changed, it would have to be enough.

She took in a few deep breaths. When her inner storm finally subsided, she hit the light switch and walked down the hallway to the doors leading to the parking lot. She stepped outside into the fading sunlight, and saw Mal sitting in his truck. She ignored him, or as much as a woman could ignore the man she'd given her entire heart to. Climbing into Baby, she started the engine and drove away.

CHAPTER
4

At sunrise the following morning, Mal lay in bed planning his day. At the top of the list: finding a job. He didn't care what it was or how much it paid. It just needed to be better than what he had now, which was nothing. He'd ruled out returning to the Dog, at least for the present, because honestly, he was too ashamed. He wasn't opposed to working in Franklin or one of the other nearby towns, though. Back in the nineties, after his veterinarian's license was suspended due to his drinking, he'd been a janitor in a Franklin bank, so he was okay with what some people called menial labor and what others saw as a livelihood. Online was a good place to begin his search, but he was reminded that he no longer had access to the Dog's computer and would have to log on somewhere else.

His eyes strayed to the blue velvet box on the nearby nightstand. He knew Bernadine was mad at him. Considering his actions, what woman wouldn't be? But he'd convinced himself that once she calmed down, she'd remember what they'd meant to each other, the good times they'd shared, and in a few weeks, she'd eventually forgive him. Now? He sat up and took the box in hand. He hadn't opened it because of what the return signified. *The end. The finale. Over. Done.* He raised the lid and stared down at the small sapphire sparkling on its delicate gold chain. Purchasing it had given him almost as much joy as the look on her face when she first saw it. She'd been both surprised and moved. He'd called it a promise necklace, and recited a litany of promises, including being faithful and dependable. From that moment forward, she'd worn the sapphire necklace daily. Last night, she'd returned it, effectively gutting him and his hubris-fed dream of a quick reconciliation. Setting the necklace aside, he put his head in his hands. All he'd wanted was the opportunity to sport her around in the manner she was accustomed to, take her on a vacation he paid for, go out to eat at a fancy restaurant where he took care of the check. What was so wrong with that? He knew stealing the money was wrong, but his intent had been honest. Unfortunately, intent didn't matter. The consequences made him want to wallow in self-pity, not eating, shaving, or bathing until he had scraggly hair and foot-long toenails like crazy Howard Hughes. Bernadine would be sorry then, he bet, but having always been vain about his appearance, he knew that would never happen.

He did know he was Black Seminole, the descendant of a people who'd never given up, no matter the odds. He'd also survived the jungles of Vietnam and stared down demon alcohol. He could do anything he set his mind to, even earning the forgiveness of the woman he loved. With that in mind, he showered, dressed, and had a quick breakfast. He was determined to have a job by nightfall because making restitution was the first step toward redemption.

He sent Clay a text asking if he could use his computer to begin his search, but Clay sent a text back saying he wasn't at home. He was at a farm checking out a couple of sows he wanted to purchase and wouldn't be back until that afternoon. With Bing in Lawrence and Mal having no key to Clay's place, going online at Clay's place was out. Lifelong friend Marie Jefferson came to mind. She owned a laptop, but she and Genevieve and TC were in Alaska visiting TC's son. Her electronics always traveled with her, so he crossed her off his list. He thought about calling Trent but didn't want to bother him while he was working. His mother, Tamar, had a laptop and a computer in her office at the recreation center, but she was still too angry at him, and he just couldn't handle it and the disappointment he'd see in her eyes. He opted to get in his truck and job-hunt the old-fashioned way.

He drove to Franklin and put applications in anywhere and everywhere he could find: the fast-food joints, the two small hotels linked to national chains, the post office, and all the small businesses lining the town's main street: from the florist to the coffee shop to the hardware store run by the family of Astrid Franklin Wiggins. Disappointed that no one was actively hiring, he took a chance and drove out to the gas station owned by an old friend. Calvin Post.

The place was a combination gas station and snack store like others nationwide. Cal's dad, Edgar, had originally owned the place, and when he passed away forty years ago, Cal took over. The place was right off the highway, and was large, clean, and profitable. Mal parked his truck and got out. Cal was helping an elderly lady inflate a tire. Seeing Mal, he called, "Hey, buddy, be with you in a minute."

Cal had been a defensive lineman for the Colts back before

the team snuck out of Baltimore in the middle of the night and made Indianapolis their home. His nose had been broken more times than one could count, he limped on bad knees, and he'd quit wearing his dentures fifteen years ago. Bald, he still had the height and size that once upon a time gave opposing quarterbacks nightmares, but the girth was now marshmallow soft.

Cal finished the lady's tire, sent her off with a wave, and came over and shook Mal's hand. "Been a while," he said, grinning, showing off the dark, toothless cave in his mouth.

"Yeah, it has been."

"You just stopping by?"

"I am, but also looking for a job."

Cal paused for a moment before saying, "I do need a clerk to take over the night shift."

Mal's hope rose. *Finally.*

"But I can't hire you, Mal."

Confused, he asked, "Why not?"

"Can't have a thief minding the register."

Shame and guilt singed him to his core.

Cal shrugged. "Sorry. Word's out that you stole from the town and your lady love. If you stole from them, you'd steal from me."

Mal wanted to explain but knew there was no way to justify what he'd done. "Okay. I understand. Thanks."

"Sorry, man."

"No problem. I'll see you around."

Making himself walk calmly back to his truck, he opened the door and got in. Smiling falsely, he gave Cal a wave and drove off. In the rearview mirror, he saw Cal watch him drive off, and shake his head as he went inside. Mal was mortified, and embarrassed. He'd assumed people were talking but had no idea the news was so widespread. Was the story of his theft known at all the businesses he'd applied to earlier? If so, he'd never find a job, at least not anywhere nearby. He wanted to be angry, but the only person responsible was himself.

Mal stopped for lunch at a fast-food place on the highway— he didn't put in an application—and drove back to Henry Adams. All the high hopes and confidence he'd had at the beginning of the day had been kneecapped by reality. Before throwing in the towel, he decided to make one last stop.

When he knocked on his son's office door, Trent, seated at his desk, glanced up from his laptop. "Hey, Dad."

"Hey. Can I bother you a minute?"

"Sure. Come on in." He gestured Mal to one of the leather chairs near the desk. "What's up?"

"Went job hunting today."

"Job hunting? What happened to the job in Oklahoma? Did you quit?"

"No, it quit me. Got laid off last night."

"Ah. Sorry to hear that. How's the hunt going?"

"I put in a bunch of applications, but nobody had anything I could interview for on the spot." He didn't tell him about his embarrassing encounter with Cal Post. "So I'm wondering if you know anybody hiring. I'll do anything: unload trucks, stock at the store, mop floors. I can't make restitution if I'm not getting a paycheck."

"No, you can't."

His son looked him in the eyes in a way so reminiscent of Tamar that Mal forced himself not to squirm. She'd done most of Trent's raising, so he supposed the apple didn't fall far from the tree.

Finally, Trent said, "There's a custodian position open at the school. The woman we originally hired fell off an ATV over the weekend and broke her collarbone."

Mal winced.

"Planned to post the opening on the website this afternoon."

"Can I apply?"

"Sure. I don't see why not."

"You'll have to get Bernadine's approval, though, right?" he asked, his voice laced with scorn.

Trent's eyes speared him, and Mal instantly regretted the belittling dig. "No, but I do need Marie's since she'd technically be your boss."

"Oh."

"Let me print out the application."

Mal wanted to apologize. Trent hadn't been obligated to tell him about the job at all. Instead of being grateful . . .

Once the printer spit out the copy, Trent passed it to him. "Have a seat at the table in the hall and fill it out. I'll send Marie a text."

Borrowing a pen, Mal sat and went to work. His eyes strayed down the hall to Bernadine's office. The door was closed, and he naturally wondered if she was inside turning the world, or out somewhere, even though he'd squandered that right. Going back to what he was doing, he realized he didn't know how much the job paid or if any benefits were attached but decided it didn't matter. Whatever the amount, it would be a blessing.

With the application completed, he returned to the office and handed it over. "Have you heard from Marie?"

"Not yet, but I'm sure I will soon."

"How much does it pay?"

"Sixteen an hour, with health, vision, and dental."

That pleased him. It was enough to live on and to pay down his debt. "Okay."

"Once I hear from Marie, I'll let you know."

"Thanks, son."

"You're welcome," Trent replied coolly.

Trent's tone let Mal know he was still unhappy with the earlier remark, and regret rode him. He fought it by changing the subject. "I stopped over at Cal's to ask him about a job. He said he couldn't hire me because he'd heard about the money I took. Does everybody know?"

Trent nodded. "Just about. It's a small town, Dad. You know there aren't any secrets."

"But you'd think—"

"Think what? That folks would want to protect you?"

Another hubris-fueled miscalculation on his part, and Mal knew it as soon as the words slipped past his lips. "Well, yeah."

"Why? You stole from your hometown!" Trent pointed out. "Be glad folks cared enough about the people you stole *from* that the theft didn't make the front page of the Franklin paper."

Once again shame singed him.

"And what Devon said about the fence? Yeah, that might go a long way toward forgiveness."

Mal's face tightened with irritation.

Trent read the response. "Then don't. But you need to make some kind of grand gesture. Otherwise you'll stay a pariah until Lily, the boys, and I put you in the ground."

Not wanting to hear any more, Mal snapped, "When's the next town meeting?"

"Thursday."

"Put me on the agenda. If folks want an apology, I'll give them one. Let me know what Marie says."

"I will."

Mal left. Angry, he blew through the doors to the parking lot and almost knocked Bernadine and the woman beside her off their feet. "Sorry," he said tightly.

Bernadine shot him a look.

The woman with her asked him, "And you are?"

"Mal July. And you?" he asked, still mad.

"Tina Craig."

He knew the name. She was one of Bernadine's best friends. "Catch me when I'm not so mad."

"Not planning to catch you at all after what you did to my girl. Thanks for allowing me to put a face to the name."

Bernadine's small smile made his anger swell, but she didn't seem to care. She and Tina entered the building without a further word, and left him outside, glaring where he stood.

"You weren't lying about Mal being tall, dark, and fine," Tina said to Bernadine as they settled into Bernadine's office.

"I thought he had the brain to go with it. Guess I was wrong."

"So sorry, girl."

Bernadine shrugged. "Better to learn about it now rather than later like I did with Leo."

"That snake," Tina said, referencing Bernadine's ex-husband. "Have you heard from him?"

"Not since my lawyers ran his company out of the county here a few years ago. No news is good news."

"Amen."

Bernadine was glad Tina had finally arrived. She'd be in town for a few days and staying with Bernadine. Her presence at the house would hopefully offset the pangs of loneliness brought on by Crystal's move.

A knock on the door drew Bernadine's attention to Trent standing in the doorway. "Hey there," she said. "Your dad almost knocked us down leaving the building just now."

"He's mad about me telling him a truth he didn't like hearing. He also wants to be placed on the agenda for the town meeting."

Bernadine admitted to being curious but didn't ask for details. Henry Adams had no secrets. "Putting him on is up to you," she said, and introduced Tina.

Trent said, "Good to finally meet you. And thanks again for the wedding gift." She'd given Trent and Lily full run of her oceanside estate in Miami for their honeymoon a few years back.

"You're welcome. You and Lily're still young and in love, I hear."

"Always and forever," he stated with quiet pride.

"I love that. Why can't I ever find a man like you?" Answering herself, she said, "Probably because I'm always looking for love in all the wrong places. Boardrooms. Palaces. Castles."

Bernadine smiled. Tina had three ex-husbands and enough discarded lovers to fill a phone book but had never found happiness. "Keep looking."

"No. I'm done searching. Going to put down roots in Henry Adams, sit on my porch, coffee in hand, and watch the wheat grow."

Bernadine didn't believe that for a minute. In spite of Tina's numerous failed attempts at love, she was a romantic at heart.

Trent asked, "Did you bring the blueprints for your bed-and-breakfast?"

"They're in my luggage, which was dropped off at Bernadine's place. Maybe we can look at them this evening?" She turned to Bernadine.

"Sure." Turning to Trent, Bernadine added, "If you and Lily want to stop by after dinner, we can see them then."

"Sounds like a plan. Almost forgot," he added. "Mal applied for the custodian job at the school. I'm waiting for a yea or nay from Marie."

Bernadine found that confusing. "He going to work both here and in Oklahoma?"

Trent told her about the layoff.

"Oh, I see," she replied. "I'm sure Marie won't have a problem with him getting the job. Neither do I. If he's not working, he can't pay us back."

"Exactly. So now both custodial jobs at the school are filled." With the community college sharing the building, two full-time custodians were needed.

Bernadine asked, "Where's the lady custodian you hired from again?" She hadn't sat in on the interviews. She was stepping back from being in on every little thing. The town leaders were excellent at their jobs and at turning the world with their own hands.

"From Memphis. Name's Lisa Stockton. I asked her to come to the next town meeting. She grew up in Hays. Came with good references from the Memphis school system, and I had the sheriff's office run a background check. Don't ever want us to be caught flat-footed the way we were with Crystal's bio dad."

Bernadine agreed. Crys's bio father, Ray Chambers, came into town posing as a drifter named Otis Miller. He kidnapped Crystal, held her for ransom. He ended up killed in a tornado instead of being paid.

Trent's voice cut into her thoughts. "If Ms. Stockton works out, we may consider letting her rent Rock's old trailer on Tamar's land. Right now, she's rooming at the motel on Highway 183."

"Okay. Looking forward to meeting her."

Tina said, "I'd like to attend the town meeting, too. Is it in the next few days?"

"Yes. Thursday evening. We can introduce you and let everyone know about your bed-and-breakfast."

Tina asked with concern, "Trent, are we really going to be able to build it before the snow comes?"

"As I said before. Depends on weather, planning, hiring workers, et cetera, but we'll look at the plans tonight and see."

"Okay."

"In the meantime, I'll head back to my office. Lily's at the Dog talking to Siz about the menu for the reunion."

"I got her text on my way to meet Tina's plane. Are you excited about the reunion?"

"I am. Looking forward to seeing the old friends I've lost touch with. Especially the guys on the basketball team."

"You were the captain, right?" Bernadine asked.

He nodded. "Captain of basketball team, baseball team, football team, and the track team."

Awestruck, Tina asked, "When did you have time for your studies?"

"When I wasn't working."

"Goodness."

"See you ladies later."

When he left, Tina quoted the old TLC/En Vogue lyric, *"I think I want to have his babies."*

Bernadine giggled. "You are so silly. Don't let Lily hear that."

"I won't, but Lord, he's as good-looking as his father."

"And loves the ground Lily walks on. He's an incredible husband and dad to their boys." Mal, on the other hand, had reverted to his snake-oil salesman ways. The pain continued to weigh her down.

"I'm sorry," Tina said softly. "I didn't mean to make you sad."

"I'm okay."

"No, you aren't, but we'll pretend until you are."

Bernadine savored the sight of her friend's familiar face. "Have I told you how much I love having you as a sister of my heart?"

"Not today, no."

Tina always had the ability to see through whatever smoke screen Bernadine threw up to mask her true feelings.

"I love you, Tina Craig."

"And I love you too, Ms. Bernadine—Mal can kick rocks—Brown."

"How about we go get something to eat?"

"I'm all yours."

When they returned from dinner, Lily and Trent joined them to view the artist's rendering and blueprint for the B&B. "Tina, this is lovely," Bernadine gushed, taking in the sitting porches, the turrets, gables, and gingerbread trim.

"It's called a painted lady. There are some in the Bay Area

near Oakland and some back east. I love the style. And they're all painted striking colors. I want this to be purple and indigo."

Lily said, "Looks like a house that could have easily been here in the nineteenth century."

Trent nodded. "How many bedrooms?"

"Five is the plan for now."

He scanned the rolled-out blueprint. "Lot of architectural detailing."

"I know. I want the exterior to be as memorable as the interior. It'll look great on a travel site."

Bernadine agreed. "I can see the rockers on the porches."

"And lots and lots of roses," Lily added.

Tina said, "Roses and hydrangeas, and mass plantings of giant zinnias. Inside, I want old-fashioned four-posters, flat screens, en suite bathrooms, gas fireplaces. I'd originally wanted real ones, but Sara, my architect, talked me out of it. Too much work. Flues, ashes, all that."

Trent said, "She's right." He continued his scan. "May take time to find the carpenters able to handle the outside trim work. This isn't a standard, suburban cookie-cutter job."

"I was worried about that, but if we have to wait for the spring to open, I'll be okay with it. I want it done right."

Bernadine agreed.

They spent the next hour putting together a task list and a tentative schedule. Trent asked questions about Tina's choices for flooring, paint colors, the number of electrical outlets per room.

At one point Tina asked, "Can we put heated flooring in the bathrooms?"

He looked up. "Sure, if your budget can handle it."

"It can."

"Adding it, then."

When they were done, Tina seemed pleased. She was the leading financial adviser for the Bottom Women's group and Bernadine knew there was no one savvier when it came to investments. If Tina felt a B&B would thrive in Henry Adams, Bernadine saw no reason to doubt it.

CHAPTER
5

Thursday evening, everyone filed into the Dog for the monthly town meeting. Amari, Brain, and the Clark sisters loaded up their plates at the buffet and settled into one of the red leather booths by the back wall. Amari enjoyed the meetings. They reminded him of a family reunion. He also liked that he and the other kids were allowed to give their opinion on whatever was being discussed. As people milled around getting food and using the gathering as a chance to catch up with others they hadn't seen for a while, he was pleased to see Rocky back from her honeymoon. Wearing her apron and a smile, she moved through the crowded diner like the boss that she was, while her new husband, Mr. James, sat talking with the new teacher, Mr. Abbott.

Preston leaned over. "Glad Mr. James is back. I like Mr. Abbott and all, but I missed him."

Amari agreed. Mr. James was family. He'd instilled in Amari a passion for learning, something he never envisioned for himself back when he was in Detroit stealing cars, and he'd always be grateful.

"Tamar's here," Tiffany said.

Amari loved every inch of his six-foot-tall great-grandmother, from the long silver hair to the wealth of white-gold bangles on her wrists. Dressed in a flowing blue-and-black caftan, she had the air of a queen. She was known for her wit and devotion to the town, and for driving like an Indy qualifier in her old truck named Olivia. Since getting a bunch of speeding tickets from the new county deputy Davida Ransom last fall, she'd slowed her roll, but nothing would keep her from being Henry Adams's Matriarch in Charge. She stopped at the front table to speak with Amari's parents and Ms. Bernadine. From the ice in her eyes and tight set of her jaw, Amari got the feeling that something or someone had set her off. He reviewed his own actions of the past few days, couldn't come up with anything that might have placed him on the hot seat, and relaxed.

Leah said, "I wonder who Tamar's mad at?"

"Me, too," Preston echoed as the conversation up front continued.

Tiffany dipped a fry in the ketchup on her plate. "After the smackdown she gave me when we first moved here, I'm never making her mad. Ever."

Truthfully, Tiff had earned that smackdown; she'd been a mouthy, unlikable mess, but Amari kept that to himself. Since none of his friends were the cause of whatever set Tamar off, he relaxed. Moving his attention across the room, he spotted Mr. Clark in the buffet line.

"Has that crazy lady with the Chihuahua been banned from the store?" he asked Leah. Amari and Preston worked there on weekends, so they knew about Monday's incident, as did everyone else in town.

"No. Just the dog," she replied. "Dad says she's eccentric, but harmless."

Preston sipped his water and said, "Eccentric. A polite word for *crazy*."

Wyatt and Zoey came into the diner with Devon, Lucas, Jaz, and Alfonso and Maria Acosta. Whose dad was the town's fire chief. They took seats at a couple of booths nearby. Now that the number of kids had increased, one booth was no longer large enough to hold them all. Amari thought that a good thing, because if Devon started the whole make-OG-paint-the-fence thing, he didn't want to be collateral damage when his brother was torched by the glares from some of the adults in the room, even if others, like their dad, agreed with the idea.

The room suddenly went quiet. Searching for the reason, he looked to the entrance and saw his grandfather. Every eye in the place was on Mal, and the way his lips tightened in response made Amari hurt inside. Amari's eyes strayed to Devon. The smug smile and the gleam in his eye indicated Devon planned to show out, and Amari wanted to reach across the room and smack him upside his round head. For a kid who once wanted to be a preacher, his little brother had a side that was all about the devil.

Preston whispered, "Look at Tamar's face."

Amari saw anger, fury, and hurt. She seemed as disappointed with her son as they all were. It made him wonder if Mal's showing up at the meeting had been the subject of her earlier conversation with his parents and Ms. Bernadine.

As the OG made his way through the room and took up a position by the kitchen doors, Amari saw sympathy from people like Mr. Bing, and winter in the face of Ms. Bernadine. Finally, the sound of the mayor's gavel opening the meeting drew everyone's attention to the front of the room.

Things began as always with his dad thanking everyone for coming, before moving on to business.

"The town-wide security system is up and functioning. The colonel has the details."

Brain's adopted dad, retired Marine colonel Barrett Payne, the head of town security, was a tall, buff, no-nonsense bad-ass, and although he and Brain had had trouble being father and son at first, they now had each other's back. "As Trent said, the new system is fully functional and proved its worth by helping us prevent what could have been a tragedy at Gemma's place a few weeks ago."

Amari remembered all the drama of that night when a crazy social worker tried to set fire to Ms. Gemma's house. He looked over at her seated on the far side of the room with Mr. Clark and could tell by her blazing eyes that she was still mad about the worker putting her and her kids in danger.

"The company that provided the equipment was pleased by the report we sent and are coming out in a few days to test enhancements that will keep it from being hacked. I doubt we'll have that issue here, but they want to use our system as a guinea pig before they offer it to companies and cities that do face hacking problems."

Zoey's dad, Doc Reg, asked, "Will we get to keep the system?"

"Yes. Thanks to Bernadine's connections, tech companies are lining up to use Henry Adams to test their prototypes, and we're here to accept all offers. Any other questions?"

No one had any, so the colonel retook his seat at the table with his wife, Sheila.

The next report was from Alfonso and Maria's dad, Fire Chief Luis Acosta. "The firehouse is up and running and ready to go." Applause greeted the news. "We'll have the ribbon cutting on Saturday at noon and everyone is invited. So far, we have nine men and women trained to be volunteer firefighters, but we're looking into hiring a couple of certified people, too. I'll keep you posted on that. Any questions?"

No one had anything for him, so he retook his seat next to his mother-in-law, Mrs. Ruiz.

Amari's dad thanked them. "Now, I want to welcome a few new people to the community. First, Sam and Brenda Miller, owners of the new coffee shop and bakery. They come to us from Vegas."

In response to the applause, the couple stood. It was Amari's first time seeing them. He didn't care about the coffee shop part. The few times he'd tasted coffee, he'd been shocked by how awful it tasted. He liked the idea of a bakery, though. It made him think about the one in Detroit that often gave poor kids like him day-old doughnuts and pastries. At the time he hadn't known the things were stale; they were filling and sweet.

His dad asked the couple, "The grand opening is tomorrow?"

Mrs. Miller responded, "Yes. Six a.m."

A buzz of excitement filled the room. Amari's eyes strayed to his grandfather, who didn't appear as impressed as everyone else. Amari wondered why. It came to him that maybe he saw the bakery as competition for the diner.

Next up was the new custodian, Ms. Lisa Stockton. Amari glanced Devon's way and saw him laughingly say something to Zoey, who gave him a scathing eye roll in return. Since their dad introduced Ms. Stockton to the class the day she was hired, Devon had been making jokes about her resembling a frog and wanted everyone to secretly call her Mr. Toad. Nobody signed on. Amari supposed Devon had said something along those lines to Zoey just now. Granted, with her acne-scarred skin, bulbous eyes, and chubby body, she did resemble a mud-brown toad. Amari liked bestowing nicknames, but not one that would intentionally hurt a person's feelings.

"Thanks for the welcome," Ms. Stockton responded to the round of applause. "I wish I could stay, but I'm on the clock and need to get back to work." With a wave she made for the exit.

Mr. Abbott was introduced next, but because he'd been eating at the Dog since taking over for Mr. James, most people had already met him and knew his story; still, he did stand and nod thanks.

"Last but not least, Ms. Tina Craig, a longtime friend of Bernadine's." The woman was tall and tan and had red hair. As she stood and smiled in response to her welcome, his dad said, "Ms. Craig is going to build a bed-and-breakfast behind the Sutton Hotel."

Amari quietly asked Leah, "What's a bed-and-breakfast?"

"It's like a hotel in a house. You get a room, but the owner just gives you breakfast."

Having stayed in hotels on vacation, he was puzzled by her explanation. "No lunch or dinner or room service?"

She shook her head. "Only breakfast."

He didn't understand why people would stay in a place where you only got breakfast. He made a mental note to ask his mom about it.

His dad added, "In a perfect world, we'd have Ms. Craig's

place built before winter so she could start taking reservations, but as I told her, a lot of things need to be done first."

Former mayor and now barber Riley Curry stood up and declared, "Sounds like a losing proposition to me. No one's going to stay in a bed-and-breakfast. Something more profitable could be built on that land."

"Oh, sit down!" yelled his boss, Kelly Douglas, and mumbles of agreement followed.

He ignored it and plowed ahead. "I'm going to run for mayor next year, and I—"

"Will get one vote this time, instead of two," Bing called out. Snickering followed.

Amari saw Ms. Craig try hiding her smile and fail.

Looking perturbed, Ms. Bernadine asked, "What do you want built instead?"

"I don't know, but when I become mayor—"

A chorus of boos rained down, as did more yells that he sit his behind down, effectively drowning out whatever else he planned to say. When the derision continued, he glared and sat.

"Eccentric," Preston cracked.

Grinning, Amari gave him a high five.

His dad then gave details on the upcoming reunion: how many people were expected and the weekend's agenda. Amari knew how hard his parents had been working to get everything locked down, and how excited they were about seeing their old crew again.

Leah said quietly, "My mom's coming for the reunion."

Amari and Preston turned to her. That she had issues with her mom was no secret. "She staying at your house?" Preston asked.

"Dad said no. Hoping she doesn't make him change his mind."

Amari looked over at Tiff. She met his eyes briefly then turned her attention to the front table without showing any reaction to her sister's comment. Tiffany was changing. Lately, she seemed less focused on being a brat, which was fine with him. She was no longer easy to read, though, and he wasn't sure how he felt about that.

His dad continued, "That's the last thing on the formal agenda. Anybody have—"

Tamar stood and cut him off. "How much does Mal still owe?"

Amari tensed. Her face was icy as it had been earlier. Everyone sent furtive looks Mal's way.

In response he pushed off the wall. "I've paid back almost half."

His scowl showed he didn't appreciate being called out, but Amari was pretty sure Tamar didn't care. Stealing the money had been stupid, and she didn't do stupid, especially from family.

"So you still owe thirty-five thousand?" she challenged.

His chin rose angrily. "Yes. And I want to apologize to you, Bernadine, and everyone else."

Amari waited for him to continue the apology, to let the town know he owned what he'd done, sincerely and humbly like the great man he, Brain, and the rest of their crew looked up to and loved. But he didn't continue. He resumed his position against the wall and crossed his arms over his chest. He was done apparently. By the quizzical looks on faces around the room, others had been expecting more, too. Amari was embarrassed, angry, and hurt. He had no name for the myriad conflicting emotions roiling his insides, but tears burned the corners of his eyes. "I have to go," he told Brain.

"Where?"

But he was already out of the booth. Crossing the now silent room with everyone watching him was one of the hardest things he'd ever done. There was concern on the faces of his parents, especially his mom's, but he kept going. Reaching the exit, he pushed open the door and stepped outside into the cool night air. Hot tears slid free and trailed down his cheeks. Furiously dashing them away, he walked home.

An hour later, he was in his pajamas brooding while propped up in bed, when a soft knock sounded on the door. "Come in." He figured it was one of his parents returning. They'd checked on him after the meeting, making sure he was okay, and reassuring him that his reasons for leaving were legit. Instead, when the door opened, there stood Tamar. Surprise made him sit straight up.

"Hey there, Amari."

"Hey, Tamar."

"Can we talk for a minute or two?"

Wondering why she'd come, he nodded. She came in and sat on the edge of his bed. For a moment, the deep concern in her eyes almost made his tears start again.

She asked, "Was worried when you left the meeting. What happened?"

Being truthful was always best when answering her questions, so he tried to explain. "I—I just expected him to give a real apology. And when he didn't . . . I had to go."

"Understood. Everyone expected more, but be that as it may, his stealing was wrong. I know it. You know it. The whole town knows it. Mal does, too."

"Then why didn't he act like it?"

She shrugged. "Pride maybe? You'll have to ask him."

Amari had no intention of asking him anything.

"Heroes can have feet of clay," she said.

"Dad's a hero. He'd never steal."

"You're probably right. Your dad is principled and very special. I wish his father was more like him," she noted wistfully. "But we all walk our own paths. Mal is Mal. Trent is Trent."

"So what do I do with how mad I am?"

"When you figure that out, let me know."

He'd expected her to have an answer that would make him feel better.

"Sometimes all we can do is wait and let the game play out."

"I guess."

"It's hard for me, too. Patience is not one of my virtues, which is why I called him out at the meeting. I probably owe him an apology for that, but I'm so angry."

"Is it wrong that I don't want to be around him until things get fixed?"

"No."

"Dad said the same thing, but I just wanted to check with you, too."

She gave him a soft smile. "You're very special also, Amari. You shine with truth, honesty, and life."

He felt better.

"You're not perfect."

He gave her a look.

"None of us are, but you're special in the way that your dad is, and that's perfect enough for me."

"Thanks, Tamar."

"You're welcome. Your grandfather will get himself together, but that doesn't mean I'm going to let him off the hook until he does, and neither should you. He hurt us all. Particularly Bernadine, and there's no getting around the consequences."

"Devon thinks he should paint the fence."

"Has he told Mal?"

Amari nodded.

"That's not a bad idea. Don't tell Devon I agree, though. I love him, but his 'insufferable quotient' is already high enough."

Amari grinned.

The concern returned to her eyes. "If you need to distance yourself from Mal, that's okay. Just don't stop loving him. He'll get it together."

"Okay."

She stood.

Amari said sincerely, "Thanks for checking on me."

"You're welcome. Bye now."

After her exit, Amari thought back on all she'd said. It was okay to be mad at Mal, but he could still love him. He wasn't sure how to separate the two, but he'd give it time. He had patience. It was one of the first things you learned as a car thief.

OUT AT THE motel on 183, the woman known as school custodian Lisa Stockton carefully pulled off the ugly latex mask that disguised her true features and studied herself in the mirror. Where Stockton had pocked brown skin, hers was brown too, inherited from her African American father and Hawaiian mother, both of whom had passed away decades ago. Due to her ancestry, she looked years younger than her true age of forty and her features were still supermodel gorgeous. She next drew off the wig with its mass of small twists and the cap beneath to let her dark short-cut hair breathe. After zipping herself out of the lightweight body suit that made her thin frame more corpulent, she donned a robe and sat down to eat the burger and fries she'd picked up for dinner.

At the town meeting she'd seen the targets in real life for the first time. They impressed her as nice people, but that didn't matter. One of the targets' federal grand jury testimony cost two powerful Russian mob bosses their freedom, and no good deed goes unpunished. The meeting also added to her concerns about getting the job done. Was the town's security system more advanced than her tech's ability to shut it down long enough to make the hit and successfully get the hell out of town? She wished the government had set the Millers up in a more cosmopolitan place. She was being paid well, but not enough to get caught and jailed because of a cutting-edge bumpkins' town in the middle of nowhere. Certain she'd find a solution, she finished her meal.

AFTER THE MEETING, the Dog was all but deserted as Mal sat in a back booth nursing a cup of coffee. The caffeine would keep him awake longer than he wanted, but he didn't much care.

"I'm getting ready to lock up."

He glanced up to see Rocky and acknowledged her statement. "I need to be getting out of here, anyway. We haven't had a chance to talk to you since you and Jack came back. How was the honeymoon?"

"We had fun. Seeing his mother was less fun, but his dad always balances out her drama. I hear you got laid off."

"Yeah. Applied to be a janitor over at the school. Trent's

waiting for approval from Marie. She's up in Alaska with Gen and TC." Rocky had always been the daughter he'd never had, and before the theft, their relationship had been one he'd treasured. Now he wasn't sure where they stood. "How mad are you at me?"

"No more or less than everyone else you know. Pitiful apology, by the way."

He shot her a look of irritation.

She wasn't intimidated. "Friends should always tell friends the truth. Right?"

He didn't reply.

"The answer is 'right,' Mal."

Lips tight, he replied, "Here's another truth. I'm getting real tired of folks dogging me about what I did."

"Then how about owning it like you should? You keep acting like it wasn't a big deal and we should all move on. Not going to happen."

"I'm not the first person around here who's screwed up."

"No, you aren't. But you're the only person who helped themselves to seventy thousand dollars that wasn't yours."

He was tired of hearing that also. "It'll take me years to pay it back on what I may be making."

"Probably, but that doesn't mean you get a pass on doing it."

He kept seeing Amari walking out of the town meeting. Although he told himself the exit had nothing to do with him, in his heart he knew it was just wishful thinking. "Any idea why Amari took off?"

Rocky sighed. "Knowing him, I'd say he was as disappointed by your feeble apology as the rest of us were, but I could be wrong. Have you talked to him or any of the other kids about this?"

He shook his head, adding, "Truthfully, I haven't figured out how yet, or what to say." He didn't share Devon's recommendation about the fence because, like Trent, she'd probably agree. He also kept to himself that Devon and Amari left the table at Trent and Lily's rather than continue dinner. The memory still made him hurt.

"What about Tamar?"

"No." Her calling him out at the meeting had been infuriating and embarrassing. He'd felt like a six-year-old. He'd have to speak to her at some point, but he wasn't ready, and if her performance tonight was any indication, she wasn't, either.

Rocky said gently, "Go home." She took his coffee cup. "Get this mess figured out so you can find some peace, and we who love you can do the same."

He wanted to tell her how hard this was on him, but didn't know how to do that, either. Instead, he slid from the booth and said, "See you tomorrow."

"Night, Mal."

Rocky watched him leave. Shaking her head at the mess he'd made of his life, she went to the kitchen to grab her things and head home.

CHAPTER
6

The following morning at six o'clock sharp, Mayor Trent July cut the big blue ribbon in front of Miller's Coffee and Things and declared it officially open. Bernadine and Tina were among the many people at the short ceremony and added their applause to Trent's announcement.

Bernadine was pleased by the large crowd. She had no worries that the coffee shop would negatively impact the Dog's bottom line. Residents who bought coffee would still walk down the street to sit down and have breakfast there. She was a bit concerned with how the shop would do once the novelty wore off. A drop-off in traffic was inevitable, but if the service was good and the pastries lived up to the hype, there was no reason the business couldn't succeed. The only competition they had was from a shop in Franklin. It offered prepackaged pastries. She didn't see plastic-wrapped products winning out over the fresh-baked breads whose scents were now wafting through the air.

As they lined up to enter, Tina said to her, "My parents owned a bakery when I was growing up in Minnesota."

"I didn't know that."

"Spent my teen years covered in flour. Hated the place at the time. I'll have to ask the Millers if they'd be a supplier for my B&B. Nothing like fresh pastries to kick off your morning."

The line moved slowly so there was time for her and Tina to chat with friends like Doc Reg and his wife, Roni, the Paynes, and Trent's assistant, Bobby Douglas. New custodian Lisa Stockton exited the shop carrying a cup of coffee and a small white bag bearing the shop's logo. Passing Bernadine, she nodded before heading off.

"Morning, Bernadine."

Bernadine turned and was surprised to see Kyle Dalton, the tall, fit, sandy-haired son of local county sheriff Will Dalton. Her sympathies rose immediately. "Hey, Kyle. How's your dad?" Vicky, his mom and Will's wife, had recently passed away after losing a long hard-fought battle with breast cancer. It had been a week or so since Bernadine had seen Will.

"Doing his best under the circumstances. I finally convinced him that Mom wouldn't want him working twenty-four/seven to cover his grief, so he and I just got back from a trip to Wyoming. We did some fishing, rode some trails. Talked."

The sadness in his sky-blue eyes pulled at her heart. "I'm so sorry."

"Thanks."

"I want you to meet my friend Tina Craig. She'll be opening a B&B here soon."

They nodded in greeting.

Bernadine told Tina, "Kyle is an agent with the Bureau."

Tina appeared impressed.

Bernadine asked him, "Are you heading back to Topeka?" He worked out of a small government office there.

"No, going to hang here with Dad for a week or two. Make sure he's okay."

"And how are you doing?"

"My heart's broken, too. Miss her so much." His grief was palpable. "Probably always will."

Having lost her own mom early in life, Bernadine knew that to be truth. "We're here if you or your dad need anything."

"I know, and it's appreciated. How are things going in town? Any issues?"

"No. It's been pretty quiet."

"Dad told me about the embezzlement. You sure you don't want law enforcement to intervene?"

"No. We'll handle it our way."

"Okay," he replied skeptically. "I hope Mal knows how lucky he is."

"I hope so, too." Although she did wonder.

"I should get going. I'm here if you need me, too. Nice meeting you, Ms. Craig."

"Same here and my condolences on your loss."

"Thank you."

Carrying his coffee and white bag, he walked away.

Bernadine and Tina finally entered the shop. Sam and his wife, Brenda, were working the counter along with two new staff members hastily introduced as Erin Gordon and Mike Dere. Erin was a tall, brown-skinned woman with glasses and back-brushing locs, while Mike, with his earring, blond

man-bun, and flirty green eyes, drew Tina's immediate interest. "You think I could hire him away as my personal towel
holder after a long soak at the B&B?"

Bernadine laughed. "Stop."

"It's a reasonable question."

"You have shoes in your closet older than him."

"Probably, but a girl can dream. And besides, it's our duty
to support the younger generation."

Bernadine paid for their purchases and led the way out
before Tina could put Mike in the bag with her croissants.

Outside was a small cleared area where a few benches, tables, and chairs had been placed. She and Tina picked a table
and sat. It was a windy fall day.

Tina said, "I like this little spot."

"Trent's idea. We're thinking of installing a few more. He
thought it might be nice to have spaces where people could sit
outside and sip their coffee, read, or just stop and catch their
breath." The area directly across the street from the church
offered an unobstructed view of Main Street, the rec center,
and the school.

"Henry Adams is lovely, Bernadine."

"I agree."

"I can't wait to move here. It's so quiet and peaceful. No
drama, no craziness."

"We've had our share of both over the years." She told
Tina about the madness tied to Riley, Cletus, and the death
of crooked banker Morton Prell, then added the story of the
deadly fire set by Odessa Stillwell that took the lives of Mike
and Peggy Sanderson. She finished up detailing all the damage set off by the riot tied to Zoey's gold. "It's not always
quiet and peaceful."

"I guess not," Tina said after hearing everything.

"But I wouldn't want to live anywhere else," Bernadine confessed. "This place gets in your blood." Her attachment had taken root almost from the moment she arrived. Back then, the town was void of modern-day perks like Wi-Fi, cell phones, and air conditioning, a luxury she'd enjoyed most of her adult life, but it hadn't deterred her. The welcoming spirit of residents like Tamar, Trent, and Bing Shepard had offset the wrongheaded protestations of Riley Curry, who had been convinced her wealth was acquired illegally. Another draw had been the town's devotion to its past. She liked being a part of an historic place steeped in the race's struggle to chart its own destiny. Her roots were now sunk deep, and she planned to be a resident until she drew her last breath.

"Bernadine?" Tina's voice broke her reverie.

"Sorry. Was just thinking about how far this place has come and how attached I am to it."

"Nothing wrong with that."

Across the street at the school, the kids were arriving to begin their day, and Bernadine checked the time on her watch. She was enjoying Tina's company, but it was time to get her day moving, too. "I'm going to head to the office. Do you want to come with me? Or I can drive you back to the house if you want."

"It's such a nice day, I think I'll sit here for a while, if that's okay with you."

"Sure. We can hook up for lunch later."

"Sounds like a plan."

Leaving Tina, Bernadine struck out for her office. Noticing Reverend Paula's truck in the church's driveway, she crossed the street to see how her trip to Oklahoma had gone.

She found the good reverend in her office. "Hey, Paula. Welcome home. When did you get back?"

"Last night. I meant to text you, but I was so worn out I went straight to bed."

"That's okay."

"Sit," Paula said, gesturing to a chair. "How's the new coffee shop?"

"Great."

"I'll run over there in a few. How are you?"

"I'm good. Stopped by to find out how the trial went?"

Paula sighed. "Aunt Della was convicted of manslaughter and sentenced to fifteen years. At her age, she'll probably die there." The aunt had been charged with the death of her daughter, Lisa.

"I'm so sorry."

"So am I. If she'd let me get her a good lawyer, things might have turned out differently."

"Did the evidence support the charge?"

"I suppose. According to Della, Lisa's death was an accident. She said Lisa and my grandfather got into an argument. He grabbed Lisa. Della tried to separate them, and Lisa fell against the edge of the kitchen table and cracked her skull."

"Oh no! Do you believe her?"

She shrugged. "When my grandfather's will was read this past summer, Della made it sound like she was more involved than that, but only she and God know the truth. At the trial, the prosecutor asked why they didn't call 911. She said my grandfather didn't think the police would believe the story about the death being accidental, so they waited until dark, buried her behind the house, and told everyone Lisa had left town—which we all believed for nearly fifteen years, until her skull was found this summer."

"And Robyn? Is she going to be allowed to stay with you?" Robyn was Lisa's teenage daughter. She'd been a toddler when her mother disappeared.

"Yes. Her father filed the paperwork giving up his rights, so she's mine to raise now."

Bernadine thought that a good thing.

"So, now," Paula said, "how are things here?"

"Good. We'll be dedicating the new fire station tomorrow morning, and my friend Tina Craig is in town. She brought the blueprints for the B&B she wants to open."

"Great. And Mal?"

"What about Mal?"

"Did you reconcile while I was away?"

"No, and I doubt we will. Not after all that's happened. He's back, though. The oil company laid him off."

Paula eyed her seriously for a moment and Bernadine tensed, waiting to be lectured to, but instead, the reverend said, "I'm not going to tell you how to handle your business, but if you need to talk, I'm here."

"Thanks," Bernadine replied, and she meant it. "I should get going." She rose from her chair. "Make sure you check out the coffee shop. The croissants will change your life."

"Will do."

Pleased that Paula hadn't pressed her about Mal, Bernadine left the church and continued her walk to the office. On the way, Mal drove past her in his truck and tooted the horn. She didn't break stride. Watching the truck drive out of sight, she threw an imaginary dart at the imaginary dartboard bearing his face that she carried in her head and wondered how long it would take to get him out of her heart once and for all.

At the office, she put him out of her mind and stopped by Lily's office. "What's on your plate for today, Lil?"

"Handling last-minute details for the fire station ribbon cutting in the morning," Lily replied from behind her well-ordered desk. "Other than that, not much. Trent heard back from Marie. She's okay with Mal taking the job at the school."

"Good. As I said before, he needs a job. When do the three of them get back?"

"Sunday, late. Trent and I will pick them up from the airport."

"Okay. Got a text from Gemma last night. She wants to take the kids to Hawaii for Christmas. Can you hook up the plane tickets and the rest?"

"I'd love to. I'll call her later and get the dates. Glad she decided to go."

Bernadine agreed. Lucas and Jasmine Herman inherited a small fortune from their late parents' estate, which included time-shares in Orlando and Maui. Gemma, having spent most of her life struggling as a single parent, had been reluctant to tap into their wealth, but Lucas's insistence on the trip seemingly changed her mind. "I'm going to meet up with Tina for lunch. Until then I'll be in the office."

"Okay."

At her desk, Bernadine booted up her laptop and checked her email. Finding nothing that needed her immediate attention, she sent a text to her sister, Diane, to say hello. Their lifelong, ugly relationship had mellowed somewhat since the divorced Diane struck out on her own and moved to Kansas City a few months ago. Bernadine doubted they'd ever be

close as sisters were supposed to be, but at least she no longer felt the urge to strangle Diane on sight. Bernadine was in
the process of reading Diane's response when a soft knock on
her open door drew her attention away from the phone. The
woman standing there wearing a nice dress and heels appeared vaguely familiar, but she couldn't put a finger on why.
"Yes? May I help you?"

"I don't know if you remember me, but I met you at Rocky's
wedding. I'm Ruth Smith. I . . . was with Mal July."

Bernadine masked her surprise.

"May I come in?" Ruth asked, her smile hesitant.

Bernadine sensed her nervousness. Curious as to what she
wanted and if drama was involved, she gestured to a chair.

She sat and looked around. "You have a nice office."

"Thank you."

As if gathering courage, Ruth drew in a deep breath. "I . . .
asked around about you and I'm told you own Henry Adams."

"I do."

"Must be nice to have enough money to own a whole town."

Bernadine didn't respond.

"I run the switchboard at the oil company where Mal
worked. Before they laid him off," she added.

Bernadine asked quietly, "Why are you here?"

"I'm sorry. I know you're probably real busy, but I came to
ask if you and Mal are back together?"

That caught Bernadine so off guard it took a second or two
to reply. "Why?"

"He's not returning my calls or answering my texts."

"Ah." Bernadine drew no satisfaction from the confession
but did wonder about Mal distancing himself. Was the relationship done?

Ruth's fingers fidgeted with the handbag on her lap. "I know you two were hooked up for some time before we met, so I just wondered if that could be the reason."

"No, it isn't."

"Oh. Okay. I think he's a good man."

Bernadine didn't respond to that, even as she thought back on how she'd thought the same once upon a time. She assumed Mal hadn't shared the reason for their breakup and she had no intention of doing so, either. "Anything else?"

Ruth shook her head and stood. "Thank you for your time."

"You're welcome."

And she exited.

Alone again, Bernadine was glad there'd been no drama. In a way she felt sorry for Ruth. It had to have taken a fair amount of courage to show up and ask the question she had, but there was also a hint of desperation. If a man was no longer returning her calls, no way would she come to his former love with questions. But seeing as how every woman dealt with men differently, she threw another imaginary dart at her imaginary Mal July dartboard and returned to her sister's text.

MAL WAS SITTING at Clay's table fuming. "I blew my horn at her and she straight-up ignored me." That Bernadine hadn't so much as paused irked him still.

Clay asked, "Why do you keep trying to talk to her when she's told you there's nothing there?"

"She could at least wave."

Clay sighed and shook his head. The doorbell sounded. "Let me get that. It's probably Ms. Langster."

And it was. Clay escorted her in. She was wearing jeans

and a nice gray blazer over a white blouse. When she saw Mal, distaste flared on her face for a moment, so he assumed she was mad at him, too. She took the seat Clay offered and set her large handbag on the floor beside her chair. "How are you, Mr. July?"

"Fine. You?"

"I'm well, thanks for asking."

With that done, she asked, "So, what can I do for you gentlemen?"

Clay explained the situation. When he finished, she looked between them and asked, "So, this David Dresden disappeared with your money, your cousin's, and the money Mr. July stole from Ms. Bernadine?"

Mal snarled silently.

She apparently sensed his irritation. "I just want to be clear on the story so I can decide whether I'm going to take your case or not."

Clay asked, "If you do, what would you charge?"

"Because I admire Ms. Bernadine, forty dollars an hour, plus expenses."

"Forty bucks an hour?" Mal echoed, surprised.

"My going rate is sixty. You're getting the town discount."

Discount or not, Mal still viewed the quote as steep.

She continued, "If we sign an agreement to go forward, you need to know that I can't do anything illegal, like break into his house, go through his bank account without his permission, or search his car. Any of that. This isn't television."

"Then what *can* you do?" Mal asked, still smarting.

"I can do my best to find him. If I do, theoretically we might get a lead on the money. I'll keep a running total of my expenses and report in as often as you'd like."

Mal caught Clay's eye. It was clear that he was concerned about costs, too. At her stated rate, twenty-four hours would cost them almost a grand. He was wondering if he could talk Trent into loaning him the money, when Bing came into the kitchen aided by his cane. He nodded a greeting at Ms. Langster and tossed a wad of cash on the table. "That's three thousand dollars, little lady, and I have more if you need it. If they don't want to hire you, I will. If only to stop the drama." His eyes locked on Mal. "And because Bernadine and the town deserved better."

Angry, Mal wanted to snap back, but knew he had no right.

Bing turned to Clay. "Sign the paperwork, Clayton, so Ms. Langster can get to work finding this crook." He left the kitchen.

She pulled out a contract. Clay signed it.

And that was that.

But as she prepared to leave, she told Mal in a serious voice, "Mr. July, if I do find Dresden and he still has the money, Mr. Dobbs and his cousin will be in a much better position to reclaim their share than you will."

"Why?"

"They'll have bank records to support their claims. Your part of the money is tied to theft. You can't claim stolen funds as your own."

Mal felt like he'd been kicked in the chest.

"Just so you know. I'll be in touch, gentlemen."

And she left.

Mal sat back and let out a deep sigh. This was getting worse and worse. His phone buzzed. It was a text from Rocky. *Ruth Smith waiting for you at the Dog. Been here over an hour.*

He dropped his head. Uttering a soft curse, he stood and

said to Clay, "Got something I need to take care of. I'll call you later."

Ignoring Clay's confusion, Mal picked up his keys and left.

On the drive back to town, he wondered why Ruth had come to Henry Adams and what she wanted. When he stopped taking her calls, he'd assumed she'd get the message that things were over between them and go on with her life. He wasn't going to be happy if she hadn't. Of course, it was possible that she was simply in town visiting a friend and wanted to say hello. Either way, she was not the woman he wanted in his life. Bernadine was; even if she didn't want the role.

He entered the Dog to the sounds of Gladys Knight singing "If I Were Your Woman," and glanced around. The breakfast rush was over. It was too early for lunch, though, so there weren't many people seated in the place. He spotted Ruth in a back booth. Before he could head that way, Rocky walked up, coffee carafe in hand. "I didn't know if you wanted to see her or not, but I got the impression that she'd sit and wait until Christmas. Seems like a nice enough woman."

He didn't respond.

"Talk to you later." She moved on and he set off toward Ruth.

Crossing the room made the few diners glance up from their plates and follow his progress, but he was getting better at ignoring the side eyes and whispers.

When he reached her, she smiled. "Hello, Mal. How are you?"

"Good. You?" Ruth was a pretty woman but not the one for him.

"I'm okay. I was told you own this place, so thought I'd

wait here until you showed up so we could talk. You have a minute to sit?"

He wanted to lie and say he had somewhere else he needed to be, but the only way to find out why she'd come was to deal with her head-on. So he sat.

She asked, "Have you eaten?"

He nodded. "I have. Why'd you stop by?"

"To find out why you're ignoring my calls and texts."

He sighed inwardly and said gently, "I'm not looking to be in a relationship right now, Ruth. I thought I made that clear the first time we went out."

"And then we went out again and again. Five times in the first two weeks, am I right?"

"Yes."

"And numerous times after."

She was correct about that too, but he didn't say it aloud.

"So, you understand why I got to thinking this was more than a casual sort of thing, especially when you took me to the wedding."

"The wedding was a mistake. The dates were, too. I'm sorry. Honestly—"

"Honestly, were you using me?"

Suddenly it was hard to breathe.

She smiled serenely. "I asked around and was told you stole a large amount of money from this place. Is that true?"

"Yes, and the oil fields were the fastest way to make restitution."

"And if you didn't want a relationship, what role did I play in this badly conceived drama?"

At that point, Mal realized Ruth Smith was way more astute than he'd given her credit for, and he wondered if this

might be how a male preying mantis felt just before the female bit his head off. "I figured Bernadine wouldn't want
anything to do with me after the theft, and I wanted to show
her I could get another lady and I was a bit lonely."

"So you were using me. I just talked to Bernadine a little
bit ago. I don't think she wants you back."

His eyes widened. No man wanted competing women in
his life talking to each other under any circumstances. Ever.

"Thanks for your honesty," she continued. "I appreciate it,
but I don't appreciate being used, especially not by a man I
had such high hopes for."

He offered the only thing he could say. "I'm sorry, Ruth."

"Yes, you are, and I'm sorry, too."

"That I played you?"

"For that, yes, and for the visit my brother will be paying
you."

Mal studied her and chuckled softly. "What? He coming to
beat me up?"

"I'm afraid so, but just enough to teach you a lesson. He
won't kill you or anything. He was a boxer back in the day.
Even made the Olympic team as an alternate, and he's very
protective of his big sister, whose feelings you admittedly tri-
fled with."

Mal froze and watched, stunned, as she got to her feet.

"You need to grow up, Malachi July. You're too old to be
stealing from people you claim to love and messing over a
woman who could've potentially loved you. Thanks for taking the time to speak with me. Good-bye."

And she walked to the exit.

Rocky came to the table. "What's wrong? You look like
you just saw a ghost."

"She said her brother is coming to whip my ass."

"Really? Anybody selling tickets?"

"I'm serious, Rocky."

"So am I. Somebody needs to knock some sense into you." She picked up Ruth's coffee cup. "Hmm. Wonder what I should wear?"

He stared with disbelief. She smiled and left him sitting there.

CHAPTER
7

Gary was packing up to leave the store for the day when his phone rang. Seeing Colleen's name on the caller ID made him want to ignore it, but he hit answer. "Hey, Colleen. What's up?"

"Goodness, Gary, you can't even say 'how are you?'"

He rolled his eyes. "What can I do for you?"

She gave him a small sound of impatience. "I want to know if I need to bring my own pillows."

"For what?"

"For when I stay with you and the girls next weekend."

All kinds of things went through his head. She was the mother of his girls, and by all rights he should be able to put up with her for a few days, but the memory of the pain on Leah's face pushed all that aside. He'd made a promise. "Sorry. We don't have room. The packet the committee emailed you has the names and the group rates for the hotels in Franklin."

"I'm not staying in a hotel."

He didn't plan to argue with her and so remained silent.

When he didn't respond, she asked, "Why should I have to stay at a hotel when I should be able to stay with you and my girls?"

"I'm sure you and Brad will be more comfortable at a hotel."

"He's not coming. He has to work."

He had yet to meet Colleen's new husband. Gary hadn't been invited to the wedding, of course. All he knew was that the man owned a landscaping company and was, according to Leah, nice. "Do you want me to make the reservation for you?"

"No. I want you to allow me to be with my daughters."

He held on to his temper. "I'm not saying you can't see them. I've never kept you from them, but you can't stay with us. There's no room."

"You can sleep on the couch."

"Make a reservation at the hotel, Colleen. You can see the girls when you arrive. Is there anything else?"

She snapped, "Stop being a jerk, Gary!"

He waited for more berating. Instead, she ended the call, and he quietly said, "Hallelujah."

The savory smells of chicken frying hit him as soon he entered the house. It was Leah's day to cook, and thanks to his uncle Terence's mentoring, she'd gotten very good. He found her in the kitchen.

"Smells great in here, Lee."

"Hey, Daddy. Thanks."

He snagged a drumstick from the done pieces waiting on a plate. "Oh, this is good."

She grinned. "I'm so glad Uncle TC taught us to cook. I didn't think I'd like it at first, but it's really just science." She paused to remove the rest of the pieces from the hot oil and placed them on the plate. "You have the mixing of chemicals, their reactions to each other, and the application of heat. Throw in weights, measures, and observation, and it all adds up to elements a scientist deals with all the time."

Savoring the drumstick, he chuckled. "Never heard cooking broken down quite like that before."

"I wonder if there are any chefs at NASA? I'll have to ask Brain's mom the next time I talk to her. I think cooking and science complement each other."

He watched her pull a casserole dish of macaroni and cheese from the oven, check the level of milk still visible, and slide it back in. "Not ready?" he asked.

"No, but almost."

"Where's your sister?"

"Upstairs packing for Zoey's sleepover."

"Oh, that's right. I forgot about that. We're meeting her at church on Sunday, right?"

"Right."

"What else are you cooking, Julia Child?"

She smiled. "Asparagus."

"Can't wait. Anything you need help with?"

"No, I got this."

"Okay. I'm going to go up and talk to Tiff for a minute."

He found his youngest angrily stuffing items in her pink overnight bag. "Hey? What's wrong?"

The glare she shot him brought him up straight. "Whoa, Tiff. What's the matter?"

She stopped packing and dropped down onto the edge of her bed. "Mom just called me."

"And . . . ?"

"She wants me to demand that you let her stay with us when she gets here next weekend."

"Demand?"

"Dad, I don't want to be in the middle of my parents' drama. She said all kinds of stuff about you deliberately keeping us from her, and that she was going to get a court order."

"What? I talked to her before I left work. I told her she could see you when she got here. There's no room for her to stay with us."

There were tears in her eyes. "Why is she such a witch? I'm a kid. I'm not supposed to have to deal with this."

Gary came over and sat beside her. He pulled her in against his side and gave her a strong hug. "You're right. You're a kid and kids shouldn't have to be pawns in whatever craziness their parents are doing. She's your mom and I've tried to be careful not to make you girls choose sides."

"I know, but she's not being nice. The whole time we were in Atlanta all she talked about was how terrible you were to her."

He didn't find that surprising. "There're always three sides to something like this: her side, my side, and the truth."

"Did Lee tell you what Mom said about her?"

"No."

"You can't let Lee know I told you, okay?"

Curious, he replied, "Okay."

"Mom told her she'll never get married if she keeps doing science."

"What!"

Gary seethed. He now understood why Leah was the way she was when he talked to her about her visit to Atlanta.

"Then she said it was too bad Lee looked like your ugly family instead of hers. Leah cried that night after we went to bed. She was quiet, but I heard her. It made me cry, too."

Gary's heart broke. "In spite of what your mom thinks, Leah is beautiful in so many ways. And you are, too."

"I know. She's going to marry Brain and be the most famous astrophysicist in the world."

"Yep."

"And I already told her I'm going to be president of her international fan club. I don't think Mom's going to get invited to the wedding."

He stifled his chuckle. "Did she hurt your feelings too, while you were there?"

"No. She just made me mad. Kept trying to get me to say you were a bad dad. When I wouldn't, she yelled at me. Said I must be stupid not to know the difference." She met his eyes. "I think you're a great dad."

Her words filled his heart. "Thanks. I think you and Lee are the best daughters a dad could ever have." He kissed her forehead. "I'll handle your mom, you get ready to go have fun with Zoey and your girls. Feeling better?"

She nodded. "Thanks."

"Good. Are you eating dinner here or there?"

"Here, and there. Zoey and her mom won't be here until seven." For someone so tiny, Tiffany could put away some food.

He stood. "Okay. And I'll be talking to your mom about this. If she has a problem with me, she shouldn't be dragging you into it." He took in her now relaxed stance. "Love you, Tiff."

"Love you too, Daddy."

As he walked to his bedroom, the idea of Colleen trashing Leah's spirit made him want to punch a wall. The urge to talk to Leah about the incident was strong, but he didn't want to betray Tiff's trust. His oldest rarely cried, and for her to do it alone with no one to comfort her or tell her not to believe Colleen's cruel words only increased his anger. Were it up to him, neither of them would ever visit Colleen again, but that would never fly. She was their mother, and until they reached eighteen she had the right to see them regardless of how they felt. As for the court order she'd talked about, he hoped she had more sense than to try that. He doubted a judge would rule in her favor if either of the girls were to testify on her own behalf. So for now, his only option was to continue to support them and their dreams with every fiber of his being. He'd also speak with Reverend Paula to find out if there was anything else he could or should be doing to help them stay strong.

A short while later, they had dinner, and as always, Leah's cooking knocked it out of the park. Everything was delicious. Once they were done, Leah was off duty, so she sat at the counter with her laptop while he and Tiff did cleanup. When they finished he said, "I want to do something as a family next summer. Any suggestions?"

Tiff asked, "Can we go to the Grand Canyon?"

That surprised him. "I like that idea. What about you, Lee?"

"I'm not sure what I want to do, but I like Tiff's idea."

"Okay," he said, "tell you what. Think about it and give me two choices each and we'll talk about them and figure it out."

They both beamed with approval.

"Do you have a preference?" Leah asked.

He shrugged. "Not really. Thought I'd let you two decide."

"You should get a choice, too," Tiffany replied. "You never do anything fun for yourself."

Leah agreed, "She's right, you know. All you do is work."

Admittedly, they were right. "Someone has to," he countered with a smile. "Kids are expensive."

"Do you need us to get jobs?" Leah asked, concern in her voice.

Sorry his quip unintentionally caused her worry, he replied, "No, not really. I make enough to keep a roof over our heads, but if you want more spending money, a job is the way to go."

"I think I might like working in the kitchen at the Dog," Leah said, as if thinking out loud. "Siz could help me be a better cook."

Tiff chimed in, "I've been wanting to learn to do hair. Do you think Kelly would teach me?"

The more he talked to his daughters, the more impressive he found them to be. "As long as the jobs don't interfere with your schoolwork."

Leah said, "Be easier for us to get around if I could drive."

Gary eyed her. "You want to drive?"

"I'm sixteen, Daddy. Everybody my age wants to drive."

He sighed. She was right again. With so much on his plate, driving lessons hadn't been a priority, mainly because Leah had never brought it up until now.

"Brain can always teach me if you don't have time," she offered.

"No, I'll make the time, and doesn't he still need an adult riding with him?"

"Yes. I forgot about that."

"Find out what we need to do to get started, like classes, costs, and all that, and we'll go from there."

Leah's smile lit up the room. "Thank you."

Tiff seemed equally happy. "You should get a Mustang, Lee. They're lit."

Gary chuckled. "No Mustangs. Nothing lit. The car will be used, but new to Lee."

Tiff did a mock pout. Leah didn't seem to mind, though.

Roni and Zoey came to pick up Tiff a bit later, and Leah left with Preston and his dad to head to the rec for movie night. As Gary watched Preston back slowly down the driveway, all he could think about was that he, too, was about to become the dad of a teenage driver. He prayed.

Later, as he sat in his pajamas in his bedroom watching television, he thought about what his life might look like once the girls were grown and gone and the house no longer echoed with their laughter, their comings and goings, or the lingering scents of Leah's cooking. He'd have nothing but the store. He'd still have Dads Inc., the town's support group for fathers, but little else in the way of social entertainment. He could remember when he looked forward to life and the future, but that changed when he gave up both to make an honest woman of Colleen. His love of reading was limited to going over the catalogs sent by automakers like GM and Chrysler so he'd be knowledgeable when speaking with customers about their potential purchases. His love of track died because there was no time for such a frivolous activity like morning or evening runs when faced with having to put food on the table for his family. And there definitely had been no way to pursue his desire to study law, because without a scholarship, he had no money for tuition. So now, two decades later, he faced a future that paid the bills and provided for his girls but offered nothing to who he was inside. Truthfully, he wasn't sure if the young man he'd once been even existed anymore. It certainly didn't feel as if he did. The girls pointed out that all he did was work—not something he wanted on his headstone. As a parent, he was supposed to set an example for his children in all aspects of life. They knew he had a strong work ethic and that he attended church, but other than the joy he found in them, no joy emanated from the Gary within for them to see or emulate. He found that troubling. Leah would be leaving for college soon and Tiff would be following a few year later. After that, he'd be rambling around the house alone. Dinner alone. Weekends alone. Going to bed and waking up alone. The thought of such a reality was depressing. He wanted more, he'd earned more, and more importantly, he deserved more. So he weighed the options. Take Door Number One and stay on his current trajectory knowing how lonely and bland the future would be, or take Door Number Two and make changes that might allow him personal joy and happiness. Gary had graduated at the top of his high school class; no one had been smarter, so he chose Door Number Two.

AMARI, BRAIN, AND Leah were handling concessions at movie night. Amari was on the popcorn, Leah was handling hot dogs, and Brain was at the nachos station. When they were younger they resented the endless list of assignments Tamar regularly volunteered them for, but now Amari enjoyed helping. Handling the orders made him feel like an adult. He knew everybody, and they knew him, so he liked the back-and-forth banter, except when he was quizzed about having a girlfriend. He wasn't sure why the older people were so interested in his nonexistent love life, but he was always grilled, albeit politely. Ever since Kyra and her family moved away, he'd had no one special in his life. He'd talked to her a few times right after the family left, but he hadn't heard from her all summer, so he assumed she'd moved on, and he wasn't putting himself out there to find out. So he was without a honey, and he had a better chance of scoring Cardi B's home address than finding another girl in a place as small as Henry Adams. In a way he envied Brain; he and Leah would probably be hooked up for life. His dad assured him he'd have a ton of ladies to consider once he got to college, so he hoped that was the truth. In the meantime, he was serving up popcorn. His first customers were Mr. James and Mr. Abbott. The new teacher appeared amazed by what was going on.

"How often do you all do this?"

Mr. James took his box of popcorn. "At least once a month."

"And anybody can come?"

"Yes. Amazed me and my son Eli the first couple of times we attended, too. Small-town fun."

Mr. Abbott took his popcorn, told Amari thanks, and the two teachers left to find seats.

Next in his line was the new custodian.

"Hi, Ms. Stockton."

"Oh, hi—um."

"Amari," he prompted.

She gave him a little smile. "Sorry, I'm still pretty new here, and I'm terrible with names."

"It's okay. Here's your popcorn. Enjoy the movie."

She nodded and moved off. Watching her search for a seat, he wondered if she'd found any friends yet. He was glad to see her, though, because movie night was a great place to meet people. She finally sat behind the Millers. In the row behind

her were the two new people who worked at the coffee shop—
the lady with the locs, and the guy with the dumb man-bun.

"Hey, Amari."

He shifted his attention to Ms. Bernadine and her friend
Tina, now standing in front of him.

"Hey, Ms. Bernadine. Hey, Ms. Tina. Would you like popcorn?"

They did, and once they had their bags, they, too, moved
away and searched for a seat. He didn't see the OG, though,
and wondered how he was doing or if he'd ever be a part of
the town's family again. The place was getting crowded. He saw
Zoey and her pajama party crew of Tiffany, Jaz, and Maria
roll in wearing matching, sparkly pink tees that said "BEING
A GIRL IS MY SUPERPOWER." He smiled and shook his head. His
mom passed behind him carrying a sleeve of drink cups and
said, "Ooo! I want one of those shirts."

He laughed.

The movies being shown were *Jumanji* and *Casablanca*.
He'd seen the old *Jumanji* and liked it, so he wanted to see
how the new one stacked up. He'd never seen *Casablanca* but
knew Bogart was a boss back in the day, and it was supposed
to be about fighting the Nazis, so he was looking forward to
watching it.

All the noise and chatter stopped as Tamar stepped on-
stage. She made an announcement inviting everybody to the
fire station ribbon cutting taking place in the morning. Once
she was done, Brain doused the lights and the opening credits
of *Jumanji* filled the screen.

An hour into the movie, the sounds of a scuffle drew his
attention. He and Brain stood up, but it was too dark to see

where it was coming from. Suddenly a male voice boomed loud enough to be heard over the movie. "THIS IS THE FBI! TURN ON THE LIGHTS! NOW!"

He and Brain froze until Tamar shouted at them, "Go!"

They flew to the switch box. The lights came on and what they saw made Amari's jaw drop. The locs lady from the café had a struggling Ms. Stockton in a headlock, and Man-Bun had a gun trained on them both. Stockton was furiously trying to fight her way free, but the locs lady, much taller and heavier, was not letting her go. Stockton was bucking and twisting, and clawed at the arm pressed against her throat, but she was finally bent down over the seat that once held Mrs. Miller, who was on her feet screaming, "We need a doctor! Please! My husband's been shot! Oh God!"

Chaos followed as *Jumanji* continued to play on the screen. Screaming people scrambled to get out of the way. Stockton was finally cuffed and dragged upright. Her wig was askew and there was something wrong with her face that Amari couldn't quite make out because of all the people in the way. Doc Reg raced up the aisle, knocking people aside. Amari saw his dad running, phone to his ear. Preston's dad and Fire Chief Acosta were sprinting, too. All hell had broken loose. Amari and Brain were speechless.

The Millers were flown by medical helicopter to the Hays hospital, and the woman they knew as Lisa Stockton was dragged out and taken into custody.

BERNADINE EYED FBI agent Kyle Dalton, who'd shown up at the end of the madness, and she wanted to scream at him for placing her people in danger. Two armor-piercing bullets had been shot into Sam Miller's back through his seat. The movie's loud soundtrack in tandem with the gun's silencer kept the shots from being heard. Stockton stood immediately and was moving out of the empty row she'd been sitting in when a quiet moment on the screen allowed Miller's cry for help to be heard, thus alerting the two Bureau agents. Given another few seconds, she might have gotten out of the auditorium and away. Holding on to her temper, Bernadine said, "Explanation, please."

Will Dalton stormed in. Upon seeing him, Kyle's lips tightened. He nodded his dad's way before replying to Bernadine, "The Millers are in the Witness Protection Program. Sam witnessed a mob hit. I'm not at liberty to say where, but two members of the Russian Mafia went to prison."

"And whose bright idea was it to relocate them here?"

"Mine."

The anger on the faces of Lily, Trent, and Barrett mirrored her own. "Why?"

"I thought they'd have a safe life here."

"But you didn't have the decency to let us know about any of it beforehand?"

"I wanted to, but my superiors wouldn't sign off."

"So, you and the Bureau placed dozens of lives in danger instead?"

"The Millers weren't supposed to be found."

"But they were," Trent pointed out. "How?"

It was obvious that Kyle didn't want to reveal the details, but his dad, Sheriff Will, who looked as if he wanted to take his son to the woodshed given the opportunity, snarled, "Tell us, Kyle!" Apparently, county officials had also been kept in the dark, or at least no one had informed the sheriff.

"One of our agents was compromised. Gambling debts."

Barrett Payne said, "So he cleared his debt by giving them up."

Kyle nodded.

Barrett swore under his breath.

"What happens now?"

"If Mr. Miller pulls through, he and his wife will be given new identities and relocated again."

"Will you let us know if he does?" Lily asked.

"No."

Bernadine shook her head.

Trent asked, "Are we going to be overrun by hit men thinking the Millers are still here?"

"We don't know."

Bernadine threw up her hands. "You don't know!"

Kyle said, "I don't and I'm sorry. We'll do our best to monitor the situation. I promise."

She wanted to yell that that wasn't good enough, but in the end, Kyle was simply doing his job, she told herself. His superiors were calling the shots, but the admission left her very unsettled. "What happens to Stockton?"

"She'll be tried for attempted felony murder and, if convicted, sentenced to a maximum-security prison. Apparently, there are international warrants out for her, too. This was not her first rodeo, but it is her first apprehension as far as we know. And she's a real pro. She was wearing a mask, a wig, and what's called a fat suit to alter the look of her body."

"A mask? That scarred face wasn't really her?"

"No."

"It certainly looked real."

"I know. Had it not been ripped during the struggle, and

she'd somehow managed to escape, we'd never know what she really looked like."

"Incredible," Will voiced.

Barrett said, "I'm surprised she took such a chance."

"Apparently, she thought she had a clear path. The movie was loud, and if our agents had been seated farther away, she might have pulled it off and gotten away."

Trent appeared confused. "But I had her credentials vetted by the county and she checked out. How did she accomplish that?"

"Not surprised. It's easy to give a phone number to a phishing service that lets you think you're talking to a real source, or place a false profile on a website, the government's included. Crime syndicates are very high tech these days. Very."

Bernadine asked, "Did you know she was here before tonight? Is that why you had the agents pretending to be employees at the shop?"

"Let's just say we knew someone was en route here."

"And you still didn't think we had the right to be informed."

He didn't respond to that, offering instead, "All I can say is I wish things had been done differently." He stood. "The agents interviewing everyone over at the auditorium should be done soon. We have others on the way to the woman's motel room. We'll need access to the school to look for additional evidence. May take us a couple of days to get out of your hair."

Trent responded: "Let me know when you're ready to see the school. I'll walk you over and open it up."

Kyle asked, "Why wasn't she at work tonight?"

"Her evening off."

"Any community college classes there tomorrow?"

"Yes."

"They'll need to be canceled."

Trent didn't hide his displeasure. "I'll call the dean."

Bernadine asked, "People are going to have questions about tonight; do I tell them?"

"We prefer that you don't."

Bernadine looked Will's way and she wondered if this was going to cause a rift in the sheriff's still-grieving household. His tight jaw showed his mood and he relayed that by saying, "This is crap on so many levels."

And she agreed.

Trent said, "As mayor, I'm going on record as disagreeing with the Bureau. We'll be having an emergency town meeting at the Dog in the morning to answer all questions. Leaving people in the dark is not how we operate here."

Bernadine wanted to cheer.

Trent turned to his wife. "Can you let the town know?"

"Will do."

Everyone looked pleased with the decision, except Kyle.

Will said, "I'll be here, too. I'm going home. Night, everybody. Night, son."

"Bye, Dad."

Will exited.

Trent said, "Let's go, Kyle."

Bernadine and the others spent a few more minutes formulating a plan for the meeting, and once that was settled, they all left for home, too.

CHAPTER
8

The next morning, while Trent and Will met in the Dog's office, Bernadine and Lily sat at the head table marveling at the sea of people filling the Dog's dining room. It was already standing room only and people were still filing in. Most of the town regulars were seated and waiting, including Tamar, Reverend Paula, the older kids, and their parents. Riley Curry was there too, trying to look important, and talking up residents from Franklin and other nearby towns who didn't appear interested in what he was saying. Bernadine guessed everybody in the county had heard about last night's drama from those who'd been there, which accounted for the sheer size of the crowd. Rocky and her crew were buzzing around like bees, serving breakfast and keeping the coffee carafes filled for those who wanted their morning jolt. Fragrant scents from the kitchen mingled with the noise of all the conversations. The dedication of the firehouse would be delayed until the meeting was over.

Bernadine nodded to Luis Acosta and his family as they

entered. Because he was a trained EMT, he'd aided Reg and the doctor on the helicopter that flew Sam Miller to Hays.

Still scanning the room, she spied Mal seated in a side booth with Clay and Bing. His eyes held hers and time seemed to stop. Everything they once shared rose to the surface, making Bernadine remember things she'd been fighting hard to forget, like the day he taught her how to fly a kite, the fun they'd had on their picnics, how new and special her attraction to him had been. Realizing she was sliding down the rabbit hole, she hastily broke the contact and turned away to find Lily staring her in the face. "Cutting those ties is going to be hard," Lily said sagely.

Bernadine didn't feign ignorance or reply.

Moments later, Trent and Will walked in. Trent came to the table. Will, dressed in civilian clothes, took up a spot nearby and the meeting began.

"As you may know," Trent said, "there was an incident here last night, and a man was shot. We were briefed afterward by federal authorities that it stemmed from their Witness Protection Program."

A buzz filled the room.

"Without informing us, Mr. and Mrs. Miller were relocated here because the authorities thought they'd be safe. They weren't. The shooter was apprehended. Mr. Miller and his wife will be moved elsewhere."

"How were they found?" Tamar asked.

"A glitch in the feds' system."

Bernadine approved of Trent's discreet response. Revealing the real reason served no purpose here, but she knew he'd tell Tamar the full story when he had the chance.

Bing asked, "Is Sam okay?"

Trent shrugged. "We don't know, and the feds won't be sharing that information going forward."

Luis Acosta spoke up. "He was alive when Doc Reg and I turned him over to the doctors."

But only barely, according to the phone call Bernadine received from Reg later.

Trent glanced around. "More questions?"

Riley had one. "How in the world did a hit man, or a woman in this case, wind up being hired as a custodian at our school? Who hired her, and will that person lose their job?"

Bernadine heard murmurs of support, and from the way Riley began preening, he'd heard them, too.

"I hired her," Trent said. "I had the background checks done. They were faked."

"You couldn't tell fake from real?"

"The references she listed turned out to be a phishing enterprise."

"Fishing? Why would you call a fishing place?"

"Phishing with a *ph*, Riley. Apparently, you don't know the difference between fake and real, either." Snickers followed.

Looking as if he had no idea what he'd missed, Riley declared, "Let me assure you that there will be no hit man hired on my watch as mayor."

Tamar countered, "Weren't you the one who told us fake news and tried to sell the town?"

Riley froze, looked chagrined, and retook his seat.

Trent asked, "Any other questions?"

Bing raised his hand. "Will whoever hired Stockton think the Millers are still here and send someone else?"

That same worry kept Bernadine awake last night.

Trent replied honestly, "We don't know, and neither do the feds."

Rumbles of concern rose. Bing said, "Then they need to come up with a plan. Or we do."

Trent said, "Your suggestion?"

"No new people in town until we're sure this has blown over."

Many people voiced support.

Trent replied, "But how will that help? We need a new janitor at the school. Do we not fill the position? We've been talking to people wanting to move into the new houses we'll be building in the spring. Do we tell them the homes are no longer available? We have a state-of-the-art coffee shop that opened yesterday, and there's no one to run the place. Should we let it sit empty?"

Security Chief Barrett Payne added his thoughts. "Bing, your concerns are valid, but the town can't spend the rest of its life hiding under the bed. Nothing will get done."

Voices both for and against filled the room.

Trent used his gavel to restore order. Bernadine agreed with Barrett. Even though one side of her wanted to put Henry Adams in a bulletproof bubble surrounded by multiple force fields to keep all of its citizens safe, that wasn't an option. To pass down all they'd achieved to the next generation, new people had to be allowed in the gates.

"How do we know the next hit person isn't already here?" Riley asked, standing again.

Bernadine wanted to punch him in the nose. His conspiracy nonsense wasn't needed or helpful.

He continued, "Is the new teacher—whatever his name is—really who he says he is?"

Kyrie Abbott, standing in the back with Jack, shouted angrily, "What!"

Trent said to him, "Calm down, man. Riley. Enough."

"But how do we know?" Riley repeated, glancing around to see if his theory had any support.

Bernadine hated the suspicious looks now directed the young man's way.

Riley said, "I say we form a committee that investigates all new people to make sure they're on the up-and-up!"

Some people actually applauded until Tamar stood up and the place went deathly still. "And I say we already have people leading this town who are smart, intelligent, and trustworthy. We don't need a man who stole from his wife, eluded the police, committed bigamy, had his hog repossessed, and is no longer homeless, courtesy of this town, calling for anything."

Jack's slow clap sharpened Tamar's icy retort, and Riley sat his totally embarrassed self down. Noting Kyrie's smile, Bernadine made a mental note to ask Sheila to plan a welcome dinner for the new teacher as soon as possible.

Trent asked, "Any other questions or comments?"

No one responded but Bernadine could tell some people weren't satisfied.

Trent said, "Then before we adjourn, Sheriff Will Dalton would like to share a few words."

Will stepped into view. "I'm just as mad and disappointed with the feds as anybody. Had we been informed, we may not have been able to prevent last night, but we would've been on the lookout for the shooter. However, I promise you, my department will keep a sharp eye on future comings and goings, not only here in Henry Adams but in the neighboring towns as well. Do we know if there are any other people hiding in plain sight? No. But I'll do my best to find that out and let your town's officials know. I don't want us blindsided by something like this again."

Applause followed. Trent struck his gavel and the meeting was adjourned.

People stayed to talk and mingle. Bernadine guessed they were discussing the situation and she wondered about their mood. Were they willing to move forward and get on with living, or did they want to build bunkers instead? Riley looked to be still trying to bring people over to his side—he was running for mayor after all—but she ignored him for the moment. Instead, she casually glanced Mal's way and found him watching her. She held his eyes for a moment and felt the battle inside rise again. Her heart was pitted against logic. She didn't want to think about Mal, or what they lost. Like her hopes for Henry Adams, she wanted to move forward and get on with living, but as Lily said earlier, cutting those ties was hard.

They held the dedication of the new firehouse a few hours later and most of the people stuck around to applaud and cheer when Trent and Fire Chief Acosta cut the ribbon. Granted, Henry Adams might never have a fire large enough to deploy the shiny red truck with its fancy equipment, but the memory of the horror visited on the town by the now incarcerated Odessa Stillwell haunted Bernadine every time she saw Bing use his cane. He'd been permanently injured in the melee that night. Should there be a similar incident, Henry Adams was ready.

The crowd began to disperse, but the sight of a caravan of black cars accompanied by a big van with the words "FBI" on the side made everyone stop. The vehicles proceeded down to the school. As everyone watched, agents and technicians left the cars and entered the building. There were also three dogs and their handlers. Bernadine wondered how long the search for evidence would continue.

In an effort to find out, she had Trent and Barrett accompany her to the building. There was yellow tape strung across the entrance and a female agent, the one who'd worked at the coffee shop, stood out front. "Good afternoon," she said. "Can I help you?"

Trent replied, "Trying to find out how long the school's going to be closed."

"That I don't know, but let me run down Kyle for you."

She stepped away and spoke into her earbud mic. Returning, she said, "He'll be here in just a few minutes."

When he arrived, she went inside.

"Hey," he said. "Gabby said you had some questions."

Bernadine wondered if Gabby was the woman's true name or just another lie. A petty thought on her part, but she wasn't feeling particularly charitable.

"How long will the school be on lockdown?" Barrett asked.

"The building's pretty large, so it's going to take a while. Maybe another three or four days. We're looking for evidence on the shooter, and we also want to make sure she didn't leave you all any surprises."

"Like what?"

"Anything dangerous."

Barrett said tightly, "He means any weapons she may have stashed inside."

Bernadine understood now and said, "Thank you, Barrett."

Kyle didn't appear happy about Barrett's plain-English explanation.

A county sheriff's vehicle pulled up and parked. Will, now wearing his uniform, stepped out. He was accompanied by Deputy Davida Ransom.

"Afternoon, everybody."

Concern on his face, Kyle asked, "Dad, why are you in uniform? You're supposed to be still on leave."

"You do your job, I'll do mine. Dispatch said the Bureau was in town. What's going on here?"

"Evidence and forensics search. We don't need assistance."

"That's what your boss said, so I talked to his boss."

Kyle tensed.

"The regional director and I go way back. Told him how I felt about not being dealt in on this little card game. I set him and his phone on fire."

His son's face reddened.

Will continued, "I respect the Bureau. I'm not here to get in your way, but the safety of this town is my responsibility. So let's start over. What's going on here?"

Kyle eyed his father and the tight faces of Bernadine and her people, and replied, "Let's go inside."

"SO WHAT ARE you going to do about the coffee shop?" Tina asked at dinner that evening. Crystal was at the table, too. She'd been working Friday night and missed the shooting.

Bernadine replied, "I'm hoping you're asking that because you want to step up and take it over."

Tina shook her head. "Sorry. I served my time under my parents. Never again."

Crystal asked, "Why not just put it up for sale?"

"I've thought about that, too. Of course, Riley Curry would have people believe anyone new in town might be another hired gun."

"Nobody listens to Riley."

"Some did today. I think because people are a bit scared." And had good reason to be after Friday night's episode.

Tina said, "I don't like him very much." She'd been at the meeting.

"Join the crowd," Bernadine cracked. "Every town has their nut and he's ours."

"Did he really do all those things Tamar accused him of doing this morning?"

"Yes."

"Even the repossessed hog?"

As Crystal chuckled, Bernadine replied, "*Especially* the repossessed hog. I'll tell you the whole stupid story sometime. We'll need wine."

Tina grinned. "I can't wait."

"But back to the coffee shop. I was really looking forward to it becoming a favorite place here."

Tina said, "Maybe one of our friends wants to buy it or knows of someone who does."

"It's worth asking around."

"I'll make some calls in the morning," Tina said reassuringly. "We'll get it open again, but I'm not changing my mind about not being the owner. I'm in town for my B&B. Okay?"

Bernadine gave her a mock pout. "Okay."

Crystal looked between them. "You two are a mess."

Bernadine countered, "But you love us."

Crystal saluted with her glass. "Yes, I do."

The doorbell interrupted the conversation. Bernadine went to the door and found the lady detective Sandy Langster on the other side. "Hi, Sandy."

"Hi, Ms. Brown. Sorry to drop by unannounced. Can I talk to you for a quick minute?"

"Sure." Bernadine stepped back so she could enter. "What's up?"

"I wanted you to know that I've been hired to find David Dresden."

The name vaguely rang a bell. "And he is?"

"The condo developer who disappeared with the money from Mr. Dobbs and Mr. July."

"Ah." That's why the name was familiar.

The detective continued, "I'm probably breaking client confidentiality, but I thought you should know, seeing as how some of the money belongs to you and the town."

"I appreciate that, Sandy. Did Clay and Mal hire you?"

"Yes and no. They made the arrangements for us to meet, but Mr. Shepard was the one to put up the money for my services. Said he was tired of the whining and the town deserved better."

Bernadine agreed.

"Do you want me to keep you informed of the progress of my investigation?"

"Yes, as long as you're comfortable with sharing the information. I doubt Bing will mind, and if you get close to solving the case and need more funding, let me know that, too."

"Okay. Sorry again for interrupting your evening."

"Not a problem. Be careful."

Sandy smiled. "I will. Thank you."

Closing the door, Bernadine stood there for a moment to

assess the new development. After learning from Tamar that Dresden had run off with the money, she'd thought long and hard about hiring Sandy herself, but opted not to. Even though Dresden needed to be found and brought to justice, she didn't feel it was her job to ride point. This was Mal's screw-up and fixing it was on him. Now that Bing had taken the reins, she could stop wondering if she'd made the right decision. Sometimes it was better if other hands turned the world.

Returning to the dining room, she retook her seat.

"Everything okay?" Tina asked.

Bernadine nodded. "Yes. Everything's okay."

AT CHURCH ON Sunday, the reverend gave a short but powerful sermon on community. Invoking First Corinthians, she spoke to what Bernadine saw as potential fallout from Saturday's meeting: divisiveness. "I appeal to you, brothers and sisters . . . that there be no divisions among you." The middle of the sermon touched on seeds sown by self-interest and their detrimental effects. Riley, seated a few pews to Bernadine's right, tightened his jaw. She was pleased that he had enough inner insight to feel called out because no one was more self-serving than Riley. The lesson concluded with words from First Peter. Paula asked that they all keep the apostle's words in their minds and on their hearts. *"Be sympathetic, love one another, be compassionate, and humble."*

The congregants responded with a hearty "Amen!" Before the reverend stepped away from the pulpit, her eyes brushed Bernadine's, and for some reason, Bernadine suddenly reflected on her own life. Had the call to be sympathetic and compassionate been directed her way for a reason? Of course, it was possible she'd imagined it. Paula had vowed not to offer an opinion on the rift between her and Mal, and Bernadine knew the reverend to be a woman of her word. So surely she hadn't used the sermon to gently prod her into offering Mal compassion and sympathy instead of tight lips and distance. Bernadine didn't have an answer, but she planned to speak with the good reverend as soon as she got the chance.

During the after-worship fellowship in the church's downstairs gathering hall, she scanned the crowd and spotted Kyrie Abbott seated at a table with Rocky and Jack. Riley had been very disrespectful to the young teacher at yesterday's meeting and Bernadine wanted to make sure he didn't have any lingering doubts about his status. Walking over, she said, "Mr. Abbott, may I speak with you privately for a minute?"

The teacher sent Jack and Rocky a quick glance before responding warily, "Sure," and rising from his chair.

"Let's find a quieter place." She offered Jack and Rocky a reassuring "I'll bring him right back," and led him to one of the empty classrooms. Seeing how uncomfortable he seemed, she jumped in. "I just want you to know that in spite of Riley, you're very welcome here. Young men like you are rare in the teaching profession and we're honored you accepted the job at our school."

"Never been accused of being a stealth hit man before," he said with a small smile.

"I'm so sorry. Riley's not a good representation of who we are."

"After the shooting, I called my parents. My mom's worried about my safety. She wants me to resign and find a place to teach closer to home."

The reply caught her off guard and she thought about how

she'd respond had Crystal called her with a similar story. "I'd probably tell my child the same, but the shooting doesn't represent who we are, either. We've never had anything like that happen before."

"That's what Jack said."

"No one will think less of you if you go, but if you stay, I guarantee you won't regret it. This place is special, and we'd like you to experience what that means."

"I promised my mom I'd think about it and let her know. I'm going to take a few days to figure out what I want to do. Is that okay?"

"Of course."

He looked her in the eyes. "Ms. Brown, I appreciate you letting me know how you feel about my being here. Up until the shooting, I was real content."

"I hope you stay."

"I'll let you know."

They went back to the hall and Jack's face showed his concern.

Kyrie said, "I'm going to take off. I'll see you tomorrow, Jack."

"Take care, Ky."

Abbott nodded good-bye to Bernadine and Rocky and exited.

Bernadine sat and sighed. "He may leave us."

Jack said, "I know."

Rocky said, "That shooting would make anybody rethink locating here."

Bernadine agreed. "I told Sheila to plan a welcome dinner for him. We may not get the chance to have it."

Jack said, "We'll keep our fingers crossed. If he does go, Marie's going to want to set fire to the folks at the Bureau. He impressed us both during his interview."

With the school year already in full swing, finding someone as qualified as Abbott would be difficult.

The hall was emptying of parishioners. Bernadine spied Paula talking with Trent and his family and decided to stay to speak with her. Jack and Rocky stood to leave. Rocky said, "Now that I'm back, let's get together and talk about the Three Spinsters."

The Three Spinsters was the new restaurant she and Bernadine planned to build and co-own. "Sounds like a plan."

After deciding on a day and a time, the newlyweds took off and left her alone at the table.

Paula walked over. "You're still here?"

"I am. Can we talk a minute?"

"Sure. Let's go to my office. First, let me tell Robyn. I'll be right back."

Robyn was across the room talking with the Clark girls. Paula said something to her, Robyn looked up and smiled, and Paula and Bernadine made their way through the now quiet building to the office.

"Have a seat, please." Paula took off her robe and hung it in the closet. "What's up?"

"Was the sermon directed at me?"

Paula paused. "Today's sermon?"

"Yes."

"No. Why'd you ask?"

Bernadine wanted to say never mind but plunged ahead instead. "The way you looked at me before you left the pulpit made me think—"

"That the words were meant for you?"

"Yes."

"I looked your way hoping you approved of my small attempt at countering the suspicions I heard at the meeting."

"Oh." Bernadine felt foolish.

Paula propped herself against the edge of her neatly organized desk and folded her arms over her chest. "Why did you think the words were directed your way?"

"Well . . ." Bernadine paused to figure out how to put her answer into words.

"Did something strike a chord?"

"Not really, but . . ."

Paula waited.

Bernadine felt like she'd stepped into a bear trap. "I thought maybe you were saying I needed to be sympathetic and compassionate with Mal."

"I wasn't, but it's interesting that you thought that, no?"

"No."

A tiny smile curved Paula's lips. "Sometimes the Person Who Really Turns the World puts things in our hearts we don't even know are there. You might want to ask yourself if you do need to show Mal sympathy and compassion."

"The answer is no. I may at some point forgive him for the embezzlement because he was just being a thin-skinned, stupid male, and I get that part, but I'll never forgive him for showing up at the wedding with another woman."

"Never is a long time."

"In this case, not long enough." Bernadine stood. "Thanks, Paula."

"Always here."

"I'll see you later."

Bernadine replayed their conversation on the drive home. It was her first time admitting out loud that she understood Mal's motivation for the embezzlement even though stealing was wrong no matter the reason. The male ego could be a fragile and sometimes dumb thing, especially for men Mal's age. They grew to adulthood at a time when gender roles were rigidly set. Men called the tune and women sat and smiled. Feeling emasculated by watching a female pay for everything was in line with that. But for him to finally return home, after weeks of being missing, with another woman on his arm? Unforgivable. The only reason she'd used the word *never* was because she didn't know a word that was stronger.

CHAPTER
9

Monday morning, Gary came down for breakfast dressed in the new running clothes he'd purchased Saturday at one of the stores in Franklin. His daughters, still in their pajamas, were at the table eating and eyed him curiously.

Leah asked, "You're really going running in the dark?"

He went to the closet and took down a lightweight jacket. "I said I was going."

"I didn't think you were serious."

"Why not?"

"Because you've never done this before."

"I ran in high school. In fact, Trent and I were on the four-by-four-hundred relay and came in second in the state our senior year."

Surprise filled the girls' faces. "You never told us that," Tiff said.

"When you get home from school, I'll show you pictures."

Leah asked, "So you know proper stretching and all that, so you don't tear any muscles?"

"I do." Even though he hadn't done it in twenty years.

"You know it takes older people longer to heal," she added.

He gave her a look.

"Not saying you're old or anything."

Both girls smiled.

He rolled his eyes. "Thanks, Lee, but I know what I'm doing." Or at least he did once upon a time. "Like I told you last night, after my run, I'm going to shower at the rec and then go to the store. Zoey's mom's going to swing by and drive you over to Mr. James's house for school since the building is still closed. Be ready so she doesn't have to wait."

"We'll be ready," Tiffany said. "Why are you doing this all of a sudden?"

He picked up his car keys. "I'm tired of watching my life pass me by, and even more tired of being boring old Gary Clark."

Leah said, "You're not boring, Dad."

"Yeah, I am, and it stops today."

The girls seemed impressed.

Tiff said, "Just be careful."

"I will. I'll see you after school." He offered both girls a quick kiss on the forehead. "Have a good day."

And he left.

Outside, it was dark and cold. The temperature was in the upper forties. After he started the car, shivering in the chilly interior, a part of him wondered if he'd lost his mind and voted to return to the nice warm house. Vetoing that, he upped the heat, backed down the driveway, and drove to town.

When he arrived, Main Street was empty. The rec, school, and church were dark. The streetlights above the track cast a bright white glow, making the red-and-green surface of the oval stand out against the surrounding darkness. He parked and had just gotten out of the car when Lily pulled up. The surprise he saw on her face through the windshield made him grin.

"What are you doing here?" she asked, getting out of her car. She was dressed in running gear, too. He was accustomed to seeing her on the track when he drove into work.

"Thought I'd run this morning."

"Really? Why?"

"I want to get back in shape. Miss running."

She reached into her car and pulled out a battered brown duffel. "How long has it been since you hit a track?"

"How old is Leah?"

She chuckled. "That long? You might want to walk for a few days to start off."

He thought back on the advice from his skeptical daughters. "Who asked you, Fontaine?"

She grinned. "Nobody, but if you keel over, you'll be still lying there when Gemma drives by on her way to the store." She saw his smile and paused a moment to assess him.

"What?" he asked.

"Just looking. Since you moved back, I've wondered if Clark Kent was still inside you somewhere."

He'd been given the nickname in elementary school because of his black-framed glasses. In middle school, contacts replaced them, but the name stuck. "He is, but he's been in hiding long enough."

"Good for you."

They walked toward the track. "How often do you run?" he asked.

"Usually three days a week. Monday, Wednesday, and Friday."

Lily had been an incredible athlete in high school. The local newspapers dubbed her the Fabulous Fontaine. During her reign, she'd held more individual track records than any other female high school student in the state's history. They sat on one of the benches and changed their shoes.

"Do you run in the wintertime, too?" Gary asked, tying his laces.

"As long as the track is clear. Trent tries to keep it open when it snows, and I love him for that."

"I think it's great that you two are together."

"I do, too. Not many men would take a girl back who treated him as badly as I did. Sometimes I don't think I deserve him," she confessed wistfully. Then she smiled. "And sometimes I don't think he deserves me."

He laughed. She stood and went through a series of stretches that worked the muscles in her legs, arms, and back. He stood and followed suit. Done, they stepped onto the track.

"Let's walk a few laps."

He whined, "Fontaine."

She whined back, "Gary. I don't want you hurting yourself, so stop playing macho man. Two laps at a walk and then we'll jog. Slowly."

"You're no fun."

"More fun than you'll be if you tear something."

He let out an elaborate sigh but did as she suggested. Side by side, arms moving, they began at a pace that wasn't fast but wasn't a crawl, either. Lily looked his way. "Next time bring your headphones. I usually wear mine, but I don't want to be rude."

"Yes, Coach."

"Don't make me hurt you, Clark."

He snickered.

After a few yards of silence, she said, "It's good having you home."

"Glad to be home."

"We had some fun back in the day."

"Sometimes too much." He thought back on the parties, the athletic events they attended and participated in, the plays they'd put on. He and Nori double-dated with Trent and Lily regularly. Thoughts of the necking sessions they'd had in Trent's Black Beauty, as his old car was known, made him smile and wonder again about Nori. "When was the last time you spoke to Nori?"

"A couple of days ago."

"Really?" he asked, trying to sound nonchalant.

"Yep. She's going to be staying with us for the reunion this weekend."

"How is she?"

"Good."

Silence settled between them. He wanted to ask if Nori'd asked about him, but realizing how self-centered that sounded, he kept his mouth shut.

In spite of the chill, he finally felt his muscles warm and loosen. After they finished the second lap, Lily asked, "Ready to jog?"

He nodded, and they started at a measured pace. He felt awkward at first and it took a few more strides to find a comfortable rhythm.

"You okay?" Lily asked beside him.

"I'm getting there."

"Just take it easy. There's no timer and no girls in the stands."
He laughed loudly at that.

She gave him a grin and they kept going. He realized how good it was having her with him this first morning on the track. Were he by himself, it probably would have been boring and not nearly as much fun, and he might have chucked the idea of continuing.

They'd done two laps when he heard a voice shout gruffly, "Hey, Clark Kent! What are you doing running with my woman?"

He looked over at Trent and grinned.

Trent called out, "Why aren't you at the store stacking cans and bread? Does Gemma know you're out here?"

Gary tossed back, "Too early for me to cuss you out, July. So just shut up!"

Trent complied, but his smile remained.

Gary told Lily, "He really doesn't deserve you."

"I know."

He and Lily ran one more lap, then called it quits. He bent over at the waist to catch his breath, glad he hadn't pushed himself like he'd initially planned because his thigh muscles were on fire. Lily, on the other hand, wasn't breathing hard at all.

"You go cool down and I'm going to get my laps in."

He hobbled over to the bench and sat with Trent. Lily took off around the track like she was back in high school running the hundred-meter.

"How you doing?" Trent asked, eyes trained on his hard-charging wife.

"I think I may have to call off work and spend the day soaking in the tub. Lord, I hurt."

Still watching Lily, Trent replied, "I was surprised to see you out here."

"My thighs are surprised, too."

Trent finally turned his way. "Do you need a stretcher? Tamar keeps a few in the rec."

Gary responded with a crisp, two-word phrase that made Trent laugh loudly. "Thought you said it was too early to cuss me out."

"For that stretcher crack I made an exception." Gary wondered how he was going to make it to his car. His muscles were turning to stone. If he didn't move soon, he'd still be sitting there when the first snow fell. Lily blew by them again and he envied her form and speed. "Do you ever run with her?"

Trent shook his head. "My knees are shot. More fun watching her."

Gary agreed because watching Lily evoked memories of the fun they'd all had at the meets. "Back in the day, did you think we'd be here?"

"No. I expected to marry Lily. You'd marry Nori. We'd move to the big city and live happily ever after."

"So much for that."

"True. I did marry Fontaine eventually, though."

"Nori and I didn't make it."

Trent asked quietly, "Still have her in your heart?"

Gary knew he could tell Trent the truth. They'd been close as brothers forever. "I do, or at least the fantasy of what could have been." He'd probably go to his grave still wondering.

"She'll be here this weekend. She isn't married. Maybe something will happen. You never know."

Gary wasn't optimistic. Other than his girls, life hadn't dealt him much happiness. "Not betting the farm."

"That's okay but keep hope alive," Trent said in a bad imitation of Jesse Jackson's voice.

Gary grinned. "I need to get going."

The sun had come up. A few cars passed by on the way to, he assumed, the Dog for breakfast. Henry Adams was beginning a new day. He wished the Millers' shop was open. A tall cup of hot coffee would taste good, and maybe resurrect his stiff leg muscles. He wondered how the couple was doing. Lily had finished her run. She was bent over catching her breath and checking her pulse.

"Thanks for the help today, Lil." Gary struggled to his feet and was trying to gather the strength in his legs to make it to his car when Gemma pulled up in her old Taurus. She got out and walked over.

"Hey," he said, taking a few steps in her direction while trying to pretend his legs weren't making him move like he was a hundred years old.

"Hey back. You feel as bad as you look?"

Trent coughed to hide his laugh.

Gary ignored him. "I'm fine, Gem."

"You're moving like somebody in leg irons."

"My first day running. It's normal. I'm going to grab my gear from the car and then shower. I'll be at the store by eight thirty."

Lily asked skeptically, "Eight thirty today or tomorrow?"

"Quiet, Fontaine."

Gemma asked, "When was the last time you took a day off?"

"I'm not missing work. I'll be fine. Besides, I'm taking vacation Friday, remember."

Trent said to him, "You know you're going to lose, don't you?"

"Nobody asked you, July."

Trent, still smiling, crossed his arms and waited.

Gary said, "Ladies, I'm a grown man. I know what I'm capable of handling."

Gemma said gently, "Grown man or not, you can barely walk. The store will still be there tomorrow. I'm sure the place won't go to hell if I run it for one day without you."

She was right, of course. She was an excellent assistant manager, and if asked, the staff would go through a wall for her. But he wasn't the type to call off work. It wasn't in him.

"Gary," Lily said. "Go home, take a nice long soak, then get some breakfast and spend the day chilling and relaxing. Watch some movies, read a book. Listen to some music. When was the last time you did any of those things?"

Admittedly, not since marrying Colleen his senior year of high school. The reality of that was like a punch in the gut. Would it kill him to have a day to himself?

Trent said, "Man, take the day off. Go do what every guy can't do once he has a wife and kids—walk around in your underwear."

The ladies turned to Trent with such astonishment that Gary laughed loud and long. "That seals it, Trent. Thanks!"

Lily and Gemma continued to stare.

"You're welcome. Now get going. I'll stay and help Lily and Gem pick their jaws up off the ground."

Gary was still chuckling when he pulled his car into the garage. Hobbling inside, he stopped, noting how quiet and peaceful the surroundings were. Low light flowed in from the partially drawn drapes and he realized he'd never seen his home this way before.

He managed to climb the stairs and make it into his bathroom. He then treated himself to a long hot shower and basked in the spray until the water ran cold.

Downstairs again, and feeling much better, he decided it was time for breakfast. He wasn't the best cook, but he managed bacon and eggs without burning anything. Grabbing a TV tray, he set it in front of the flat screen and placed his plate and glass of juice on top. After using the remote to fire up the TV, he searched the movies until he found what he wanted. *Black Panther.* Faced with no worries, Gary Clark, in his underwear, smiled and settled in for his very first daylong home-alone.

MAL SAT EATING breakfast in his apartment, debating whether to contact the sheriff about Ruth's threat. Of course, she might have been joking and nothing would come of it, but something told him she'd been serious. Will Dalton would probably tell him there was nothing law enforcement could do unless the threat was carried out, which meant Mal might be on his way to the hospital by then. He ran his hands down his eyes. His life was spiraling out of control, making him so dizzy he couldn't see straight.

There was a knock on the door. He went to answer it and found Marie Jefferson, cat-eye glasses and all, standing on the other side. She didn't appear happy. "So, you're back," she said.

"Yeah."

"Can I come in?"

Assuming he was in for more lecturing, he wanted to tell her, *No, go home!* Instead, he stepped back, and she entered.

She looked around the neatly kept space with its artwork on the walls. "Trent said you got laid off and applied for the custodian job. It's yours. You can start as soon as the FBI is done with the building."

"Thank you, Marie."

"You can't pay back the money standing in line at the unemployment office."

Mal thought if he had a dime for every time someone said something along those lines, he'd be able to clear the debt and move to Maui. "How was Alaska?"

"Breathtaking. How are you and Bernadine?"

"All the king's horses and all the king's men, blah blah blah," he recited.

Marie folded her arms and sighed. For a few moments she didn't say anything, just eyed him with disapproval and disappointment. "And you're going to fix it, how?"

He snapped, "I can't fix it if she doesn't want it fixed, Marie. And don't tell me it's all my fault because I already know that."

"At least you're admitting it."

"Doesn't seem to make a difference. Everybody is still pissed off. Trent. Lily. Even Amari. Only person not rubbing my nose in it is Clay."

"Last spring, when I lost my mind, what did you tell me to do?"

He sighed aloud. "This is not the same thing."

"If I remember, I pissed off a lot of people, too. Wouldn't even open the door for you."

After a heated altercation with Trent's mother, Rita Lynn, Marie dug a hole for herself and jumped in. She'd wallowed and wailed so long that Genevieve, her best friend and then housemate, threatened to move out.

Marie continued, "Part of what you told me was to apologize to everyone I'd hurt."

He didn't respond.

"It was sort of like the twelve-step program you used for your alcohol issue."

Mal tossed out, "Little Mr. Round Head is telling everyone I should paint the fence."

She chuckled. "I take it you're meaning Devon. I kind of like that idea."

"I don't."

"Okay. Suit yourself. Are you still seeing Ruth?"

"No. She was here a few days ago rubbing my nose in things, too. Apparently, her brother's a former boxer and wants a piece of my hide."

"Could be worse. He could want pieces of your manly parts."

He thought back on Rocky saying she wanted to buy tickets to the fight. "Why do people think this is funny?"

"I don't, but I do think you need to start your Come to Jesus twelve-step program and put your life back together."

"Thank you," he said sarcastically. "And thanks again for the job."

"You're welcome," she replied in a similar tone. "I'll let myself out."

At her exit, Mal shot an irritated look at the now closed door. He was sick of people telling him what to do. As the old folks used to say: the only thing he had to do was stay black and die. *And get Bernadine back.* He ignored that inner voice.

Although it had only been a few days since Sandy Langster took on their case, he wondered if she'd found anything. According to Clay, she'd met up with his cousin Jimmy to learn what he knew about David Dresden's relatives and habits. Did he gamble, cheat on his wife, have a passport? Mal supposed it was a reasonable way to start sniffing out a trail, but he wanted the man and the money found yesterday. There'd be issues reclaiming his portion, but he'd cross that bridge when he got to it.

Now that Marie had okayed him for the job, he was no longer in financial limbo. The sooner the FBI turned the building loose the sooner he could start earning a paycheck. According to the rumors, the feds were looking for stashed weapons, so he didn't mind if they took their time. Like everyone else, he wondered how the Millers were doing. Had Sam survived? Convinced that the coffee shop the Millers had set up would negatively affect the Dog's bottom line, Mal had been against its opening, but he hadn't wanted them harmed. Never in a million years would he have imagined Henry Adams being embroiled in something like this. From what he'd seen at the Saturday meeting, Bernadine seemed to be handling things, though. He could tell she wasn't happy with the government for setting the whole thing in motion. She didn't like being blindsided and he didn't blame her. Even though he'd done that to her as well. Deciding not to think about that, he went into the closet and got his kites. Since his return last week, he hadn't talked to Tamar about the embezzling, but it was time to get that out of the way. Watching his dragon kite dance on the wind had always calmed his spirit, and he'd probably need calming after Tamar finished giving him the tongue-lashing he knew he deserved.

As he drove up July Road to the house where he'd been

born, having to face his mother, even at his age, made him feel like a child again. Clay told him she'd opened fire on him with her legendary shotgun to get the truth about where Mal had disappeared after the theft. Scared him so bad, he said he screamed like a little kid coming face-to-face with Godzilla. The Julys may have descended from train robbers, but Tamar always set high standards of conduct for him and Trent, a concept passed down and embraced when the family stopped breaking the law.

When he reached her place, he drove through the open gates and up the winding dirt road to the house. Turning off the ignition, he got out. When she stepped through the door onto the porch, he expected a snarky welcome. Instead, she said simply, "I've been expecting you. Come in."

He climbed the steps and followed her inside.

The house had been in the family for generations and, thanks to Bernadine's generosity, had been given a major makeover. Air conditioning had been installed, rooms expanded, plumbing upgraded. A state-of-the-art furnace replaced the old wood-fed boiler, and the appliances in the kitchen were sleek and modern enough to be the set for their own TV show. He took a seat at the kitchen table.

"There's coffee if you want some," she told him.

He went over to the carafe, poured the piping-hot brew into a mug, and retook his seat.

"I need to apologize," she said.

He paused. Eyeing over his raised mug, he asked warily, "For?"

"Calling you out like I did at the meeting on Thursday."

"No big deal. But you might want to apologize to Clay for shooting at him."

"Clay should be glad I shot at his feet and not higher. He knows better than to lie to me."

Having raised her temper, he thought it best to leave it be. If Clay wanted an apology, he was on his own.

She asked, "So outside of paying back the money, how do you plan to atone for what you did, Malachi?"

Her tone brought his eyes to hers, and the hurt they displayed was startling. Shame grabbed him. "I don't know," he replied quietly. He'd been expecting rage and fury, not this show of raw pain. He couldn't remember his mother exuding such anguish before, not even when he'd been drinking. The force of that knowledge hit him harder than rage and fury ever could. His stupid pride had reduced his warrior mother to revealing an inner vulnerability he never knew she had. "I'm so very sorry." And he meant it. His apology was the most genuine one he'd given to anyone so far. He knew his embezzlement had crossed a line, but not how deeply it cut into the heart and souls of those who cared about him. He'd convinced himself that a simple "I'm sorry, please forgive me" was all he needed to put himself back into their good graces. Now he began to understand the need to do more—the need to atone. He couldn't sweep his actions under the rug and go on his merry way.

Tamar was watching him.

"Never meant to hurt you like this."

"I know."

"Never meant to hurt anybody, but being with Bernadine in Key West hurt me. Bad. Not being a man, you wouldn't understand that."

"No, I wouldn't." And her icy tone let him know the dynamics had changed.

"I'm just trying to be honest here, Tamar."

"And I appreciate that, but you don't seem to see the flaw in your justification."

"I saw myself sitting on the sideline while she paid for everything from drinks to suntan lotion, and people around us thinking I was a gigolo."

"What other people think of you is none of your business, Mal. Who cares what they think."

"I cared!"

"So you came home and stole a bunch of money, and what do people here think of you now? Do you care about them?"

He snarled inwardly.

"And there's your flaw. You cared more about the opinions of a bunch of strangers you'll never see again so that down the road you could pretend to be someone you aren't?"

"I should be the one taking care of her."

"Bernadine can take care of herself. That isn't why you're in her life. She wanted you for you, Mal. Not for what you have or don't have in the bank. And I get the man thing. It's another flawed theory, but I get it. The question remains: How are you going to atone for what you did?"

He pushed back from the table and stood. "I'm too old for this."

"So am I. You're my son and I love you, but you're going to have to answer that question sooner or later."

He placed his nearly full coffee mug in the sink and left.

Instead of going home, he drove down to the creek on Tamar's land and took out his long-tailed Chinese dragon kite. He knew she could see him from the kitchen window, but he didn't care. Earlier, on the drive from town, he'd been disappointed by the lack of a breeze. Now the wind was blowing briskly. Looking upon that as a gift, he walked the kite across the flat land until it caught the current. He fed it string until it climbed, twisting and bobbing high in the air. He chose to concentrate on it and not his mother's question about atoning.

CHAPTER
10

Amari decided he liked having school at Mr. James's place. One, he only had to walk across the street to get there, and two, the atmosphere was laid-back. The students were sprawled out on couches and chairs, and seated on the floor, with their laptops, while Mr. James guided them through a lesson on the Constitution. Mr. Abbott and the younger kids like Zoey, Devon, and their crew were in the basement. Mr. James said he initially thought about having school in the rec, but it, too, was a crime scene, and the FBI weren't done doing whatever they were doing. Amari was still blown away by what happened Friday night. A hit woman? In Henry Adams? There'd never been anything that crazy since they all moved there. He'd asked his mom how Mr. Miller was doing, but she said the FBI wouldn't be releasing any information, and that people in town would probably never know. He understood the reasonings behind this decision, but he still wanted to know if he pulled through.

At lunch, everybody gathered outside. The big kids got the

porch. The young ones took the steps. Amari noted the dark circles beneath Zoey's eyes and recalled that she'd been real quiet all day. As she opened her lunch bag, he asked, "Zo, you okay?"

She didn't respond at first and took her sandwich out of her green bag. She finally looked at him. "Had a stupid nightmare last night."

Concern filled her friends' faces.

Brain asked gently, "You want to talk about it?"

She gave a quick shake of her head. "No. I'm good."

Leah said, "Maybe talk to the rev. You look really tired."

"I am. I couldn't get back to sleep."

Lucas asked, "Did you dream about Ms. Stockton?"

She met his eyes and, after a long pause, nodded yes. Amari thought they'd keep Lucas around.

"You should talk to Reverend Paula," Leah said quietly.

A tear slid down Zoey's cheek and she angrily wiped it away. "I'm such a damn baby! Jeez."

A chorus of denials went up.

Amari asked, "Have you talked to your mom or dad?"

"No. Mom's recording her new CD and Dad is trying to get all the stuff moved into his office. It was just a stupid dream. I'll be okay. Can we move on, please?"

Amari shared a look with Brain.

Devon said, "Okay, but if the dream comes back tonight, tell your mom."

She nodded.

Amari was proud of Devon for offering a good piece of advice. Maybe there was hope for him after all. As Zoey suggested, they moved on, but for the rest of the lunch period, the atmosphere was quiet and subdued.

After school, Amari was in the kitchen with his mom. It was her turn to cook and he was watching her make jambalaya, one of his faves.

"How'd school go?" she asked.

"It was kind of fun until lunch."

She paused while stirring the roux. "What happened at lunch?"

He told her about Zoey.

She blew out a breath. "That poor baby. Did she say what the dream was about?"

"Just that Ms. Stockton, or whatever her real name is, was in it."

She shook her head. "She finally stops dreaming about those rats that attacked her when she was little, and now this. It's a wonder we all aren't having nightmares after what happened, though. I'll let Roni and Reg know."

"Mom, I didn't tell you so you could snitch."

She gave him a look. "They should know. If you had something weighing on you, Dad and I would want to know."

"I guess."

"Her parents won't give you up. Promise."

Amari hoped she was right. Having Zoey, aka Ms. Miami, go off on him was the last thing he wanted. "Is the FBI going to be done in time for your reunion?"

"Hope so. They're supposed to be through tomorrow afternoon."

Amari was pleased by the news. He and Brain were hooking up videos for the gathering and needed to have access to the rec to set things up. Turning his attention back to the jambalaya prep, he watched her put the chopped onions in the silky brown roux and stir them around. The great smell that filled the kitchen made him groan with pleasure. Smiling at his reaction, Lily added the rest of the ingredients—the rice, the andouille sausage, and the chicken broth. Once it started boiling, she put a lid on the pot and turned down the heat.

"We'll be able to eat in an hour or so."

"Yay!"

She put the cutting board in the sink to wash. "How are you feeling about what happened Friday night? Any worries, nightmares?"

"No nightmares, but yeah, concerned. Suppose the people who hired Ms. Stockton do send somebody else. What do we do?"

"Rely on your dad, the colonel, and the sheriff to keep us safe."

"Are they strapped?"

She paused. "As in armed?"

"Yeah."

"No."

"If somebody starts shooting at us, we're going to need to shoot back, don't you think? By the time the sheriff gets here, people could be dead."

"This isn't Detroit, Amari."

"Bullets don't care what a place is called, Mom. They just do their job."

She assessed him silently for a long moment, then agreed. "You're right, and I apologize for my flippant dis of your hometown."

"That's okay. Detroiters are tough. Being dissed goes in one ear and out the other. We're used to it."

"Have I told you lately how lucky I am to have you as a son?"

Embarrassment heated his cheeks and his heart filled up. "You're pretty dope too, Mom."

She inclined her head. "Pretty dope is high praise, so thanks."

His dad came in a few minutes later along with Devon, who'd been over at Zoey's doing band stuff. As they ate dinner, Devon said, "Mom, did Amari tell you about Zoey?"

"He did."

Seeing the confusion on his dad's face, Amari told him the story, adding, "She wouldn't tell us what the dream was about."

Devon said, "She told me and Wyatt at practice. She said she dreamed she was under the highway in Miami and everybody in town was on the ground shot and dead."

Amari felt bad for her.

Their mom said, "That sounds really scary."

Devon nodded.

Amari said, "Everybody in town should be carrying in case those people send somebody else."

His dad asked, "Carrying . . . guns?"

Amari nodded.

"I don't think that's a good idea, son."

"Then how are we going to protect ourselves?"

"I thought you didn't like guns."

"I don't. This isn't shooting for fun, but for protection."

His dad shared a look with his mom. She gave him a tiny shrug.

Devon said, "Don't worry, Amari. Dad and I will protect you and Mom."

Amari narrowed his eyes. "I don't need you protecting me, Devon, but thanks."

Devon said, "Aren't you scared of guns? Isn't that why you don't go hunting with me and Dad and OG?"

"No, I just don't like guns."

"I think you're scared," Devon tossed back, looking smug.

Dad said, "That's enough, Devon."

But Devon was still smiling, so Amari asked, "Have you ever seen anybody get their head blown off, Devon?"

Devon looked his way and froze.

"I have. I was seven. The people in the foster home where I was living got into a fight and they started shooting. Ever seen brains splattered on a wall, Dev? Ever seen a person with no face? Or eyes?"

Devon looked on the verge of throwing up and Amari took perverse pleasure in the reaction. "Don't ever come at me again about what you think I'm scared of because you don't have a clue!" He turned to his dad. "May I be excused?"

"Sure, son."

His mom said softly, "Take your plate, babe."

He gave her a nod, picked up his plate, and climbed the stairs to his room.

After finishing his dinner and sending Brain a text about needing bail money because he planned to kill Devon, there was a knock on his door. "Come in."

He expected it to be one of his parents, or both. Instead, it was Devon. "What do you want?"

"I just came to say I was sorry."

"Mom and Dad tell you to?"

He shook his head. "No. I asked them if they thought it was a good idea and they said yeah."

"Okay. You said it. Bye." Amari was not in the mood.

"You're supposed to say you forgive me."

"But I don't, so beat it."

"Why not?"

"Because you're a smug jerk, Devon, and I'm done with you today. Tomorrow doesn't look any better."

Devon had the nerve to look hurt.

"Oh, now you want to act all sad? Stop saying dumb shit, then. You get off on stomping people's feelings, especially mine, and I'm done. From now on, every time it happens I'm calling you out, and I don't care where we are or who we're with. Got it?"

Devon nodded.

"Good. Bye."

"But—"

"Get away from my door!"

Devon left.

Amari glared at the now empty space.

His dad appeared. "Heard you yelling."

"We should've traded him for a draft pick when we had the chance."

His dad smiled. "Can we talk?"

"As long as it doesn't include me being told to be nice to the butt-head, sure."

Trent came in. "Devon earned being told off. Just wanted to let you know that Mom and I aren't mad at you about what happened."

Amari appreciated it, but it didn't matter if they were. He kept that to himself of course.

"Son, you never said anything about seeing someone murdered."

"Yeah. Another highlight from the wacky world of foster care." It had taken him years to rid himself of the awful memory. It was still with him, but no longer showed up every time he closed his eyes.

"What happened after?"

"Police came, arrested everybody, and I was moved to a new place—with the lady crackhead."

Trent sighed. "You ever talked to anyone about all this stuff, son?"

"No."

"You might want to talk to Reverend Paula about some of it."

"Maybe. Being here in Henry Adams helped me put a lot of it behind me. Never thought I'd have a real family with love and stuff, you know? It's like my life back then was just a bad dream, so I don't need Devon in my face about who I am."

"No, you don't. He has his own issues."

"Yeah, he does. Told him I'm calling him out on them, too. No matter where, no matter when. If you and Mom think that's wrong, I'll take my punishment. I'm tired of him."

"A bit of brotherly tough love may be what he needs, occasionally."

"More like twenty-four/seven/three hundred and sixty-five. Me trying to be kind and not right doesn't mean anything to him. Although he did give Zoey some good advice at lunch."

"What did he say?"

"That if her dream came back tonight, she should let her parents know."

"That *is* good advice."

"He can be a good kid, but he likes thinking he's lead dog and he's not. I'm so done with him."

"Your mom and I talked to him when you left the table. He seems remorseful, Amari."

"Seeming and the truth aren't the same. I know I'm not perfect, but I don't try and hurt people on purpose."

"Your brother still has a lot of growing up to do. Your mom and I aren't giving up on him and we hope you won't, either."

"I never had a brother; I want us to be buds, but he's got to start thinking about what comes out of his mouth before it does."

His dad appeared to agree, and Amari was glad he'd come up to check on him. Whenever things sucked, his parents always made him feel better.

Trent stood. "I don't want you to worry about the gun thing, though. Kyle Dalton says there's very little chance we'll have anyone riding down on the town and shooting up the place. And if they do, there are more than enough weapons here to keep us all safe."

"This is the same FBI that thought the Millers were going to be safe, right?"

Trent dropped his head and smiled.

Amari did, too. "I'm going to need you to do like Tamar and put a weapon in the gun box in your truck. Okay?"

His dad studied him for a moment, then nodded. "Okay."

"Thank you." Because something was coming. Amari could feel it.

THE NEXT MORNING, Bernadine was in her office when Kyle Dalton knocked on the frame of her open door.

"Morning, Kyle. Hopefully you're here to tell me your people are done."

"We are. The school and rec center are yours to use again. We also cleared the Millers' personal effects out of their apartment."

"Good. Anything else?"

"Just another apology. I'm sorry this whole thing went sideways."

"I appreciate that. Hopefully, wherever the Millers wind up, they'll be okay."

"And so you'll know, Sam did make it. Can't tell you where they are—"

She threw up her hands. "I don't want to know anything else. That he pulled through is enough."

"You'll, of course, keep that under your hat."

"Yes."

"Good. Now, to work on getting my old man to speak to me again."

"Good luck with that."

"Thanks, Bernadine. I'll see you."

"Bye, Kyle."

Sam Miller had survived. That was good news, but the question remained, would the people who wanted him dead continue to stalk him? Bernadine hoped he and Brenda weren't betrayed again, and had the opportunity to live out the rest of their lives in peace. She also hoped the shooter got her just deserts. Getting herself hired as a custodian to carry out her evil plan was like something out of a Hollywood movie. Bernadine still found the whole episode incredible. Now, with all that behind them, the people of Henry Adams could get back to the business of living.

Trent appeared in her door. "Hey."

"Morning."

"Did Kyle stop by?"

"Yes. He said they're done."

"Yes. They took the seat Sam was sitting in as evidence. I'll have Lily order a replacement. We'll have to tear out the tiles in that section of floor too, because of all the blood."

"Okay."

"I'll start looking for another custodian and be smarter about checking the references."

"Don't beat yourself up about that, Trent. You did what you were supposed to do. It's the sheriff's office that should be ashamed; they did the background check."

"I know. Still feel bad, though."

"Well, don't. Anything else?"

"No. Just want us to get back to normal."

"Amen."

After his exit, she sent Rocky a text to make sure they were still on to talk about the new restaurant. Because they both wanted more input, it was to be a topic of discussion at the Ladies Auxiliary gathering that evening at Tamar's. Tina would be joining them but was presently at Bernadine's home calling club members about potential new owners for the Millers' coffee shop. Receiving an affirmative reply from Rocky, Bernadine looked up to see Mal in the doorway. She steeled her heart. "Morning."

"Hey. Just on my way to Lily's office to turn in the payroll paperwork for the custodian job. Marie gave me the green light. Thought I'd stop by and see how you are."

"I'm fine."

"I miss you, girl."

"I miss you, too," she said, keeping her tone nonchalant. "Things didn't work out, though, so, we move on."

"If I could go back—"

She didn't want to hear it. "Lily's probably waiting on that paperwork." The interruption tightened his jaw, but her shredded emotions took precedence. "Have a good day, Mal."

They viewed each other over a gulf filled with loss and regret. She felt it and supposed he did as well.

He finally replied: "You, too."

Alone again, she printed out the info she wanted to share during the restaurant discussion. Paula's sermon brushed the edges of her mind, but she refused to second-guess sending Mal on his way.

THAT EVENING, BERNADINE and Tina arrived at Tamar's for the Ladies Auxiliary meeting and were greeted warmly by the members already there: Lily; Gemma; Genevieve, Marie, Anna Ruiz, Luis's mother-in-law; and, of course, Tamar.

"Did you bring the wine?" Lily asked Bernadine. "You know you can't come in without it."

A smiling Bernadine handed over the two bottles from her cellar, and Lily went to the kitchen for a corkscrew.

Next through the door were Rocky, Sheila, and Reverend Paula, all bearing trays of snacks from the Dog. A few minutes later songstress Roni Garland arrived much to everyone's surprise and delight. Accompanying her was her producer, the always-leather-clad Irishwoman Cassie Sullivan, aunt of Roni's adopted daughter, Zoey.

"Didn't expect to see you," Bernadine said to them. "I thought you were recording?"

"We are," Roni replied. "Cass and I needed a break."

Cass said, "Besides, I love hanging out with you ladies."

"And we love having you with us," Bernadine told her. As

the noise level rose, along with the laughter, Bernadine introduced Cass to Tina.

"Roni said you'll be opening a bed-and-breakfast?" Cass asked Tina.

Bernadine left them to chat while she moved to the other side of the room, where Gen and Marie were holding court about their Alaska trip. She'd never been to Alaska. The pics Gen had on her phone showing the mountains and beauty cemented the idea of going. She thought it would've been a perfect getaway for her and Mal, but not now. The only thing she and Mal were good for was keeping their distance from each other.

Reverend Paula pulled her aside. "Anything on the Millers?"

"No, and we won't be hearing anything, unfortunately." Bernadine didn't like lying, especially to a woman of the cloth. Although she knew Paula could keep a confidence, secrets had a way of becoming news in Henry Adams and she didn't want to risk word getting out that might jeopardize the safety of the Millers and the people in town. The last thing they needed were rumors surrounding Sam Miller's fate and having more bad people show up demanding to know the truth.

Sheila Payne was the town's VP for special events and the auxiliary president. Once the opening chitchat died down, she opened the meeting. "Okay, ladies, we need to narrow down our choice for the family outing. The Dads are meeting at Lily's house and I told them I'd text them our decision." The auxiliary, in conjunction with Dads Inc., was planning an all-family outing.

Sheila continued, "We have Anna's suggestion of the Costa Rica rain forest and my museum trip to New York City."

Gen said, "Can I add an Alaskan cruise?"

Laughing groans were heard and Tamar said, "Gen, it took us weeks to whittle it down to just these two and now you want to add another choice at the last minute?"

Gen hung her head in mock shame. "Okay, sorry. Scratch that. We just had such a great time there. I think the kids would love it."

Roni said, "I think they would too, but how about we save Alaska for maybe next time? I'd definitely be open to going."

Lots of verbal support followed that.

Rocky said, "I'm more inclined to vote for the rain forest. I think it would be more fun for the kids."

"I agree," Gemma said.

Sheila's disappointment was plain. She'd been beating the drum for the museums. Seeing her reaction, Marie offered, "How about we do the museums as an auxiliary trip? That way we won't have to be concerned about whether the kids are having fun or not."

Tamar said, "I like that. And once we're done in New York, I want us to go to DC so we can tour the new African American museum."

Bernadine thought that was an excellent plan. Like every other person in the room, she'd been sending the museum money for years to help make the dream of the place become a reality, and she was really looking forward to touring the outstanding exhibits. She and Mal had planned to visit. She realized it was the second time she'd brought him up to herself that evening. Chastising herself, she turned her attention back to the vote.

Gen said, "And while we're in DC, we have to do the night-time double-decker tour of the monuments. I took it when I visited, and it's amazing."

Sheila said, "Okay, let's vote. All in favor of suggesting Costa Rica to the Dads, say aye."

Support rang out.

"Opposed?"

Silence.

"I'll let them know." She took out her phone.

They then spent the next few minutes talking about Lily's class reunion set to kick off on Friday.

Tamar asked, "Is everything in order?"

Lily replied, "I think I have everything pretty much locked down, but if something goes off track, I'll let you know." She shared the agenda, how many people were expected, and when the Dog would be closed to the public.

"Which is a great segue to the new restaurant," Rocky said, smiling. "Bernadine, you do the honors."

Bernadine shared her thoughts on the new eatery she and Rocky planned to call the Three Spinsters. "As most of you know, it's going to be named after three women who helped found nineteenth-century Henry Adams: AME church secretary Daisy Miller, town telegraph operator Rachel Eddings, and milliner Lucretia Potter. All three were unmarried and were vital forces to the town's establishment and growth."

Gen said, "I think it would be wonderful having a place we could get dressed up and go to for special events like anniversaries and birthdays, or just a night out with someone you love."

Bernadine saw nods of agreement.

"Where are you going to build it?" Marie asked.

"That's the question. Trent and I are thinking about adding

another street behind Main and maybe building it there, but that means delaying construction until we get the infrastructure installed, like water mains, lights, and sidewalks. Not sure I want to wait that long."

Rocky said, "An alternative is to place it across the street from the Power Center. There's nothing on Main down that way except Roni's studio."

Anna asked, "But does Roni want the traffic and noise it might bring so close to her?"

Everyone turned Roni's way.

She shrugged. "Something to think about, I suppose, but I sort of enjoy leaving a session and going out back, where it's quiet and peaceful, and just sitting. If there's a parking lot next door and people coming and going . . . not sure how I feel about that."

"Fangirl here," Gemma declared, raising her hand. "Then we need to put it someplace else. We're all waiting for more music. We need you relaxed."

There was laughter.

Roni smiled. "Thanks, Gem."

Bernadine said, "Okay. Rocky and I will think this over and keep you in the loop. Just needed some feedback."

Tamar said, "I think a new restaurant is a great idea. We need something fancy here."

Marie said, "But will it affect the Dog's business? Have you run this by Mal?"

Bernadine said, "We have. He votes no."

Rocky said, "The Dog is a diner. This will be a restaurant. It'll open in the evening. I don't see it competing at all. Mal and his opinion can kick rocks."

A quiet settled in. Bernadine knew they were all thinking

about her and Mal, so she spoke up. "Okay. Elephant in the room. Mal and I are done. Kaput. Over."

Gen said, "That's too bad. You were so good for him, Bernadine."

"Not good enough, apparently."

Marie said, "He's remorseful, if that helps any."

"It should, but it doesn't. How am I supposed to trust him again? First the money, and then another woman." Her eyes brushed Paula, who showed no response.

Rocky said, "Update on Ruth. She's not happy with him, either. She turned up at the Dog and they talked. When she left, Mal said her brother was coming to kick his butt."

Bernadine couldn't hide her surprise. "Really?"

"I asked if I could buy a ticket."

Smiles showed.

Marie said, "He told me the same thing. He's torn his pants with people far and wide."

Bernadine agreed, and she was curious about the information Rocky shared. During her visit to Bernadine's office, Ruth revealed that he was no longer taking her calls. Why? she wondered. What happened? Not that she cared, or at least that's what she told herself.

Tamar said, "Thanks for giving him the job, though, Marie."

"You're welcome. Like I told him, he can't pay back what he owes standing in the unemployment line."

"Amen," Gen said.

Roni asked, "So what's going to happen with the coffee shop?"

Bernadine said, "Tina and I are calling friends to see if anyone wants to buy it, but in the meantime, I guess it'll just sit empty."

Marie said, "The community college has a culinary program. Can they run it until you find a buyer?"

Bernadine stared. "That is a brilliant idea. Why didn't I think of that?"

Marie grinned.

Bernadine said, "Marie, you're a genius."

"I try."

"I'm calling the dean first thing in the morning."

Rocky said, "We need to plan a going-away party for Siz. I got his two-week notice today."

Cries of sadness filled the room.

Rocky continued, "His mentor is back from Asia and wants our baby boy there as soon as he can make the arrangements. Not happy losing him, but happy he's chasing down his dreams."

Sheila said, "I'll take care of the party. Anyone who wants to be on the committee, let me know."

Roni asked, "So, who's going to be in charge of the kitchen now?"

Rocky replied, "Randy."

Tamar said, "The one with meat-and-vegetable tattoos?"

Rocky nodded. "He may be a bit odd-looking, but the young man can cook. We'll be in good hands, I promise."

Bernadine had no reason to doubt Rocky's judgment but Siz was like one of their kids. He'd been feeding them since she purchased the town. He'd be sorely missed.

DADS INC. WAS meeting in Trent's basement. There was beer, snacks, and the trash talk that always accompanied their get-togethers. Composed of Henry Adams's dads, the group met monthly to talk about life, plan events, and enjoy themselves away from the children and womenfolk. Mal came in during the opening happy hour and all eyes turned his way.

In the silence, he asked, "So, I'm not welcome?"

Trent replied, "No one said that."

Reg quipped, "I don't know about anybody else, but I'm surprised you're here."

"Why?" Mal knew what was coming.

"After the way you dragged me about my being upset because Roni made more money, I'd've thought you'd be too ashamed."

"Cut me some slack, doc," Mal said, crossing the room and taking a cola out of the old-fashioned box-style cooler Trent had in a corner of the room. "Everywhere I go, people are giving me a hard time."

"Well earned," Barrett Payne pointed out. "If I remember correctly, you didn't have much pity for me when Sheila left, either."

Mal rolled his eyes and took a swallow from the frosty bottle. "Tell it to the Marines."

Jack said, "Pretty feisty there, OG."

"You'd be too, if you were in my shoes."

Reg said, "Which are probably fitting rather tight. Yes? No?"

Mal glared.

Barrett asked, "When are you painting the fence?"

"People need to stop asking me that because I'm not doing it."

Trent sighed. Mal glared his way.

Mal took them all in, then said, "Look, I came here to get away from the finger-pointing and lectures, so let's have the meeting."

Reg said, "We can't sweep what you did under the rug,

Mal. What kind of example does that set for our kids? You know, the ones who used to worship the ground you walked on? I admit it. I had issues with Roni's career and how much money she makes, but I was never dumb enough to steal to make up for it. What the hell were you thinking?"

"Obviously, I wasn't, okay. I'm from a different generation."

"A generation that helps themselves to seventy thousand large that isn't theirs?" Luis asked coolly.

Angry, Mal blew out a breath. He didn't want to have this conversation.

Luis said, "I'm just trying to understand, because my son asked me if it was true that you stole a bunch of money. I had to tell him yes. And when he asked me why, I told him you thought it would make you a better person."

The room went still.

Luis continued in a cold voice. "We know the world was a different place, gender-wise, back in the day, but stealing hasn't changed. It was illegal then, it's illegal now. We're all raising sons in a world that is dangerous to them just because of who they are. Do you know how angry I am at you for making my son think stealing is how you solve a problem? None of us is perfect, but you just trashed one of the basic lessons a father teaches his sons—and his daughters: be honest in all things. Society already thinks they're thugs and thieves, and here you are, living up to that stereotype. How could you, Mal?"

The outrage Luis exuded shook him. Mal had no quick clap-back. His face hot, he noted Trent's clenched jaw, mirrored by Gary, Jack, Barrett, Reg, and Bobby. Since coming back last week, Mal had been vacillating between being defiant one minute and shamed the next. Now shame and humiliation owned him completely in the wake of Luis's incensed words. "I'm sorry, man," he said quietly. "I was just thinking about me. It never crossed my mind how it might look to the kids—especially not in that way."

Reg seethed, "And that's one of the most messed-up things about what you did—how the kids see it. Not sure how you're going to fix this, but you need to come up with something. Soon."

Mal glanced around the room again, taking in men who were not the stereotypes society assumed them to be. Men both trustworthy and strong, faithful to their wives, loving with their kids, educated men who contributed to society in positive ways every day. As a boy who'd grown up without a dad, he knew how special they were. "Okay. I will. I don't know what it'll be, but I will." He'd made a similar pledge before, but this time he planned to follow through. He owed these men for what they represented. They looked skeptical, however. Not a one showed a lick of support, and that was even more painful and embarrassing, so he snapped, "You don't believe me."

After a few moments of silence, Trent said, "Actions, Dad. Actions."

Calling upon anger to hide the sharp sense of betrayal he felt inside, Mal said, "Okay, if you don't think I'm a man of my word, then I don't need to be here. From now on, meet without me. I'm no longer a member."

He waited for someone, anyone, to tell him differently, but no one spoke up. Furious, he left.

The only place he knew to go was Clay's. Bing answered his angry knock.

"What're you so hot about?" Bing stepped aside so he could come in.

"Got a lecture from the Dads and I'm not happy about it."

Bing, like Tamar, often doubled as a mind reader. "Gave you hell about the bad example you set for their kids, I bet."

Mal didn't reply.

The old man chuckled bitterly. "Be glad they didn't set you on fire."

"Can it, Bing. Where's Clay?"

"Out. Black Farmers' meeting."

Mal belatedly remembered Clay saying something about that a few days ago. "Okay."

Frustration added itself to the sea of emotions swirling inside him.

"Can I give you a piece of advice?" Bing asked.

"No, but since you're going to do it anyway, go ahead."

"Stop dealing with this like what you did is no big deal. Use whatever it was you had inside to kick the alcohol and make amends. And if you have to crawl from here to Kansas City through glass to get Bernadine to forgive you, do it. You're a better man having her in your life."

Having heard all this before, Mal offered the only response he could.

He left.

CHAPTER 11

Friday evening, Gary checked himself out in the mirror to see what Nori would see. Tall, still relatively slender, clean-shaven, fresh haircut, going bald. Glasses. Not exactly the description of Denzel or Idris, but he had on a great-looking charcoal-gray suit, a crisp white shirt, and a nice blue patterned tie. After so many years, he didn't know why he wanted to make a good impression, but he did, and if Nori spoke to him only once during the reunion, he'd take it. After what happened between them, it was more than he deserved. His thoughts moved to Colleen. Knowing his ex-wife as he did, she would do her best to sabotage whatever fun he tried to have, but he was determined to keep her at arm's length whether she wanted to be there or not.

Downstairs, his daughters were waiting to critique his attire. When they saw him, their faces lit up and both raised their thumbs.

He smiled. "I look okay?"

Tiff grinned. "Wow!"

Leah said, "You look really good, Dad. So good Mom might ask you to take her back."

"Then I'm going back upstairs to put on some old jeans and a hoodie."

They laughed.

"Who are you hoping to see?" Leah asked.

"The guys I ran track with and played with on the basketball team."

"No honeys?" Tiff asked slyly.

He hesitated, and because he did, she said, "Okay, spit it out. Who?"

"A girl I dated before I married your mother."

As if something about his manner was evident, Leah asked in a serious tone, "What's her name?"

"Eleanor. We called her Nori."

Tiff asked, "Why'd you break up?"

He offered up a small smile. As far as he knew, the girls didn't know the details surrounding their parents' marriage. "I'll tell you the story sometime."

Leah asked plainly, "You loved her, didn't you?"

Once again he hesitated, then replied, "I did, or at least what I thought passed for love in high school."

"Is she married?" Tiff asked.

He shook his head. "No."

The girls shared grins.

He laughed. "Don't start thinking we're getting back together. I don't even know if she'll remember me. High school was a million years ago."

Leah countered, "If you two loved each other, she will remember you. If Preston and I ever split up and met again a million years later, I'd remember him, and he'd better remember me."

Tiff said, "This is like one of those movies on Lifetime or the Hallmark Channel."

He loved his girls so much. "No, it isn't. I'm going to head over to the reception."

Leah said, "Have a good time."

Tiff added, "And we'll want answers about Ms. Nori at breakfast; just so you know."

Amused, he gave them each a kiss on the forehead. "I'll see you later."

Gary entered the Dog to the up-tempo sounds of Whitney Houston on the jukebox asking *"How will I know?"* The music mingled with the laughter-spiked conversations of the well-dressed crowd. Seeing familiar faces, like the tall Jud Wealthy, who'd played center on the basketball team, widened his eyes, and he rushed over to give him a brotherly hug.

"Clark Kent! How are you, my man?"

Jud had been a string bean in high school, but appeared to have added quite a few pounds in the years since. He resembled a baked potato now, but his smile was the same.

"I'm doing good. How are you?"

"I'm making it. Good to be back. Henry Adams has changed. A lot."

"Yeah, We're real proud of it, too."

"I guess so. Saw the new school driving in. Amazing."

As they chatted, other classmates came over to greet him. Sam French, who played guard and was on the wrestling team; Ike Kramer, a hurdler whose mom taught high school math; and Howie Pratt, an arrogant jerk no one really liked but was tolerated because his love of chemistry helped more than a few people pass the class.

"Well, if it isn't Gary Clark?"

"Hey, Howie. How are you?" Gary discreetly searched the crowd for Nori but didn't see her.

"It's 'Howard' now, and I'm a law professor at Stanford."

"Ah. Do you enjoy teaching?"

"Much better now that I have tenure. Was just telling July on the phone last night that I'm in the running for departmental chairman."

"Congrats. Hope you're chosen."

"Too bad you weren't able to take advantage of that scholarship to Notre Dame. July says you run the grocery store here in town?" Howie's—Howard's—tone was as smug as the look on his light brown, freckled face.

"Someone has to do the heavy lifting."

Jud and Ike laughed.

Howard added, "You know, I'm still simmering over you having a higher SAT score than mine. Are you sure you didn't cheat?"

Gary said, "No. I was just smarter. Always was, always will be. I'm going to go say hi to some folks. I'll see you all in a bit." He knew Jud was going to cuss him later for leaving him with Howie "It's Howard now," but Gary wasn't in the mood for his sneering.

He said hi to a few people, spotted Lily but not Trent, and stopped off at the buffet table to grab something to eat. He was reaching for a cup of punch when a soft manicured hand sporting sparkling gold nails covered his. "Is that for me, Superman?"

The purring voice belonged to Val Joyce, former head

cheerleader. She'd been a short, curvy, gorgeous ball of fire back then. Now she was still gorgeous. The hair blond instead of black. The brown eyes flirty as ever, and the body high school boys once dreamed about remained something to behold in a tight black dress with a low neck and a short hem. In answer to her question, he replied, "Of course," and handed her the cup. "Hey, Val." He leaned over and gave her a peck on the cheek. "Looking good."

"You're looking real good too, son of Jor-El. Glad to see you're still avoiding the Kryptonite."

He chuckled, "Doing my best."

As the party flowed around them and they nodded and smiled at people they recognized, he and Val talked about what they'd been up to since graduation. She'd gone to LA to be an actress. "I didn't have half the talent I thought I had," she confessed with a smile. "But I did have a head for business, so I ended up becoming an agent." She reeled off the names of some of her A-list clients.

"I'm impressed," Gary said.

"It pays the bills. Also keeps me from needing money from a husband, especially since the only one I wanted is taken."

She'd been in love with Trent since kindergarten. The two might have married eventually had Lily Fontaine not showed up at track practice one day after moving to Henry Adams. The moment Trent saw her, he lost his mind and his heart.

Val sipped her punch. "Fontaine's my girl, but I hate her. In fact, I call her once a month just to let her know I still do."

He laughed.

Val said, "I heard you and Cruella are divorced."

He choked on the appetizer he'd taken a bite of and coughed and laughed. He hadn't heard Colleen called that in years.

Val playfully slapped him on the back a few times. "Sorry. She did you dirty, Clark."

Gary agreed but didn't want to talk about it. "Water under the bridge now. I got two amazing daughters out of the deal, though."

"Good, because you were way nicer than most guys would've been. Everybody knew you were being railroaded."

He did too, but had Colleen's father made good on his threats, Gary would probably be just getting out of prison.

Val added, "And the question you've been dying to ask? Nori's on her way. Trent picked her up at the airport about an hour ago. They should be arriving shortly."

Anticipation did crazy things to his heart rate, so he forced himself to calm down.

"She just retired after teaching high school algebra. Never married, though."

"Lily told me that the other day."

"And now that Cruella is no longer in the way, maybe you two can finally find your happily-ever-after."

"Val?" he said warningly.

"Fontaine stole mine, I can root for you and Nori," she said in defense.

He chuckled.

"Don't look now, but there she is, just coming in the door."

"With Colleen behind her," Gary added. His elation died.

"Ignore her. Do this right and I'll have a screenwriter I know turn it into a movie. Let me know who you want to play your part." She raised herself on her toes and gave him a peck on the cheek. "See you later. Good luck."

He nodded but all he could see was Nori. She was, of course, still tall, wearing silky black pants, a top, and a long-sleeved jacket made of the same silky material. There was silver around her neck and matching hoops in her ears. Her hair was worn natural, framing her gorgeous dark brown face with a mass of curls. Numerous people surged forward to greet her, Lily included, but he hung back and watched. He watched Colleen, too. No one surged up to greet her and he saw her cut an irritated look Nori's way. Colleen spotted him and waved like they were long-lost friends. He didn't return the wave, but as she moved in his direction, he prepared himself for an encounter he knew wouldn't go well.

"Hi, Gary."

"Colleen." As always, she was fashionably dressed in a well-fitting red dress, her favorite color.

"You could at least act happy to see me."

"It's too late in the day for lying, Colleen. How was your flight?"

She pouted. "And here I was all excited to tell you I'm taking you back."

He froze. "Back where?"

"As my husband."

"Bigamy is against the law."

"Brad and I are getting a divorce. He says I'm too high maintenance, but he's just cheap. I got the papers when he moved out a few days ago."

"Sorry to hear that." All he could think about was her ugly treatment of Leah and it gave him one more reason not to be around her any more than necessary. Watching Nori holding an animated conversation with Jud on the far side of the room, he excused himself to Colleen. "I think Lily needs my help. Have a good time this weekend. Let me know when you want to see the girls." And he walked away.

As he did, he shook his head. That Colleen somehow believed he'd agree to marry her a second time was insane. He'd
initially thought new husband Brad nuts to marry her too, but
now that the man wanted out, after less than two years, Gary
guessed Brad was smarter than he'd given him credit for.

Gary joined Lily and Trent at the front of the room for the
official welcome. As Lily spoke and relayed what the committee had in store for the weekend, he discreetly scanned
the room and his eyes met Nori's. She gave him an almost
imperceptible nod and turned away. He'd been prepared for
that, but still found the impersonal acknowledgment disappointing. Chastising himself for expecting more, he was glad
when the lights dimmed for the viewing of the slide show.

It strung together all the photos sent to the committee by
the attendees. Juxtaposed with a soundtrack of the music they
had listened to, they saw themselves as high schoolers again,
much to everyone's delight. There were pictures of people
posing after school, during athletic events, at graduation, and
at the proms. With each new reveal, the classmates laughed
and commented on the clothing and hairstyles. A picture of
the teenage Lily and Trent grinning and seated side by side
on the trunk of his car, Black Beauty, drew a loud "Aw." A shot
taken during the fight Lily got into at a track meet after being
punched by a girl from another school during a race evoked
cheers. Someone yelled, "And the winner! The Fabulous Fontaine!" Laughter rang out. The next picture showed Gary
standing at the free-throw line during a basketball game, and
he marveled at his skinny legs in his very short shorts. The
next slide, taken of the girls' and boys' track teams, showed
them all huddled together and smiling. Gary picked out himself along with Lily, Trent, and Nori. The pictures flooded him

with memories of a more innocent, carefree time, when life had been simpler, and in some ways kinder. The boy in the pictures had no idea of the struggles he'd face in the years ahead.

When the lights came on again, applause filled the room and people were wiping their eyes. Gary guessed he wasn't the only one moved by the images and remembrances of their shared past.

They spent the rest of the evening playing bid whist, dominoes, and spades. They drank, ate, talked smack, and caught up on what everyone had been doing since graduation. As one of the hosts, Gary floated between the tables and booths and even took a beating during a game of whist. He'd forgotten what a terrible player his partner, Val, was. Colleen and Bebe Carter, one of Colleen's mean-girl friends, were in a booth in the back. He avoided them. At 10:00 p.m., the fun ended. They would reassemble tomorrow morning for a tour and a cookout at the rec. Calling good-byes, some people drifted out to make the drive back to hotel rooms in Franklin, while others stayed to gallantly help put up the chairs and fill trash bags with the discarded plates and cups.

Gary was clearing a table when he spotted Howie aka Howard talking to Nori. By his unsteady sway, Howie'd had too much to drink, and whatever he was trying to run on Nori, she wasn't feeling it. Her jaw was tight and her smile fake. Lily appeared at her side, and the encounter ended as the women moved away. Howie watched them go with angry, glassy eyes. Gary suddenly remembered that Howie had taken Nori to their senior prom. She and Gary were supposed to be going as a couple, but Colleen and her outraged father killed that plan. When the dust settled, Gary was forced to take Colleen. Nori, left with no date, had gone with Howie. Prom night was the last time he'd seen her, until this evening. Drawing his mind away from that, he watched Lily and Nori walk to the exit and felt the sadness tug at him again. Throwing it off, he focused on helping Trent and the others finish the cleanup.

Colleen came up behind him. She had her coat over her arm and Bebe Carter by her side. "How about I have breakfast with you and the girls tomorrow and we can talk about us reuniting as a family?"

"You're welcome at breakfast, but we aren't having a conversation about reuniting."

"I think the girls would like it, so—"

He cut her off. "Listen to me. You and I are not getting remarried. Ever. No discussion needed. Good night, Colleen. Drive safely." He walked off toward the kitchen doors to dispose of his trash bag and left her and the embarrassed Bebe in his wake.

Seething, he was leaning against one of the counters, when Trent walked into the quiet kitchen. He took one look at Gary's angry face and asked. "You okay, man?"

"No. Colleen is getting divorced and wants to get remarried."

"To you?"

"Yeah."

Trent's jaw dropped.

Gary quipped, "Insanity is a helluva drug."

"Wow. Is she serious?"

Gary nodded. "Wants to come to breakfast in the morning to talk about it. Thinks the girls would like the idea."

"Would they?"

"No. Leah would run away from home for sure." He told Trent about Leah's dealings with her mother over the summer. Trent looked appalled. "That's awful."

"Yeah, it is. So, no, Leah doesn't want anything to do with her mother, and frankly neither do I."

"I'm sorry, man."

"She screwed up my life enough. The only good thing that came out of our marriage was Lee and Tiff." Gary wanted to punch a wall. Sunday night, when Colleen flew back to Atlanta, couldn't arrive soon enough.

"Are you going to let her come for breakfast?"

"Yes. No choice really. I don't want her accusing me of keeping the girls from her and wind up in court. I'll let them know when I get home so they'll be prepared." He wondered if NASA needed volunteers for a Mars mission. He had a candidate named Colleen Ewing. "And in other news, I got nothing but a cold shoulder from Nori. Wasn't this reunion supposed to be fun? I want a refund. Who do I see about that?"

Trent chuckled. "At least you still have your sense of humor."

"Beats cussing and crying. As long as Colleen goes home on Sunday, I can put up with her for a weekend."

"That's the spirit."

Gary pushed off from the counter. "Let's get this place cleaned up so we can go home."

As Trent went out the door, he tossed out casually, "Just so you know, on the ride from the airport, Nori did ask if you were here."

Gary stopped. His eyes widened. He viewed the grin on Trent's face and responded with a grin of his own.

After the cleanup, Gary drove home thinking about Trent's

revelation. He'd been ecstatic at first, but the more he thought it over, the more he wondered what it meant. Had Nori asked because she was interested, or so she could avoid him? From the brush-off she'd given him this evening, the latter seemed a likelier answer, but was it? Like most of his gender, he found women hard to read, and now, with Nori, he felt as clueless as the guy in the old Switch tune who wanted to know if the girl liked him, could he call her, and if it was her real phone number. Rather than make himself crazy wondering about it, he set the issue of Nori aside. The reunion would continue tomorrow and hopefully he'd have answers by the time everyone went home on Sunday. The more immediate problem lay with Colleen. As he drove up the driveway and into the garage, it was a bit past eleven thirty. He hoped the girls were still awake. They needed to know their mother was coming for breakfast.

He found them in the spare bedroom they'd converted into their media room. It held gaming equipment, beanbag chairs, a pair of old but reupholstered recliners, wireless speakers, and a huge fifty-five-inch flat screen he'd gotten for a song from a former employee who was moving out of state. Each girl claimed two walls. On one of Leah's were the planets of the solar system laid out against a blue-black background representing space. Using stencils and poster paint, she had needed nearly a month to get the proportions and colors of each planet the way she wanted, and it turned out magnificently. On her other wall were pictures of her heroes and sheroes: Einstein, Dr. Neil deGrasse Tyson, Mae Jemison. In the center was the woman who most held her heart, the late Claudia Alexander. She was the last project manager for NASA's Galileo Project to

Jupiter, and a force of nature in planetary physics and space exploration. Ms. Alexander passed away in 2015, and Leah had been inconsolable for days knowing they'd never meet.

Tiff's walls were a tribute to popular culture. One was covered with pictures and posters of her queens: Serena and Beyoncé. The other was devoted to her king: Chance the Rapper.

Both girls had their earbuds in. When they finally noticed Gary standing in the doorway, their warm smiles made his heart swell. They were the only thing he and Colleen had gotten right.

Leah removed her buds. "Hey, Dad. How'd it go?"

"I had fun."

Tiff asked, "Did you see your old girlfriend?"

He nodded. "I did. She basically ignored me, though."

"No!" Tiff cried, eyes filled with concern.

Leah added, "Then forget her. She's not worth your time."

He didn't respond to that, but instead said, "I saw your mom, too. She's coming to breakfast in the morning."

Tiffany fell back against her beanbag and threw up her hands while Leah asked, voice cool, "Why?"

"She wants to see you."

"Did you tell her it wasn't necessary?"

"Lee . . ." he said with a warning tone.

"I'm serious, Dad. Her seeing us is unnecessary."

"She's coming anyway. And you may as well know, she wants us to get married again."

Tiff's face creased with confusion. "She can't have two husbands, can she?"

Leah answered: "No. It's called bigamy. She could go to jail. Is she divorcing Brad already?"

"He's divorcing her, apparently. She just got the paperwork recently."

Leah said, "I'd divorce her too if she yelled at me the way she does him."

"She thinks reuniting the family is something you girls would like."

"Was she drunk, Daddy?" Tiff asked.

He hid his smile. "I don't think so, babe."

Leah said, "She had to be. You didn't agree with her, did you?"

"No."

"Good, because that's a totally messed-up idea. We like our family just the way it is now."

He agreed. "I expect you to be respectful to her while she's here."

Tiff said, "Okay."

He looked over at his oldest. "Lee?"

"I always am, Dad, but someone needs to tell her the same thing. Just because I'm her daughter doesn't mean she can be nasty to me whenever she feels like it."

"I'll have your back. Promise."

Tiff turned to her sister. "Can we have waffles?"

"If you fry the bacon."

"Deal."

He enjoyed their sisterly camaraderie, and for the hundredth time wondered what it might have been like to have a sibling of his own. "I'm going to my room. I'll see you in the morning."

They called out good night, went back to their earbuds, and he walked down the hallway to his bedroom.

The next morning he came down to a kitchen fragrant with the sweet scent of bacon. Tiff was standing over a skillet filled with it, and Leah was giving a bowl of batter a last few stirs with a wooden spoon.

"Morning, ladies."

"Morning."

He sat down at one of the counter stools. "Did you sleep well?"

They nodded.

"How about you?" Tiff asked

"I did." Truthfully, he'd flipped and flopped all night long. He didn't really fall asleep until a few hours before dawn. He wasn't sure why but guessed it might have stemmed from the uncertainty surrounding Nori and the certainty of Colleen. As a result, he was dragging and wanted to go back to bed.

Leah asked, "Are you going to the reunion dance tonight?"

"I am."

"Too bad you and your old girlfriend didn't hook up. You could go together on a date."

He agreed. Not that he knew a thing about dating at his age.

The doorbell rang.

"I'll get it," he said.

He opened it to find Colleen on the doorstep. "Good morning."

"Good morning," she replied. She was wearing jeans, a black turtleneck, and a leather jacket. Looking past her at the driveway, he didn't see a vehicle. "How'd you get here? Someone drop you off?"

"Uber. I was floored that I could get a driver in Franklin," she replied, coming in. "I figured we could go to the tour together and then to the dance tonight."

"Did it occur to you that I might have other plans?"

She smacked him playfully on the arm. "What else would

you have to do?" She removed her coat, handed it to him, and walked into the living room. Fuming that she always made plans for him without asking him first, he hung her coat in the closet and followed.

"Ah, here are my girls," she said cheerily. "How are you?"

"We're fine," Tiff said.

Leah said, "Hi." She then poured some batter onto the opened waffle iron.

"Why are you cooking?" Colleen asked her.

"It's what I do."

Colleen turned to Gary. "Why aren't you doing the cooking?"

"Because Leah enjoys it and is way better at it than I am."

"But you're the parent."

He didn't respond.

Leah said, "You're a parent, but you never cooked breakfast for us in Atlanta."

Colleen glared. "I have a maid."

"And Dad has me."

Tiff took the last of the bacon from the skillet. "And me."

Colleen's lips tightened. "So, how's school?"

"Fine," they replied in unison, but didn't respond further.

Visibly irritated by their brevity, Colleen nonetheless pasted on a smile and said sweetly, "Tiff, I love your hair."

"Thanks."

"Where are you getting it done?"

"In town." Her hair was elaborately braided in a way that took shop owner Kelly Douglas hours to do.

Colleen eyed Leah critically and asked, "Is someone doing yours, Leah?"

"Yes. Me." Leah wore her hair in a loose curly 'fro that

reminded her father of Nori's. He wondered what Nori was doing this morning.

"It's a bit unkempt, don't you think?"

"No." And she took another done waffle from the appliance and placed it on the plate in the warming drawer.

Colleen persisted. "I know all the young women are wearing their hair that way, but—"

Gary cut her off. "Her hair is fine, Colleen. Leave her alone."

"You're a man, you don't know anything about this."

"Maybe not, but I know you're hurting her feelings, so stop."

As though he knew nothing about that, either, she waved him off. "Leah, am I hurting your feelings?"

"Yes."

Colleen drew back sharply. She sat silently for a moment, then said, "I just want you to be more attractive."

"I know," Leah said sarcastically.

"Well, if you're going to get all offended . . ."

Gary said, "Let it go, Colleen."

"I'm her mother—"

"Then act like her feelings matter."

Leah said softly, "Thanks, Dad, but I'm good. Waffles are ready. Let's eat."

The meal was a tense, silent affair. As they ate, he saw Colleen glance questioningly Leah's way a few times, but Leah avoided the eye contact. It made him wonder if Colleen was feeling remorseful. Had the lightbulb finally come on that maybe her badgering was causing her daughter pain? Tiff was watching Leah too, and her concern was plain. He wanted to make Colleen leave so he could enfold his girls in his arms and hold them both close to his heart. The last thing they needed was Colleen in their lives full-time, and he included himself in that.

Colleen said, "Gary, since you don't want to remarry, I'm going to petition the court for a change in custody."

He saw the girls tense and share a look. "And that means what?"

"I want full custody."

"Not going to happen," Gary replied bluntly.

"With Brad leaving, I'm alone, Gary."

He didn't see how that had anything to do with the girls.

Apparently, Leah didn't, either. "You didn't want us after the divorce, and now you do?"

"Yes."

Leah shook her head. "No."

"You don't get to be in this conversation, young lady."

"Yes, I do. You want to disrupt our lives, make us change schools and move in with you, because you're lonely? Get a pet."

"Don't you dare talk to me that way!"

Leah stood and turned to her father. "May I be excused?"

Colleen snapped, "No, you may not."

"Dad?"

Gary didn't hesitate. "Go on, Leah."

Colleen took her last shot. "When the judge gives me custody—"

"You aren't going to get custody, Mom, because I have receipts." And she left the dining room. Gary heard her run up the stairs.

He looked at Tiffany and saw a tiny triumphant smile flash across her lips. It disappeared just as quickly.

A confused Colleen asked, "What does she mean, receipts?"

Gary didn't know. He was very curious, though. "No idea."

"Tiffany?" Colleen snapped. "What does that mean? What did she buy?"

Tiff shrugged.

Gary said, "You should call your Uber driver, Colleen."

"You're supposed to be taking me back to town."

"No, you are supposed to be taking yourself back to town. I never agreed to play chauffeur. You decided without asking me, as always." The entire time they were married, he was invariably the last person to know what she had planned for him.

"It's not like you have anything else to do."

He wasn't going to argue with her. There'd been enough tension and raised voices. "Okay. Let's go, then. I'll drive you to town and drop you off."

"Fine. Get my coat."

"I'll be right back, Tiff."

"Okay."

Initially, the drive to town was as silent as breakfast had been. He kept his eyes on the road. Colleen stared out her window at the passing landscape, until finally saying, "I don't appreciate you turning my girls against me."

"You did that all by yourself, Colleen."

"We were fine until they began living with you."

"Believe what you want. I'm not here to argue."

"I'm serious about the custody change."

He shrugged. "Okay. We'll let a judge sort it out."

"I don't want you challenging me in court. Just let me have them."

"What you want isn't the issue. It's what the girls want, and I'll be advocating for them."

She looked his way. "You're enjoying this, aren't you?"

"Enjoying what?"

"Me being alone and in pain."

"No, Colleen. I'm not." He wanted to point out that she hadn't cared about his pain when her lie disrupted his life, but he didn't. It served no purpose. She'd always been the center of her own world, and those on the fringes hadn't mattered. Even now they didn't. All she cared about were her own circumstances, and if screwing up the lives of her daughters served her purposes, she was okay with it.

"I think we should go to counseling and try and work things out so we can remarry."

"I don't."

"You won't even try?"

He was so outdone with her illogical fixation on this fantasy that he pulled over to the shoulder and stopped the car. "Listen to me," he said, trying to keep from screaming at her. "Your lies railroaded me into a marriage I hated for over twenty years. When you told your father I got you pregnant, he threatened to have me charged with rape if I didn't marry you. I was seventeen years old! You and your father stole my life! I'm not marrying you again. Ever." He remembered how scared he'd been the night her father showed up at his parents' door, voicing his demands. Colleen was with him, eyes red and puffy from crying. Her father, Milton Ewing, was a rich, powerful man. Gary's parents were poorly educated farmers who'd spent their lives making sure his life would be better than theirs. Colleen's lie turned their dreams to ashes.

"Why did you lie?" he asked. It was a question he'd been trying to get an answer to for years and he must have asked it a thousand times when they first married, but each time she responded with tears and accusations that he was being mean to her. Out of frustration, he simply stopped asking; now he wanted the truth. "Tell me. Why? Wasn't being the richest girl around enough for you? I had dreams, Colleen. A future." *Nori.*

She finally turned and said coolly, "Because I wanted to be your girl. You were the smartest, cutest boy in class."

"But I had a girl. You and I never even dated, let alone had sex."

"I know," she sneered. "Nori. Everybody loved Nori with her perfect grades and perfect smile. No one gave me the time of day."

"Because you were spoiled and mean."

Anger flashed in her eyes. "And spoiled mean girls get what they want, don't they?"

Filled with disgust, he steered the car back onto the road and continued the drive into town. When he pulled up to the rec, she got out without a word.

Back at home, he swallowed his bitterness and found the girls cleaning up the kitchen. "Lee. Can I talk to you for a minute?"

"Sure."

He led her into the living room. "First, I know one person can't apologize for someone else, but I'm sorry you had to endure your mom's attitude."

"Par for the course, I guess, but thanks for letting me go back to my room."

"You're welcome. Talk to me about these receipts."

Leah paused, eyed him for a moment, and replied, "I'd rather keep them to myself for now."

"Can I ask why?"

"I just would. I'm not trying to be disrespectful to you or anything, but I think a judge will be interested if she tries to make us live with her. And it's better if you don't know. That way no one can say you put me up to it."

He had no idea what to say next. His mind fumbled for a second or two until he finally came up with, "Does Tiff have receipts, too?"

"Yes."

Now he was even more curious. He knew what the teens of the day meant by the term *receipts,* but what possible evidence could they have on Colleen that needed to be kept secret? He was raising them to be forthright, honest young women, and it didn't feel right for him to demand they share what they had, so he supposed he had to trust them. "Okay. If you think it's necessary to keep it to yourself, I'm not going to push."

"Thanks. But can I say one thing?"

"Sure."

"Get a good lawyer. Tiff and I don't want to live with her."

He smiled. "Gotcha."

To his surprise, she came over and gave him a big hug. She didn't say anything, but her action meant the world to him after dealing with Colleen. She returned to the kitchen and he went up to his room to get ready for the rest of his day.

CHAPTER
12

Waiting for Clay to join him at the Dog for breakfast, Mal sat in a booth sipping coffee and musing again on the mess he'd made of his life. Since the Dads Inc. meeting, he'd been unable to get Luis's words out of his head. Of all the finger-pointing, ragging, and lecturing he'd received since returning to town, none had hit him harder. As a descendant of a proud people, he'd always done his best to be seen in a positive light. Even when he was drinking, he'd been committed to that scenario. Whether it was founding the county's Buffalo Soldier reenactment group to keep the memory of those brave black soldiers and their service to the nation alive, or being a member of the Kansas Historical Society to ensure the history of the Dusters remained in the forefront, no one had ever called him a detriment to the race until now. And although Mal didn't want to admit it, the fire chief was right. The burden of that knowledge was heavier than being labeled a drunk or a thief, because his people had spent two hundred years trying to dispel the myths that they were less intelligent, lazy, untrustworthy, and inherently violent. He wondered how many people outside Henry Adams attributed his theft to his race rather than the simpleminded failings of a stupid old man. Probably not many, but he was sure there were some who said, *See? They can't be trusted—they even steal from their own.* He hated being tied to such damning conversations.

"You want more coffee?"

He looked up to see Rocky beside him, carafe in hand.

"Yeah. Warm me up. Clay's running late."

She poured. "You're looking pretty gloomy."

"Gloomy times."

"Jack said you stormed out of the meeting the other night."

"And men say women can't keep a secret."

She ignored that. "He told me how angry Luis was and what he said."

"And Luis is right."

Rocky sighed sympathetically. "Wish I could tell you how to fix it."

"I know. It's on me, though."

She nodded. "Here comes your buddy."

Clay walked through the crowded room and sat down. "Morning, Rock."

"Hey, Clay. You two want your usual?"

They nodded. She poured coffee into the empty mug in front of Clay and went to put in their orders.

"Sorry I'm late. Got hung up on the phone. Sandy Langster called."

Mal perked up. "What'd she say?"

"She got a call from Dresden's wife. He's in Jamaica with his nineteen-year-old girlfriend. Wants a divorce."

Mal shook his head. He'd run with the young ones before meeting Bernadine. He hoped Dresden had lots of Viagra.

"The wife told him we wanted our money back and she'd be calling the cops if he didn't return it and make it worth her while to say yes to the divorce."

Mal stared. "She wants a cut of our money?"

"Sounds that way."

"How much does she want?"

"Sandy doesn't know, but said the wife was so angry at Dresden it was hard to get a word in with all the cussing and yelling."

Mal didn't believe this.

Their meals arrived shortly thereafter. They'd just dug in when Clay's phone buzzed. He looked at the screen. "It's Jimmy. I'm going to take this. Be right back."

Mal watched him talk on the phone as he walked to the deserted area by the door. Standing there, he conversed for a few long minutes before lowering the phone and returning to their booth.

"Well," Clay said, retaking his seat, "Jimmy just got a message from Dresden. He's going to wire back Jimmy's portion and mine."

"And what about me?"

"He said he's paying his wife off with some of the rest."

"Some? How much is some?"

Clay shrugged. "Jimmy asked about that, but Dresden said he'd heard you got the money illegally, and since you can't call the cops, he's keeping it so he can pay off his wife."

Mal was floored. "How does he know? Did Jimmy tell him?"

"Since I didn't tell Jimmy about it until after Dresden disappeared, my guess is no, but Dresden's wife has family in

Franklin, maybe they heard it through the grapevine. Didn't you tell me that's how Ruth found out?"

Mal fell back against the booth. Ruth did say that. The hole he was in kept getting deeper and deeper. How many more uppercuts did he have to take before he could leave the ring? "I need that money back, man."

"I know, but I don't know what to tell you. Sandy said you might not get it back the day she met with us, remember? Maybe Dresden will get religion and send it all."

The way things kept spiraling down, Mal didn't hold much hope.

He and Clay finished their meals, paid the bill, and walked outside to the parking lot. Down the street they saw a crowd of people assembled in front of the church.

Clay asked, "Is that Trent and Lily's reunion group?"

"Yeah. They're doing a walking tour to show off all the new stuff in town."

Someone tapped Mal on the shoulder. He turned to see a younger man about his height. He looked vaguely familiar, but Mal wasn't sure why.

"Are you Mal July?"

"Yes. Who are you?"

"Ruth's little brother."

Mal didn't have time to get out of the way of the fist that exploded in his face, or the one that crashed into his gut. Thunderous pain was the last thing he remembered before everything went black.

When he opened his eyes, he didn't know where he was, but he was propped up and his vision was so hazy that he had trouble focusing. Someone was moaning. It took a few seconds to realize he was the source. His nose felt plugged up and his stomach and ribs were on fire, reminiscent of the time he'd been head-butted by an angry Cletus. He closed his eyes again and heard someone say, "He's awake." *Was that Tamar?* He tried to sit up straight so he could look around, but his head hurt so badly that another moan rose, and he slowly eased himself back against whatever was propping him up.

Reg Garland shimmered into view. "How you doing, Mal?" The doc placed a hand against his forehead.

Mal croaked, "What happened? Where am I?"

"You're in my clinic. Clay said you were sucker-punched by Ruth's brother. Do you remember?"

Mal fought to make his memory work. For a moment it refused, too much fog, and then his mind replayed the punch in the face and the lower one that followed. "Yeah, I do. Clay bring me here?"

"Luis did. He said to tell you thanks for allowing him to use the town's ambulance for the first time. He had the sirens and flashers going the whole half block it took to get you here."

"Jesus," Mal whispered. He'd never live this down, but he was more concerned with the pain in his head. It felt like someone was using it for an anvil. "Why's my head hurting like this?" He belatedly realized he was propped up against a partially raised hospital bed covered by a white sheet.

"The punch broke your nose, and when you fell, you hit your head on the asphalt. I straightened the nose while you were out, but it's going to hurt for a few days."

"Great."

"Now that you're awake I'll get you some ibuprofen, and here, put this ice pack on your nose to keep the swelling down. You've got a busted rib and may have one or two black eyes before this is all said and done."

Double great. The ice pack gave him some relief. The cold felt good. Only then did he notice Trent, Tamar, and Clay standing at the foot of the bed.

Trent said, "You scared us, old man."

"Yes, you did," Tamar said, her voice filled with concern. "Will wants to know if you want to press charges?"

"No." He didn't want to see Ruth or her brother ever again, and in truth, he'd earned the knockout for treating her the way he had.

"You sure?" Clay asked.

"Yeah. I am. Did he get away?"

Clay said, "He tried, but Rock was in her truck getting ready to run some food down to the rec. When he jumped into his car to drive off, she grabbed her shotgun out of the bed's locker and blew out his back window."

Trent took up the tale. "By the time Luis and the rest of us ran down the street to see what was going on, he was face-down on the ground with his arms stretched above his head. Rock had her foot on his back, the shotgun pointed at his head, and he was crying like a baby."

Mal smiled for the first time in what felt like weeks. Rock to the rescue.

Clay said, "I'm glad she's on our side."

Mal was, too.

Reg returned with the pain meds and a cup of water. "Drink slowly. You may have trouble swallowing because of your busted nose."

Reg was right, but Mal managed to drink without choking too badly. He handed the cup back. "When can I go home?"

"You're going home with me," Tamar informed him. "Reg said you need to be watched in case you have a concussion."

He didn't want to go to Tamar's. He wanted to go to his own place, but he was in too much pain to argue.

Reg said, "I'll keep you under observation here for a few more hours, then we'll let Luis transport you to Tamar's."

"Okay." He saw the worry in Trent's face. "I'm fine, son. Go on back to the reunion."

"I can stay if you want."

"I appreciate that, but Reggie's got my back. You go ahead. Check on me tomorrow."

"You sure?"

"Positive. You go home, too, Tamar. I'll see you at your place."

She nodded.

Mal could feel the pain meds kicking in. He'd be asleep soon. "Clay, thanks."

"You're welcome, but it's Rock you need to be thanking."

"I will." As soon as the thunder in his head subsided. He owed Luis thanks too, but not for the sirens and flashers.

Reg said, "Okay, everybody, visiting hours are over. Let him rest. Anyone wanting to see Mal can do it at Tamar's in a few days. No more visitors today. Doctor's orders."

Clay, Trent, and Tamar gave Mal a final call of good-bye and left the room.

As Mal was drifting off to sleep he heard what sounded like an argument outside his partially closed door. It was Reg and Bernadine!

"What do you mean I can't see him?" she snapped.

"You can't. Not today. He's sleeping."

"I just want to put my eyes on him," she said firmly.

"No. It's not like you two are a couple anymore. I'll let him know you stopped by."

"Get out of my way, Reggie Garland."

"Or what? You may turn the world in your office, but here, I'm the hand on the wheel. No visitors."

She didn't respond.

"He's fine, Bernadine. You two are beefing. I don't want my patient yelled at or upset."

"I'm not going to yell at him or upset him."

"Doesn't matter. Go home. See him at Tamar's. Luis will be transporting him there in a few hours."

The hallway quieted after that, so Mal assumed she'd left, realizing she wasn't going to get her way. Very few people said no to Bernadine Brown. He had to hand it to Reg for standing his ground.

Reg stuck his head in the door. "Mal? You awake?"

"Yeah."

"Did you hear that?"

"I did."

"Interesting?"

"Very."

"Okay. Go to sleep now."

"Thanks, Reg."

"You bet."

Mal thought the conversation interesting indeed. Did the visit mean there was a thaw in the cold war? He hoped so, because he wanted to explain everything to Bernadine—from why he'd taken up with Ruth and gotten punched to how bad he felt not having Bernadine in his life. And sometime soon, after his ribs and nose healed, he needed to make a run to

Franklin's hardware store to buy a couple of gallons of paint. He was musing over color choices when he drifted off to sleep.

AFTER TRENT RETURNED to the reunion and explained what had happened with his dad and assured everyone he was okay, Gary and the other reunion attendees got ready for the cookout. The grills were manned by Rocky's employees Siz and Randy and they soon had the air filled with mouthwatering scents. There were hot dogs and sausages, steaks and chicken, along with fajitas, burgers, and succulent chunks of lamb on skewers. Gary, still in a mood from dealing with his ex, found a place at an empty table and sat. He wasn't intentionally being antisocial, but he needed a minute or two to himself, until . . .

"Mind if I join you?"

Nori startled him so badly he knocked over his can of cola. The drink went everywhere. Embarrassed, he hastily jumped up and grabbed his napkins to mop up the mess, all the while chastising himself for being such a clumsy fool.

"Here," she said, smiling, offering him her napkins. "I think you may need more." She set her plate down in a clear spot. "I'll grab some."

"No, I—"

But she'd already started back to the main tables, and he wondered if he could've done anything more stupid. He felt like a boy in junior high interacting with the prettiest girl in school. When she walked back, it gave him the opportunity to silently relish just how beautiful she was in her loose-fitting red blouse, black jeans, and red high-top Chucks—the sight of which made him inwardly chuckle. Like last night, there was silver around her neck and matching silver hoops in her ears.

"Think this will be enough?"

He took in the large stack of napkins in her hand and shot her an amused quelling look. He took them from her. "I see you still got jokes."

"Always."

For a moment time seemed to stop as their gazes held. Only then did he acknowledge to himself how badly he'd missed her.

She must have read his thoughts. "Been a very long time, Gary."

"Yes, it has been."

"Is your car here?"

"Yes, why?"

"I thought maybe we could go someplace quiet. Sit, talk, eat."

He was so caught by surprise he was sure his eyes looked ready to pop from their sockets.

"No?"

"Um, yes, sure," he replied quickly. *Is this really happening?*

"How about I grab some foil for our plates and we can go."

"Okay." He was nodding like a bobblehead but couldn't help himself.

She took off again. He was left staring stupidly, his brain scrambled.

They wrapped up their plates and walked to his car. Passing the main group, he girded himself for the smack talk and good-natured heckling sure to follow the sight of him and Nori sneaking off, but instead, applause rang out and then cheers. A couple of people broke out singing the old Shalimar tune "Second Time Around." Nori grinned and looked a tad embarrassed. Gary didn't know what to do, but his smile was wide.

In the car, she said, "They play way too much."

He chuckled and agreed. "Where do you want to go?" He stuck the key in the ignition.

"Where do the teenagers go these days?"

He stopped with his hand on the key and realized he had no idea. "I don't know."

"Lily said you have two teenage daughters. And you don't know?"

He laughed. "I don't."

Nori shook her head. "C'mon, Dad, you need to be doing a better job."

He supposed she was right, but it wasn't like he could just come out and ask Leah where she and Preston went to hang when they wanted to be alone. He wondered who would know. Rocky? Jack? His generation used to sneak inside what had been the abandoned Sutton Hotel movie theater. Realizing he was wasting precious time, he started the car and headed for July Road. He hoped Tamar was home by now.

She was. Answering his knock, she smiled seeing him. "Hey, Gary. What can I do for you?"

"Is it okay if Nori and I sit on the bank for a while and eat our lunch?"

She peered around him to get a look at Nori in the car. "Of course. Glad to see you two together finally."

"Thanks."

"Second time can be sweeter. Don't let it slip away."

He nodded, not sure what else he was supposed to do, but he did wonder if this would be a second chance for him and

Nori. He was walking back to the steps when Tamar said quietly, "Gary?"

He stopped and turned back.

"I'm sorry no one here had the power to help you back then. What happened weighed heavily on all our hearts."

He was moved by the sincerity in her eyes. "Thanks for that, Tamar."

"You're welcome. Go have some fun."

He parked as close as he could to the bank of what he and Trent called Seminole Creek, and he and Nori got out and walked the rest of the way. The old picnic table was still there, making him wonder how often it was used these days.

"It's so nice out here," Nori said, looking out at the water and the bank on the other side. The area had some of the only trees for miles around. "Beautiful sunny day. Been a long time since I've been here, too. This is just perfect."

He thought her perfect as well. Back in the day, he and Nori and Trent and Lily had come out to the spot often, using the picnic table for cards, laughter, sneaking beer and smokes. Kissing, too. He turned his mind away from that.

Gary sat and watched her. He didn't want to crowd her and spoil the moment. He removed the foil covering his plate and was glad to find his burger still warm.

"What's it like living here now in the twenty-first century?"

"About like it was in the twentieth but with better infrastructure, more money, and a new school."

"I promised myself I'd never come back."

That surprised him. "Why?"

She shrugged. "I was so unhappy. My mom dying sophomore year. Daddy marrying so quickly after because he was lonely. And then there was us." She viewed him over her shoulder for a moment before turning back to the creek. "I heard later that she lied."

"Yes."

"And yet you stayed with her." She stated it as fact, not a question.

"I wanted to divorce her after I learned the truth, but her father wasn't having it. Once again threatened me with jail. Said he'd make it look like I was embezzling from the dealership."

"Lord," she whispered.

"I know. And having two daughters, I can almost forgive him for the forced marriage. Almost. Of course he'd believe his daughter over me no matter how many times I denied being with her. I hope he roasts in hell for holding the embezzlement thing over my head to make me stay married to her, though."

"I'm so sorry you had to deal with that."

"So am I, but I had no choice. Then, after the girls were born, my responsibility was to them, even though she didn't let me have much say in their raising. Colleen had never worked a day in her life. If I'd left after her father died, my daughters would've probably starved."

"Were you at least happy?"

"No."

She turned his way again.

And he confessed honestly. "Never."

"Damn," she said softly.

He whispered, "I know. Had she not divorced me, we'd probably still be together because I'd given up. I figured I'd stay married to her until I went to my grave."

"Are you happy now?"

"I am. My daughters are the only good thing to come out of the marriage. It took me some time to adjust to being a single parent, but we're doing well."

She walked to the table and sat down.

He said, "Your turn. How's life been for you?"

"Pretty good," she said, opening her foil and extracting her burger. "Taught algebra, retired, have a good pension."

"Never married?"

She shook her head. "Couldn't find anyone who could keep up."

"What do you mean?"

"I like adventure. Travel. Mountain climbing. White-water rafting. Camping. Everything society says black women have no business doing, and many of the guys I hooked up with seemed to believe that, too."

"What mountains have you climbed?"

"Denali. Kilimanjaro. Even some of the peaks in Nepal." She glanced at him and laughed. "Close your mouth, Clark, before a fly goes in."

"The Himalayas, too?"

"Yes. Didn't get close to summiting but I wanted to check it off my list."

"Wow."

"After I did Denali and started planning a trip to Tanzania to prep for Kilimanjaro, the guy I was dating got really snippy."

"Why?"

"He didn't understand why I wanted to climb another mountain. He said one should've been enough. I dumped him immediately and went on with my prep."

Gary was impressed. "So how did you fit all this in while teaching school?"

"Used my free time during summer vacation."

Of course. He felt like an idiot for asking such an obvious question. "Blown away here, Ms. Algebra."

She smiled and chewed. After taking a sip of her cola, she placed the can off to the side. "Don't want you knocking it over."

"More jokes. You surprised me."

"Surprise is good."

"Last night you were so chilly, I didn't think you even remembered my name."

"Oh, I did. I was chilly because . . ."

He waited.

"Truth?"

"Please."

"I got overwhelmed by all the feels, as the kids say. The feels and the memories, and how much seeing you again made me wonder if a second chance was possible. Silly, right?"

"No, Nori. Not silly."

She whispered, "I've missed you my entire life."

"Same here," he whispered back, his tone just as emotional.

Next thing he knew, she was in his arms and they were holding each other like the lost souls the past had forced them to become. "Missed you so much, baby," he confessed. "So much."

She was sobbing, and he held her and prayed for the chance to love this woman the way he was meant to love her thirty years ago.

They eased apart a bit, and he wiped at the tears on her cheeks and she did the same for him. She said, "The night you called me and told me why you couldn't take me to prom . . ."

"I died that night, Nori. I spent the entire dance watching you."

"I did the same and hated Colleen with the heat of a thousand suns."

"She wants us to remarry."

"What!"

The anger and shock on her face made him smile a little. "My sentiments exactly, but not a chance."

"Good. It's my turn."

He paused. "You mean that?"

"Am I being too real? One of the many duds I dated said I didn't have any filters and it scared him."

"You've never had any filters. You and Fontaine are the most filter-free women I've ever known."

She chuckled.

He asked, "Do you really want us to try again?"

"Yes. If that's not too scary. I would've contacted you after the divorce, but I wasn't sure if I should or how you'd feel if I did. I don't want anything formal. Definitely not a ring. I just want to be able to call you. Send you a text. Come visit. Have you visit me when you can and see if a second chance is doable."

He couldn't believe how right this felt. "I'd like that, too." So many years had passed them by and he'd didn't want to lose a second more. Life was too short. He refused to be leery of jumping in with two feet so quickly because the payoff was worth giving it a shot.

She continued, "And I don't have to meet your girls this

weekend. Let's just do us. A month from now we may decide this isn't a good idea after all and I don't want them to feel jerked around."

He agreed. They were jerked around enough by their mother. "The dance is tonight. Would you, Ms. Algebra Mountain Climber, do me the honor of being my date?"

"Yes."

He traced her lips with a slow finger. "Can I kiss you now?"

She grinned. "Always the gentleman. Yes, son of Jor-El, you may kiss me."

And so he did.

After another hour or so of reconnecting, he finally dropped Nori off at Trent and Lily's but not before sharing a few more kisses in the car in front of the house. "I'll be back to get you later."

"Okay," she said softly, and opened the door. "Bye, Gary."

When he entered his house he was walking on air. He had his Nori back. He couldn't have asked for a better afternoon.

He heard the speakers in the media room and stuck his head in. Tiff was playing with Mario on the big screen and Leah was on her laptop with a book open, making him think she was doing homework. "Ladies."

Tiff paused her game and Leah looked up. Both wore huge grins.

Tiff said, "We hear you and your lady had a good time."

He froze.

"Brain said you were so engrossed in PDA you didn't see him walk by the car."

"PDA?" he asked warily.

"Publicly displayed affection."

Gary's jaw dropped. "He didn't take pictures, did he?" He knew nothing was sacred with his daughters' generation.

Leah shook her head. "No, Dad. Brain has more respect than that."

Relief filled him.

"So," Tiff said, "tell us about this woman who has my daddy so turned up he's kissing her in public."

He laughed. Knowing he was caught, he sat and told them all about her.

When he was done, Leah said, "She climbs mountains?"

He added, "Yes, and wears red Chucks. And as you say, I have receipts." He took out his phone and showed them the pic he'd taken of Nori's high-tops.

"Sweet!" Tiff said.

Leah studied the footwear and said, "Mom wouldn't be caught dead in a pair of Chucks." She handed him back his phone. "I like this lady."

"I do, too," he said.

The girls grinned at each other.

"Are you taking her to the dance?"

"Yes."

"Can we meet her?"

"Probably not this weekend. Let's see if this works out first. She may think your dad is too slow to roll with."

"If she does, she doesn't deserve you . . . or us," Tiff declared.

Leah said, "I hope you do work out. You deserve some happy, Dad."

He agreed. "Any plans tonight?"

Leah said, "Physics test prep."

Tiffany said, "Bingeing on *Star Trek,* I'm half a season behind."

"Okay. I'm going to shower and get ready for my date."

The girls nodded, and he let them get back to what they'd been doing.

THE REC'S GYMNASIUM was decorated in the high school's colors of purple and midnight blue. There were streamers and balloons and tables circled around the open floor where the dancing would take place. Along the back wall was the food for the fancy dinner they'd be having later. Gary, dressed in a new black suit, had Nori on his arm as they entered. She looked heavenly in her midnight-blue gown complete with wrap, and he felt like the luckiest, happiest man in the world. They joined Trent and Lily at a table near the middle of the room. The place was filled with formally dressed classmates, laughter, and conversations.

Lily, wearing a black dress as beautiful as Nori's, said, "You two are making me cry. It's so good seeing you back together."

Trent said, "She's right. Tamar said you were out at Seminole Creek?"

Gary shook his head. There were no secrets in Henry Adams. "Yes." And left it at that.

Lily said, "Oh Lord. Check this out." They all turned to see Colleen walking in on the arm of Howic "It's Howard now" Pratt. He had on a white tuxedo complete with tails. Colleen was dressed in a beautiful ruby-red gown.

Gary shook his head. "She's in the market for a new husband. If Howie's not careful, he may wind up as number three."

Nori said, "They deserve each other. Prom night, I wound up punching him in the nuts because he couldn't keep his hands to himself."

Surprise showed on their faces.

"And on Friday night he tried to convince me I should come to his hotel room. Like maybe I was dumb enough to go anywhere with his drunk behind."

Gary remembered seeing the drunk Howard having a conversation with her.

Howard and Colleen stopped at their table. Howard said, "Evening, everyone."

They politely returned his greeting.

Colleen said, "Howie and I are dating." She met Gary's eyes and cuddled closer to Howie's side. Gary didn't care.

As if he hadn't heard Colleen's boast, Howie said, "Eleanor. Looking lovely as ever. Remind me to give you my card before you leave tomorrow. If you're ever in Dallas, we could have dinner."

Gary saw full-blown fury erupt on Colleen's face.

Nori said, "Thanks for the offer but I won't need your card."

"But—"

Colleen practically dragged him off. "Hon, let's find a seat."

In their wake, Lily cracked, "Oh yes, they're going to do real well together."

Again, Gary didn't care.

The rest of the night was great. They ate, danced, had an old-fashioned *Soul Train* line, exchanged phone numbers, addresses, and business cards. As he slow-danced with Nori to the last song of the evening, Gary didn't want their time together to end. "I'm so glad you came," he told her.

"So am I."

He loved dancing with her again, the scent of her perfume and the idea that they'd thrown the dice on a second chance. "You want me to take you to the airport in the morning?"

"No."

Surprised, he drew back so he could see her face in the dimmed lights. "Why not?"

"Because I may not get on the plane."

He chuckled and eased them close again. "Is that such a bad thing?"

"Yes. I have to pick up my dog from the kennel tomorrow afternoon."

"You have a dog?"

"Yes, a three-year-old Rottweiler mix named T'Challa. He's grown so big he's eating me out of house and home. I keep telling him he needs a job."

"Can't wait to meet him."

They finished the rest of the song in silence. When it ended, the reunion was officially over. Lily walked up to the mic to offer a few parting remarks and she was thanked for her extraordinary organizational skills with a rousing round of applause and cheers. The group then spent a few more minutes saying their good-byes to each other with hugs, pecks on the cheek, and promises to stay in touch.

Gary drove Nori back to Trent and Lily's and stayed to talk, reminisce, play cards, and bask in the force of nature that was Eleanor Christine Price. Around 2:00 a.m., Lily and Trent headed to bed and Nori walked Gary to the door. Holding her close, he said, "Text me when you get home so I'll know you got there safely, okay?"

She gazed up at him. "Will do. I had a great time."

"Ditto, and thanks for wanting to ride the Second Chance Train with me."

"Ditto."

Their grins met, they shared one more kiss, and Gary stepped out into the night.

The girls were asleep when he got home, but he looked in on them anyway because that's what good dads do. As he went from Leah's room to Tiffany's he was overcome with how blessed he was having them in his life, and now Nori was with him, too. Entering his bedroom, he changed into his pajamas and got into bed. As his eyes closed, he smiled, content.

CHAPTER
13

At church on Sunday, everyone was buzzing about Mal's encounter with Ruth's brother. Although no one knew the true reason for the knockout punch, rumors were rife, everyone citing everything from his being caught with another woman to having helped himself to Ruth's life savings. Moving through the crowded fellowship hall after the service, Bernadine tried to turn a deaf ear to all of it but found it difficult, because in a small town, gossip and drama were the main sources of entertainment, so she didn't linger as she usually did and drove home.

The house was quiet. Tina had flown home yesterday morning and would be back soon, but Bernadine missed her presence. Going up to her room, she got out of her church clothes, put on a pair of soft comfortable sweats, and turned on the television. She was still miffed about her standoff with Reggie yesterday. Yes, he was a doctor protecting his patient, but she wasn't accustomed to being denied; his citing her breakup with Mal as one of the reasons for his decision had been particularly irritating. Learning that Mal had been knocked out cold had filled her with concern. And now she had to decide if she should try to see him again. She didn't want him or anyone else to think visiting him meant more than it did. *And what* did *it mean?* She wasn't sure. In some ways, she felt like Dorothy in *The Wizard of Oz.* Did she want to look behind the curtain for the truth? She was supposed to be strong, confident, tough. Mal had wronged her by taking up with another woman, and clinging to that as her defense salved her hurt and punished him, allowing her to step out of his life. Would she be undercutting her strength and betraying herself by admitting she was also punishing herself? Did acknowledging that as the answer behind the curtain make her appear weak, or worse, desperate? Would it appear as though she was willing to accept his failings in exchange for his love? She'd been having this inner debate since his return to town. Now that some of the heat had boiled off her anger and she could deal with the issue rationally, it was time to look behind the curtain and honestly confront the real answer waiting there.

Crystal stopped by to have dinner. She'd made new friends at school and when not working her shifts at the Dog had been spending her free time with them. Bernadine admitted to feeling neglected but would never be so selfish as to bring it up.

On the menu were shrimp tacos, something they both loved, and it added to Bernadine's joy having her daughter all to herself.

"So, have you seen Mal since he got knocked out?" Crystal asked.

Bernadine hoped Crystal never lost her bluntness. "I tried

yesterday, but Reg wouldn't let me. He said Mal needed his rest."

"Is he okay?"

"I think so. He's recuperating over at Tamar's. I may swing by tomorrow."

"Between the hit lady and Mal, there's been a whole lot of serious drama."

"I know. How's your new place working out?"

"I love it. I realized this is the first time I've ever lived alone. Has taken me a minute to get used to that, but I'm okay. Everybody keeps asking me if I know anything about the Millers, though."

Bernadine could tell Crystal was fishing for information, so she replied, "FBI hasn't shared anything, and they don't plan to, so your friends will have to be in the dark with the rest of us." No way was she going to share what she knew with Crystal. It would be all over the county as soon as Crys got in her car. "Have you heard from Eli?"

"Talked to him last night. He's coming home for Thanksgiving. Says he's homesick, which I found kind of surprising. He said it surprised him too, but he misses everybody."

"Glad to hear he's coming. I'm pretty sure Jack misses him, too."

They spent a few minutes talking about how Eli was adjusting to being back in California, where he and his dad lived before Eli moved to Henry Adams, and how he was doing living with Trent's mom, Rita Lynn, and her cardiologist husband. "He likes them a lot. He's working in Ms. Rita's art gallery. He says they're like really cool grandparents."

Bernadine was glad to hear that.

Crystal said, "I was talking to Leah last night and she said Mr. Abbott is thinking about leaving?"

"Yes. The shooting has his parents worried, but according to Marie, he's going to stay."

"Good. Mr. James could use the help and Abbott's really cute. All that dark chocolate. Yum."

Bernadine chuckled. "Any chocolate in your life?"

"No. The guys I know are all looking for booty calls, and I am way too fabulous for that."

"Good for you. Wait for somebody worthy."

"That's the plan."

When it was time for Crystal to leave, Bernadine walked her to the door. They shared a parting hug. "I'll see you soon," Bernadine said.

"Yep. And you go see Mal and fix your life, Mom."

Bernadine drew back. "What brought that on?"

"Just how sad you look."

Bernadine's lips tightened.

Crys kissed her cheek and said softly, "I'm just saying." She added, "I love you."

And she departed.

In her office on Monday morning, Bernadine made a follow-up call to the head of the community college's culinary department about the coffee shop. He thought the idea of having the school temporarily take over the abandoned business would be a great opportunity for his students. Not only would they be given practical, hands-on experience by making the breads and pastries, they'd also receive college credits. He'd proposed contacting his counterpart at the business school to see if any of their students wanted to work the registers and take charge of the books and orders. She was on the phone with the dean of the business school when a woman knocked on her door. She was tall, dark-skinned, and wearing a gray business suit and heels. She had the air of an impatient Fortune 500 executive and appeared displeased to find Bernadine on the phone. Needing to finish her conversation with the dean and seeing as how the woman didn't have an appointment, Bernadine gestured her to a seat, raised a finger to intimate she'd be with her in a minute, and finished up her conversation. Once she was done, she said to the woman, "Sorry, but I needed to finish that. May I help you?"

"Yes, I'm Janet Roxbury and I'm trying to locate my sister, Cynthia Hale."

Bernadine took in the arrogant attitude and matching tone of voice and drew an instant dislike. "I don't know anyone by that name."

"You know her as Brenda Miller."

Alarms went off in Bernadine's head, but she kept her cool. "She and her husband left town."

"Under what circumstances?"

"They were here one day and gone the next. I have no further information."

"We both know they were moved here by the government."

"Do we?" Bernadine surreptitiously pushed the small button on her desk to turn on the security camera. She wanted a record of the conversation and the woman's face. "Ms. Roxbury, I have no other information. If you believe the government is involved, you might want to contact them."

"I'd like to see where she and Sam were living. There might be a clue there."

Bernadine had no intention of giving her anything, especially when she'd offered no verification as to her identity. "I

can't help you, Ms. Roxbury. If you'd like to leave your contact information—"

"No, I'll keep looking."

Bernadine found that telling. Sharing her contact info
would be a no-brainer if Janet Roxbury was really who she
claimed to be.

"Thanks for your help," the woman tossed out sarcastically,
and swept out.

Bernadine simply smiled. "You're welcome."

Bernadine quickly clicked on her laptop's security app to
view the parking lot. The camera kicked in just in time to see
Roxbury entering a black SUV. A burly white guy dressed in
black was behind the wheel. Bernadine grabbed a screen shot
of him and the license plate. As the SUV exited the lot, she
picked up her phone and called Kyle Dalton.

He called back an hour later and said his techs had run the
plate and it came back as registered to a Honda hybrid belong-
ing to an elderly retired postal clerk in Boise, Idaho. They were
still trying to determine how it wound up on the SUV. As for
Roxbury and her driver, their faces were being run through
databases worldwide, but so far, no hits. She asked him, "So,
should we be concerned here?" She had him on speaker so the
rest of the people in her office— Trent, Lily, Luis, and Barrett—
could hear the conversation.

"Not sure."

"You're not filling us with confidence, Agent Dalton," Trent
said.

"I know and I'm sorry. The woman you knew as Brenda
Miller did have a sister, but she died at the age of fourteen.
Once we find out who this Roxbury woman really is, we'll
be better able to assess the situation and offer advice. In the

meantime, keep your eyes open. If any more strangers show up asking questions, call me right away."

They assured him they would and Bernadine ended the call.

"So," she asked her people. "What do you think?"

Barrett replied, "We do as Kyle suggested and keep our eyes open."

Lily said, "And let's hope the Bureau can figure out who this woman is before something ugly happens."

Barrett said, "Should we alert the town about this?"

Luis replied, "I think we have to. Trent, what do you think?"

"I agree. The more eyes looking out the better. I also don't want people thinking they're in an innocent conversation with a stranger concerning the Millers that might not, in fact, be so innocent."

Bernadine agreed. "I put in a call to Will, but Deputy Ransom said he left this morning for a conference in Boston. He'll be back later in the week. I did let her know what happened and sent her the screen shots. She promised to let the sheriff know and asked to be kept in the loop. She's going to call Kyle to make sure they are."

Luis said, "Sounds like we have all the bases covered for now."

Barrett added, "Keeping fingers crossed that it's enough. I'm going to run a diagnostic on all the cameras. We'll keep them running twenty-four/seven for the next thirty days. If anything jumps off it'll probably be within that time frame."

Bernadine was comforted by their plans but there were troubling uncertainties. They had no idea what might happen in the days ahead. She'd like to think Roxbury would move on and look for her alleged sister elsewhere, but she sensed they might not be that lucky.

An hour or so later, Gary Clark showed up at her office. "Hey there," she said, "are you just stopping by on your way to see your buddies, or are you here to see me?"

"Here to see you, if you have a minute or two?"

"For you I have at least all day. Have a seat. What's up?"

"I need a lawyer. My ex-wife wants custody of Leah and Tiffany. The girls and I were hoping you could recommend someone."

She was surprised. Knowing Gary's ex-wife hadn't wanted the girls at all after the divorce, she wondered what had changed Colleen's mind. "If you're looking for a lawyer, I take it you aren't down with the change. What about the girls?"

"They aren't, either."

"Then let me make a few calls. I know how much your girls mean to you and to their friends. My Bottom Women's group has a slew of legal beagles on retainer for cases like this, and I'll take care of the fees."

"I can't let you do that."

"Sure you can. You save your money to send your girls to college. I have your back on this."

"Are you sure?"

"Positive. Give me a call tonight after work, and I'll have the name of someone you can speak with about your case."

He nodded. "Thank you, Bernadine."

"You're welcome. That's how we roll here, you know."

"I do, but it's still surprising and humbling." He smiled and got to his feet. "Well, that was easy. Guess I'll get back to the store."

"I'll talk to you tonight."

He left. She flicked on the intercom. "Hey, Lil?"

"Yeah?"

"What's going on with Gary and his ex?"

"I'll be there in a half a sec to tell you all about it."

"Thanks."

After hearing about Gary's ex-wife, the reunion, and his rekindled love affair with his high school sweetheart, Bernadine bit the bullet and drove over to see Mal. Getting out of the car, she walked up the steps to the porch and knocked. Tamar answered, smiled, and stepped back to let her in.

"I'm assuming you're here to see Mal?"

"I am, and please don't say it's about time."

"Wasn't going to say that, so drop your gloves, missy."

Embarrassed, Bernadine apologized. "Sorry."

"He's in there."

Bernadine went to the open door of the bedroom Tamar indicated and stood there a moment observing Mal. He was in bed with his eyes closed, and it surprised her how fragile he appeared with his two shiners and swollen nose. "Hey, Mal," she called quietly.

His lids rose, and he looked her way. "Hey."

"Wanted to come check on you."

He wiped the sleep from his face. "Appreciate it. Not looking my best, but you're welcome to come on in if you like."

He sounded like a person plugged up with a bad cold. She guessed it was the broken nose. She took a seat in the rocker near the bed and set her handbag beside it. "How are you?"

"Been better. Head still hurts like crazy; nose, too. Reg said it will stop soon. Hope he's right."

"I won't stay long. I know you need your rest."

"What I need is to tell you how I ended up like this, and

if I could get on my knees to apologize for the pain I caused you, I would."

Silent, she held his bruised and regret-filled eyes and allowed herself to be touched by the sincerity he exuded. That allowance wasn't a weakness. He'd hurt her on more levels than she ever thought anyone capable of doing since Leo, and it took strength to acknowledge that vulnerability, and to step out from behind the curtain anyway. "Tell me everything."

So he did: about how he felt after Key West, his ill-thought-out plan to make himself feel better, the way he'd used Ruth as a placeholder for Bernadine, and Ruth's response once she realized the truth. "I used her," he confessed. "I didn't think about her feelings, or her hopes for a committed relationship with me. None of that. I started seeing her because I didn't think you'd forgive me for the stealing, and I missed you. I thought it would be easy for an old broken-down player like me to replace you, but you're irreplaceable, baby, and Ruth became collateral damage." He added, "I dogged Reggie for being upset about all the money Roni made, and I fell into the same stupid trap. And now it doesn't look like I'm going to get any of the money back to repay you." He told her about Dresden. "I'm still committed to paying you back, though."

She replied, "I appreciate that, but the happiness you gave me had nothing to do with how much money you had or didn't have. Who has a picnic in the back of a pickup? That first time, I thought you were totally insane, but I had so much fun. Just as I did when you taught me to fly a kite, and the Santa hat you wore on our sleigh ride. How could you think none of that meant anything to me, Malachi July?"

"Men get things real twisted sometimes."

"You think? I wouldn't know a raptor from a raft were

it not for you. Honestly? I want to shake you for destroying what we had. It was precious to me. *You* were precious to me."

He looked grim. "I'm so sorry."

She sighed. Hearing him out did help clear some of the issues, but now what?

"So where do we go from here?" he asked.

"I was asking myself that same thing. I don't know. I wish I did. I can't say okay, let's try it again."

"Why not?"

She went still. It was a hard question, whose answer lay hidden behind the curtain. If she pulled it aside, what would she see? Let bygones be bygones and go forward? That seemed easy enough, but was reconciliation supposed to be easy? Her pain and heartache had mattered; it still did. Was she supposed to pretend that it didn't? But what did she gain by continuing to cling to the hurt?

"Not trying to put you on the spot."

"That's how it feels," she replied honestly.

"I love you, Bernadine. If you want to kick me to the curb permanently, I'll understand, and it'll be my loss for causing this mess. But let me try to show you that I won't hurt you again and you can trust me again."

Both were major concerns. No one wanted to step into a bear trap twice.

"We can start small," he said. "No dates or dinners or big stuff. Let me call you every now and then, that's all I ask for now."

She met his eyes and he whispered, "Please."

She looked away. He wasn't asking for much, she told herself. She'd concede him the small boon. Maybe it was the way to go.

He added, "And I promise not to blow up your phone every hour on the hour. Just one call a day. That's all."

Needing to distance herself from the emotions welling up inside, she stood and shouldered her handbag.

He waited.

She gave him a tight nod. "Okay. Call, and we'll go from there. No guarantees, though."

"Understood."

I need to get back to work. I'll check on you in a few days. Take care."

"I will. You, too."

She said good-bye to Tamar and got the side eye she'd earned. On the drive back to town, her phone sounded. She glanced over at it lying on the seat and saw a red heart. It was from Mal.

AFTER BERNADINE DEPARTED, Mal slid back into sleep until midafternoon. Hungry, he forced himself to get up and eat the food Tamar had waiting for him in the kitchen. He could've easily taken it to bed on a tray, but he wanted to get back on his feet as soon as possible and lounging around with a tray wasn't the way to go. His head was still pounding, but the pain meds helped.

Seated at the table, eating soup and a turkey sandwich, he was glad Bernadine had come by. He was also glad he'd confessed everything. Although she hadn't been overly en-thusiastic about his desire to call her, she had accepted his proposal, and he looked upon that as a beginning.

Tamar came into the kitchen. "You have a visitor."

"Who?"

"Your real girlfriend."

Confused by that, he asked, "My real girlfriend?"

And when Zoey walked into the kitchen, he grinned. "Hey, Ms. Miami."

Tamar left them alone.

"Hey, OG." Zoey stopped and took in his face. Hers turned serious. "Does it hurt?"

He nodded and even that slight movement made his face throb.

"It looks like it does."

Putting her backpack on the floor, she took a seat. "I wanted to see how you were doing."

"I'm okay. Got a busted nose, though."

"I busted Devon's once; it only gave him one black eye, though."

He chuckled. "I remember."

The concern on her face made his heart swell with affection. She appeared genuinely concerned.

"Did you come all this way on your bike?"

"No, Mama Roni drove me. I asked her if she'd bring me after school, and she said yes. She's talking to Tamar."

"Oh, okay."

"I brought you something." Zoey bent down to her pack and handed him a purple Crown Royal bag.

He laughed. "You drinking Crown now?"

She giggled. "No. Daddy Reg likes it. I think the bags are pretty, so he lets me have them. Open it."

He noted the slight weight of whatever it held, and as she watched, he opened it, and what he saw inside dropped his jaw. "Zoey?"

"Don't say you can't take it. My aunt Cass says when someone gives you something from the heart, you can't turn it down."

He poured the contents onto the table. There were ten gold coins. Each worth a small fortune. They originally belonged to the outlaw Griffin Blake, who'd buried stolen railroad gold in Henry Adams back in the 1880s. The cache was found a hundred years later by Old Man Patterson. When Patterson died last year, he left the gold to Zoey.

"Do you think that's enough to pay Ms. Bernadine back?" she asked.

Mal was speechless and moved to tears. "Baby girl, I—"

"When I first came to live here, I had really bad nightmares, and you brought me Tiger Tamar. You helped me, OG. You're having a nightmare too, sorta, so it's my turn to help you."

He still didn't know what to say. He heard movement and saw Roni standing in the doorway. "Zoey came to me with the idea. And we all know she doesn't like hearing no, especially if it's something on her heart. Take the coins, Mal."

He looked to Zoey again. And what else could he say but "Thank you, Zoey. Can I get a hug?"

She smiled and returned the embrace with a strength that equaled his. "Thank you," he croaked through the emotion in his throat.

Roni wiped at her tears. Looking on, Tamar did, too.

Mal was so overcome his hands shook as he put the coins back in the bag. "I'll make sure Ms. Bernadine gets these."

"Okay." Zoey added, "And if there's anything left over, get you some boxing lessons." She pointed at his eyes. "It's not a good look, OG."

He laughed.

Roni said, "Come on, Miss Girl, let's go. You have homework."

Zoey picked up her backpack, waved, and followed her mom out the door.

Mal looked at Tamar and said, "She's something, isn't she?"

Tamar nodded. "Yes, she is, and I know you're grateful."

"I am."

She exited, leaving him alone.

Mal felt as though his world was finally realigning. He cast his bruised, swollen eyes to the heavens and whispered, "Thank you."

CHAPTER 14

Over at the garage, Amari was working alone. Ms. Marie's car was all but done, and with his dad at a meeting in Franklin, he was given the task of handling the final details like vacuuming out the interior, cleaning the windows, polishing the finish, and putting a shine on the chrome. The 1969 Camaro was now midnight blue, fully restored, and it looked amazing. Had it been up to him, tinted windows would've been added, but his dad nixed the idea. He said Ms. Marie wasn't going to enjoy being pulled over by the police every time she got behind the wheel, and Amari understood that. Tinted windows would've had the police going through the trunk with a warrant and dogs. With clear glass the car looked classic. All a cop would want to know was how fast it rolled.

After finishing the waxing, he was admiring the shine when Tiffany walked in. Surprised, he blurted out, "What're you doing here?" She'd never come to the garage before.

"I need to talk to you."

"About what?" She was the last person he expected to see. "How'd you get here?"

"I walked."

He shook off the fumbles in his brain. "Okay. So, what do you need to talk to me about?"

"My mom wants to change the custody arrangements."

"You mind if I finish this last window while we talk? My dad wants this done today."

"No. Nice car. Whose is it, yours?"

"Not a chance. Belongs to Ms. Marie. Dad and I restored it."

"It's sweet."

He agreed and then remembered his manners. "You can sit on the couch if you want." Although he hoped she didn't plan to stay long because he needed to get his work done and she was a distraction. "There're drinks in that old fridge over there."

"Thanks, but I'm good." She sat.

He picked up a spray bottle holding cleaner solution and a paper towel. He sat on the edge of the Camaro's front seat and started in on the window on the driver's-side door.

"So like I said, my mom wants to change the custody arrangements and we'll probably have to go to court. What am I supposed to say?"

Confused, he paused. "Say about what?"

"If the judge asks me who I want to live with, what do I say?"

He scanned her face for a second or two, noted how pretty she'd gotten lately, heard himself, and moved away from that real quick. Truthfully, he wanted to blow her off. This was Tiffany Adele after all, and even though she was way less of a brat than she once was, she'd never come to him for any kind of advice before. "Why ask me?"

"Because, Amari. Just help me, okay?"

"Okay. Do you want to live with your mom?"

"No. Being with her all summer made me crazy. She whined all the time. Everything we did was wrong. She even dissed Leah about not being pretty enough and liking science."

"Then what's the problem?"

"I don't want her to be alone."

"So you'd rather pack up and move to Atlanta to stay with her and be miserable for the rest of your life?"

"No, but—" Her lips tightened, and she looked off into the distance.

Giving her advice was way more than he'd signed on for. He resumed cleaning the window. "Have you talked to Reverend Paula about this?"

"No."

"Why not?"

"I don't know. I thought talking to somebody closer to my age would be better." She looked so confused Amari almost felt sorry for her.

She asked, "Suppose your bio mom asked you to come and live with her? What would you say?"

"To kick rocks. She showed me who she was when Dad and I visited her and her husband. I like my life the way it is."

"I like mine the way it is, too."

"Then what's the problem?"

"She just seems so sad."

"Did she act happy when you and Leah were there?"

She shook her head.

He wanted to throw up his hands. "Do you like living here?"

"I do."

"Then why move away and add a bunch of drama to your life you don't want?"

"I don't know. I feel as though I owe her."

"Owe her what? Didn't she say she didn't want you and Leah when your parents broke up?"

Her reply was soft. "Yes."

"Sounds like an easy decision, but I'm not you."

"I know."

"You should talk to Reverend Paula. Or maybe Crystal. They're both way better at this advice stuff than I am."

"Okay, but you helped. Thanks."

He found himself staring at her from where he was sitting, and she was staring back. He felt kind of weird, like he was seeing her for the first time: her face, the way she wore her hair, the shape of her lips. Something was going on, but he wasn't sure what. He looked away and there stood his dad, watching. Amari jumped, startled, and hit his head on the door frame above him.

His dad smiled. "You okay, son?"

"Ow. Yeah."

His dad said, "Hey, Tiff."

"Hi, Mr. July. I needed to talk to Amari about something. I'm sorry for keeping him from getting his work done."

"You're fine."

She turned to Amari and said, "Thanks for the help. I'm going to go. I told Dad I'd come by the store so he could take me home."

"Is the car done, Amari?" Trent asked.

"Yes." Amari got out, rubbed the sore spot on his head, and surveyed Ms. Marie's ride. "She's going to love this."

"Then how about you drive it out to the pump and fill it up and we can run Tiffany home. You drive."

Amari stared. "You're going to let me drive? This?"

"Did I forget to tell you this is going to be your car?"

"WHAT!" Amari's heart was beating so hard and fast he couldn't breathe. "You're punking me, right?"

"You ever know me to punk you?"

Amari looked at Tiffany and her shining dark brown eyes were as wide as his. It was at that point that Amari "Flash" Steele July began jumping up and down like a little kid getting his first Xbox. He didn't care if it blew his image of cool, or if Tiffany told everybody he'd acted insane. His dad just gave him the dopest car in the state of Kansas! And when he stopped jumping, he walked around it, viewing it in an entirely different light. The beautiful, perfectly restored, midnight-blue Camaro was his! Brain was going to be so jealous! He jumped up and down a few more times. His dad threw him the keys and Amari got in. Adjusting the mirrors, he carefully backed out of the bay and steered over to the old pump.

After filling the car with gas, he sat and waited for Tiffany and his dad to get in. Because of the law, she had to be in the backseat, his dad up front.

"Let your dad know we're taking you home, Tiff," Trent said. "Do you have your house key?"

"I do." She sent a quick text. "Okay. He said he'll meet me at home."

Amari had been driving since he was a little kid, so he had no idea why he was so nervous pulling out onto Main Street, but he was. Willing himself to calm down, he concentrated on his steering and staying under the speed limit, hoping he'd relax.

His dad looked over. "You okay?"

"Yeah."

They passed the Dog and the rec and the church. In a way, he wanted everyone to see him driving. But he didn't want a swelled head to make him wreck his new ride before it was a day old, so he went back to concentrating. Everyone in town would know about the car soon enough. Impressing Tiffany was playing into his nervousness for some reason too, and he refused to delve into why. He passed the Power Plant and turned onto the road leading past Mr. Bing's farm.

"You're a good driver," Tiff said behind him.

A glance up into the mirror showed her smiling and he quickly focused on the windshield, wondering what was wrong with him. "Thanks."

His dad said, "When you get your license and you're allowed to drive alone, we'll put a Bluetooth hookup in here for your music."

"Do I have to wait that long?"

He received that patented parent look in response, so he kept driving and didn't argue.

When they reached the Clark house, he slowed and turned into the driveway. The car was a two-door with bucket seats, so his dad opened his door and stepped out to allow Tiffany to do the same. But before exiting she said, "Thanks, Amari."

"You're welcome."

She removed her seat belt, then leaned between the two front seats and gave him a quick kiss on the cheek. "Thanks for the advice." And she hustled out.

He must've blacked out for a minute, because when he

came to, his dad was back in the shotgun seat looking quietly amused. "You okay to drive?"

Amari snarled inwardly and backed down the driveway. He had nothing to say the entire way home.

After dinner, he was in his room brooding at his desk, when his mom peeked in on him. "You were awfully quiet during dinner. Are you feeling okay?"

"I think I'm coming down with the flu again."

She paused for a moment and eyed him. "Flu as in sick, or flu as in girls." When he first started liking Kyra, he'd been so jumbled up inside he thought he was coming down with something. His mom had helped him figure things out.

"Girls."

She walked over to where he was seated at his desk and rested her hip against the edge. "Anybody I know?"

He blew out a breath. "Tiffany."

Her eyes widened. "Tiffany Clark?"

He nodded unhappily and told her about Tiffany showing up at the garage and the conversation they had. "When I drove her home, she kissed me on the cheek, and I think I passed out."

"Really?"

"I'm seriously thinking of running myself over with my new car." He glanced up and saw the soft smile on Lily's face. "It's not funny, Mom."

"I'm not laughing at you, sweetheart. I'm just surprised."

"How do you think I feel?"

"Do you like her?"

"I think so, but I don't want to. It's Tiffany."

"I understand, but sometimes the brain doesn't control affairs of the heart."

"Jeez, don't call it that." He put his head down and bounced it against the edge of the desk. "I don't want to like her."

"She's grown up a lot in the past few years."

"I know, and she's cuter, too." Hearing himself, he groaned. "I can't believe I said that." He bounced his head again.

"I won't tell anybody. Promise."

"What am I going to do, Mom? Do I ignore it and hope it goes away?"

"You can try, I suppose."

"This is a nightmare."

"Whatever you decide, please don't be mean to Tiffany hoping that will scare her away."

"I won't." He sighed. "Maybe I should talk to Dad."

"I think that's an excellent idea. He's watching TV. I'll send him up."

"Thanks."

She kissed him on the forehead and left him alone.

His dad came up a few minutes later. "Your mother said you wanted to talk to me."

"Yeah. It's about Tiffany."

"I was wondering about that. What's going on with you two?"

"I wish I knew, but I think I like her." Amari told him what he'd told his mom and how he felt.

Trent listened and said, "You're at the age where girls are starting to look real good, and your job is to keep yourself under control."

"You mean physically?"

His dad nodded. A few years back they'd had what his dad called the birds-and-bees talk, so Amari knew about condoms and STDs, porn addiction, and the rest.

His dad added, "When things get hot and heavy and your body starts overriding your brain, you can lose yourself."

"But how do I not like her?"

"Tough question, because a lot of times love comes at you fast, and you don't have any control over liking a girl. But whatever you do—whether it's a kiss or just holding her hand—make sure she's okay with it. And if she says no, respect that. Don't try and wear her down so she'll change her mind. No means no. Always."

Amari understood consent, it was all over the news and the Internet, but he didn't think that would be a problem. He was looking for a way out, not how to get closer.

His dad continued, "And who knows, Tiffany may be the one for you."

Amari glared, and his dad chuckled in response. "You'll figure it out, son."

"I hope so. Thanks again for the car."

"Thank Marie. It was her idea."

"Really?"

"Yes."

"Okay. I will."

"Are we done here?"

"I guess."

His dad gave him a pat on the shoulder. "You'll be fine." And he left the room.

Sitting alone, Amari wondered why life had to be so complicated. In truth, this mess with Tiffany was a small problem. It wasn't like being in foster care and wondering if there'd be anything to eat, or if the next home you were moved to had heat or not. He'd survived that, so he guessed he'd survive this, too.

Devon appeared in the doorway. Amari looked up. "What do you want?"

"Zoey gave OG some of her gold so he could pay back Ms. Bernadine," he said excitedly.

"When?"

"After school. Her mom drove her over to Tamar's."

Amari's relationship with their grandfather was still unsettled, but he knew Zoey loved the OG just as much as he did. "I'm glad she helped him."

"Me, too, but I still think he should paint the fence."

"Bye, Dev."

Devon stuck out his tongue and went back to his room.

Wondering how much it might cost to send his brother to Madagascar, permanently, Amari picked up his phone and sent Zoey a text. *Heard about the gold. Awesome.*

She replied. ☺

CHAPTER
15

By midweek, Mal had had it with his confinement. Four days had passed since his altercation with Ruth's brother and he was ready to go home. The throbbing in his nose and head only bothered him occasionally and the bruising around his eyes was fading. When he walked into the kitchen for breakfast that morning, he asked Tamar, "Can you run me home?"

She looked up from reading the day's news on her laptop. "Eat first."

He didn't want to, but was in no mood to argue, so he sat and helped himself to the grits, scrambled eggs, and bacon.

On their ride into town, he glanced away from the cold rain drenching the countryside and said, "Thanks for taking me in."

"You're welcome. Glad life is looking up."

"Me, too." And he was. With Zoey's gift, he could finally make restitution and, depending upon what Trent and the others decided, maybe return to work at the Dog. Paying the money back might also aid in his quest to regain Bernadine's love. Time would tell.

As Tamar pulled into the Dog's parking lot, he thought about all that had occurred since he'd last been home and how his life had changed. In a way, he felt as if he were starting over, and planned to take advantage of this second chance. "Thanks, Tamar."

"No problem. Call me if you need anything."

"Will do." He got out of the truck and moved quickly through the rain to his place. Fitting the key into the lock, he gave Tamar a quick wave. Inside, warmth and silence greeted him. Removing his damp jacket, he hung it on the closet doorknob and savored the relief and gratitude that filled him.

Taking a seat on the couch, he sent text messages to Clay, Trent, Marie, and Rocky to let them know he was home. He wanted to contact Bernadine to give her the gold, but hesitated. So far, he'd stayed true to his promise to text her only once a day. Most of his texts had consisted of a simple how are you, or have a good day. He'd steered clear of asking to see her, take her out, or come on her in any way that might jeopardize their fragile truce. Giving the coins to Trent would be a better idea. That way the distance she wanted could be maintained. And who knew, maybe she'd call to say thanks.

Trent stopped by a few hours later to pick up the gold.

Mal confessed, "I wasn't sure who to give it to."

"I'll make sure it gets where it needs to go."

"Thanks."

An awkward silence followed, and Mal searched for words to repair the breach he'd created. "My apologies again for what I put you through. You've always been a better son than I deserved."

"I appreciate that."

Mal knew it would take time to repair their relationship and he was willing to do whatever it took to again have Trent's respect. "Going to take Marie's advice and apologize to everybody, including Amari. Luis's son, Alfonso, is on my list, too."

"Glad you're ready to fix things," Trent replied. "It'll mean a lot."

"I hope so."

"It will, and it does—especially to me." When Trent extended his hand for a shake, Mal, filled with surprise and emotion, extended his own and shook firmly.

"Let's go back to being family. Okay?" Trent said softly.

His heart full, Mal nodded.

They broke the connection and viewed each other in the silence. For the first time in weeks, Mal felt no shame meeting Trent's eyes. "Thanks for being my son."

"I've always loved you, old man, and always will. That's never been at issue."

"Do I still have a job?"

Trent smiled. "Yes. I have a temp filling in for you, so take the weekend to finish recovering."

"Okay."

"I need to get back to the Power Plant. I'll call you later."

Trent departed. A humbled Mal sat down. Once again he noted how blessed he was to have Trent as his son and was glad his apology had been taken to heart. He thought maybe he should have leather jackets made with "Mal July Apology Tour" written across the back. He wondered if he could convince Clay to be a roadie.

The next morning, he woke up at dawn and had his coffee outside on his small deck. The rain had stopped sometime during the night, and although the air was chilly, it felt good to sit and sip and watch the sunrise. He also thought about the day ahead. Missing Bernadine continued to resonate inside like the quiet tinkle of a delicate wind chime, but there was nothing he could do but sigh and move on. He'd sent Rocky a text last night asking to see her, so when he heard his doorbell a short while later, he answered it, and there she stood.

"Morning," she said, coming inside. "What's up? Are you okay?"

"I'm fine. Just making sincere apologies to everybody I hurt during this whole stupid affair and that includes you."

"Okay," she replied with a hint of doubt.

"I mean it, Rock. I'm truly sorry. And thanks for taking down Ruth's brother."

"You're welcome. He needed it after sucker punching you that way." She viewed his eyes. "You look like you're healing up."

"I am. Head has stopped hurting, but my nose is still a little sore."

"I heard about Zoey's gift. What a big heart."

"I know. She'll probably rule the world one day. I just hope I live long enough to see it."

She looked him up and down and, as if she could see the truth in him, said quietly, "Welcome back, Mal."

Hearing that meant so much, he choked up. "I still have a long way to go to be trusted again, but thanks for not putting me out with the trash."

"It was real close, believe me."

"I know, and it was what I deserved." And he based that on how he'd've reacted had someone illegally helped themselves to his bank account. Being happy wouldn't have been on the list.

Rocky said, "I'm glad you mentioned trust, though, because that's going to remain an issue for now. You're welcome to come back and work if you want, but the passwords, and handling the books, are still off-limits."

"Understood. I think I'm going to stick with the custodian job for now." He needed the solitude the position offered to help put him back on track.

Their eyes met. Over the years, Rocky had stuck with him through everything. He never wanted to disappoint her, ever again. "Thanks, Rock."

"You're welcome. I need to get to work. We'll be having Siz's going-away party two weeks from Saturday. Make sure you're there."

"Wouldn't miss it."

"I'll see you later." And with that she was gone.

The Mal Apology Tour continued for the rest of the day. He spoke to Marie, Gen, and Barrett Payne, who was in his office at the store.

"Finally come to your senses, have you?" Payne asked.

Mal knew the retired Marine wasn't going to give him a break and it was okay. "Yes, I have."

"Good. Leave the dumb stuff to the kids from now on, how about it?"

Mal gave him a crisp salute. "Yes, sir!"

Barrett returned the salute. "Carry on."

Leaving the store with a smile, Mal stopped by Reg's office to clear the air with him and thank him for his care. Reg evaluated his nose and eyes. "You're healing nicely. Try to avoid being punched out in the future."

Mal nodded.

"You mean a lot to my daughter and to this town. And as she would say, 'No more being a dumb ass, okay?'"

Mal chuckled. "Got it."

After lunch, he walked into the fire station and found Luis at his desk. "Can I bother you for a minute, Chief?"

Luis, apparently still upset, didn't hide his displeasure at seeing him but gestured to a seat. "What can I do for you?"

"Came to thank you for the verbal slap in the face you gave me at the meeting. I earned it. Never had anyone accuse me of being a detriment to the race before. You woke me up."

Luis studied him silently for a moment before saying, "Glad to hear it."

Mal added, "And if it's okay, I'd like to talk to Alfonso and Maria, so I can apologize to them, too."

Luis seemed caught off guard by that. "You're serious?"

Mal nodded. "I want to make things right. I don't ever want your son to question the way you've raised him or deal with a problem the way I did."

"I was so angry with you."

"And you had every right to be, Luis. Every right." His fury at the meeting had been memorable.

"When do you want to talk to him?"

"Can I stop by the house this evening after you're home?"

"How about I send you a text when we're ready."

"Sounds good." Mal stood. "I'll let you get back to what you were doing. Thanks, Luis."

"You're welcome."

Mal started to the door.

"Mal?"

He turned back.

"Thanks."

Mal nodded. Buoyed by the positive day, he stepped out into the sunshine.

That evening, after receiving Luis's text, he drove out to the doublewide the Acostas were occupying until their new house in the subdivision was finished. Luis ushered him in. Mal nodded at Anna and the children, then they all took seats in the kitchen.

Alfonso, looking professorial in his black-rimmed glasses, said, "My dad said you wanted to talk to me and Maria."

"I do. It's about the money I stole."

The two kids shared a quick look of surprise.

"I set a bad example when I did it, and I wanted you to know it didn't make me feel better about myself. In fact, I feel pretty stupid."

Maria asked, "But why did you think it would make you feel better?"

"Because I thought it would turn me into somebody else."

"Who?"

"I don't know. Somebody richer and cooler maybe. Pretty dumb, huh?"

Alfonso shot his dad a quick glance. "We're not supposed to call adults dumb."

Luis said, "You can make an exception this one time."

"Then, yeah, OG. It was pretty dumb. Stealing is always wrong."

"You're right," Mal replied. "And that's why I came to apologize. I don't ever want you or any of the other kids to think you can fix a problem by choosing the dumb way out."

Maria asked, "Is Tamar going to put you on punishment?"

"No, but I'll be putting myself on punishment."

Alfonso's eyes widened. "Really? Whoa. What are you going to do?"

"First, apologize to everyone I hurt because that's what you're supposed to do when you mess up. Then I'm going to do some other things I don't want to talk about right now."

"Devon says you should paint the fence. I don't ever want to do that. Zoey said it's really hard."

"Zoey learned that firsthand this summer, so make sure you stay away from the dark side. And always talk to your dad or your grandmother Anna if you have a problem. They'll steer you right."

"Okay."

"You have any questions for an old man who did something real dumb?" Mal asked.

Alfonso showed a small smile. "No, sir."

Maria said, "No, sir."

"Then thanks for listening."

"You're welcome."

And after receiving a nod from their dad, the kids left the adults alone.

Anna said, "Mal, I don't know too many people who'd put themselves out there for some children the way you just did."

"It was owed—to them and to Luis." Done with this portion of the Apology Tour, he stood. "Luis, thanks for allowing me to clean things up. I'm promising everyone it won't happen again."

"Holding you to that." Luis walked him to the door and Mal drove home.

The next morning, although Trent told him to take the day off, Mal went to the school, not to work but to talk to the kids. His unannounced entrance into the classroom grabbed everyone's attention.

Face puzzled, Jack said, "Hey, Mal. What's up?"

"Stopped by to talk to the kids about the theft, if I may."

Jack went silent for a moment, then said, "Um, sure."

Mal added, "Can you have Mr. Abbott bring the young ones in, too?"

"Yeah. Hold on."

He left and returned with Abbott and his small class, which included some Franklin kids and Jaz and Maria.

While they were getting settled, Mal eyed Amari, seated at his desk, arms folded, eyes skeptical. Mal had earned the skepticism and it pained him. Having Amari's respect meant as much to him as having Trent's. He wanted Devon's as well, even if the boy was a pain in the behind most of the time. In fact, Mal thought of every kid in Jack's classroom as one of his grandchildren, and he'd let them down. Terribly.

He realized they were all quietly waiting for him to do whatever he'd come to do, so he began, "I came to apologize to you for being a thief and a liar." Mal saw Amari's eyes widen, but continued, "Sometimes, adults make excuses for their bad behavior, but I have none. Zip. Zero. What I did was selfish, stupid, and hurtful, and it cost me your respect. I'm sorry. As your OG, I'm supposed to set an example of how to handle life the right way. Instead, I set one that none of you should emulate. Ever. Hopefully, sometime in the future I can re-earn your respect, and the respect of your parents and teachers." He looked to Jack, who gave him an approving nod. "And as my way of showing how serious I am, I'll be painting Ms. Marie's fence, first thing in the morning."

He heard gasps. "I know it's only been a punishment for young folks, but I think my crime fits."

The kids stared at each other with wonder-filled eyes. Amari had his fingers steepled against his lips, watching. Mal wished he knew what was going through his grandson's mind.

Amari asked, "Do you mean it? I mean really?"

Mal knew his response would color their relationship for years to come—maybe forever—so he replied with genuine, heart-driven sincerity, "Yes, Amari, I do. This isn't like that half-baked apology I gave at the town meeting. This is the real deal, and I hope, one day, you'll forgive me."

He sensed Amari weighing both him and the answer. As if coming to a decision, Amari stood, smiled, and began applauding. The other kids followed his lead, and soon the room rang with cheers, shouts, desk poundings, and roars of "OG! OG! OG!"

Mal cried. He couldn't help it.

Later, on his way down the hallway to the exit doors, Mal heard Amari call his name. Wiping the lingering dampness from his eyes, he turned and waited.

When Amari reached him, the boy just eyed him, before saying, "That was a big thing you did."

"Big screw-ups demand big things."

"I was so mad at you. At least when Devon was stealing it was for a good reason. Yours didn't make sense."

He nodded. "I know, and losing the respect of you, your dad, and everyone else? All the money in the world couldn't make up for that." He studied the boy who'd brought nothing but joy into his life. "I hope one day soon you'll be proud to be my grandson again."

"I think we're going to be okay."

Mal opened his arms. "Can an old man get a hug?"

Amari didn't hesitate.

As Mal held him close, tears stung his eyes. "Thanks for giving me a second chance."

Amari looked up. "We're family. It's how we Julys roll."

That evening, Mal had one more tour stop to make. As he rang the doorbell, he thought this one might be the most difficult. When Crystal answered the door, she gave him a puzzled look. "Hey, Mal."

"Hey, Crys. Can I talk to you for a few minutes?"

"Sure. Come on in."

He stepped inside and followed her into her nicely furnished living room with its neutral color palette and art-filled walls.

"Have a seat," she said, gesturing to the couch.

He sat. "I stopped by because I'm going around apologizing to everybody for being such a dumb ass."

"'Bout time."

He hid his smile. She never pulled any punches and he loved her for it. "And I wanted to apologize to you, too."

She appeared surprised. "Why?"

"For hurting your mom."

"Ah yeah. Broke her heart and all that." She studied him for a moment before saying, "Instead of being here, you need to be apologizing to her while kneeling in two inches of broken glass and barbed wire."

He winced.

She asked, "Have you talked to her?"

He nodded. "Yes. She visited me while I was healing up at Tamar's."

"Oh yeah. I heard about the big fight with the lady's brother."

She peered at his eyes. "You look like you're better. Zoey said you had two black eyes."

"I did."

"I admit, I thought you getting a beatdown was a good thing, but Mom still loves you. Not sure why after what you did, but she does."

"I still love her too, probably more than before. She makes me better."

"And you used to make her better. I worry that all that turning the world is going to make her stroke out, but you helped her relax. She needed that, and then your dumb behind tried to kill her anyway. Who does that to someone they're 'posed to love?"

"I know, Crys."

"I put her through hell when I ran away. I never thought I'd see her that sad again, but you topped me."

Shame returned, and he looked away.

She continued, "Because I know how much she cares about you, I've been telling her to try and work things out between the two of you, but me? It's going to be a long time before I stop wanting to cuss at you every time I see you."

He met her angry eyes.

"I'm being honest. I accept your apology in the spirit it's given, but that's as far as I go. When you fix things with Mom, we'll talk." She stood. "Thanks for coming by."

Mal had no other choice but to take his dismissal and leave. On the drive back to his place, he sighed. He'd been right. The final stop on the Apology Tour had been the hardest. He was lucky to have gotten out alive.

Bright and early Saturday morning, he showed up at Marie's door. "Came to paint."

She smiled. "So I hear. What color?"

"Green, in honor of Zoey." It was her favorite color.

"Well, have at it. And remember to take breaks. You're an old man."

"I love you, too, Marie."

He was walking back to the fence when the peanut gallery showed up. Tamar, Trent, Bing, and Genevieve. Whenever the kids had to paint, the adults gathered on Marie's porch to drink coffee and watch, mostly to make sure the punished kid or kids stayed hydrated and didn't pass out in the sun or drown themselves by falling into a paint can. In his case, however, they'd come strictly to razz him, and he supposed it was what he deserved. Bernadine wasn't with them, but there were no secrets in Henry Adams, so he knew she'd heard about his painting. He hoped she approved of his self-chosen penance.

He was opening the cans when Clay drove up. "Morning," Mal said.

"I can't believe you're doing this."

Mal looked at the nearly mile-long pickets that made up the fence. "Truthfully, I can't, either, but it's part of reclaiming my self-respect. You want to help?"

"No."

"Then go sit in the cheap seats on the porch. They've got coffee and doughnuts."

Reverend Paula drove up, slowed, and yelled from her window, "Awesome decision, Mal!" And drove on.

He smiled. "And that's why I'm doing this."

Clay shook his head. "Have fun, then." He returned to his truck and drove away.

Disappointed with his friend's attitude, Mal watched the truck disappear, sighed, and pried open a can.

By the end of the first hour the repetitiveness of dragging the brush up and down began taking its toll on his right arm and shoulder, and he didn't even want to talk about what the prolonged bending at the waist was doing to his back and spine. He couldn't imagine how the kids did this. They were younger, of course, but this was no joke—especially for an OG like himself.

Trent walked down to join him. "How's it going?"

Mal wiped the sweat from his face with a towel. "I can't believe we made you kids do this."

"And remember I was dumb enough to have to do it twice one summer. After that second time, just the sight of paint made me nauseous."

Mal looked at the fence and how much more there was to do. "At the rate I'm going, it'll be spring before I'm through."

"Or summer."

Mal shot him a glare. "You got jokes for your old man now?"

Trent smiled and sipped at the coffee in his cup. "I'm just saying. You can invoke the Zoey Rule you know. After three days you can call a friend. I'll help." The rule was put in place over the summer by Roni Garland when Zoey's potty mouth earned her paint time. Her friends wanted to help, but Roni made Zoey paint alone the first three days so the punishment would be taken seriously. For her part, Zoey had helped Devon paint after the mini crime wave that saw him stealing money from Mal and Lily.

Mal didn't want to admit needing help, even though he did. Having always been one of the watchers from the peanut gallery, he never imagined the job would be this difficult. "I'll let you know."

"Don't let pride put you flat on your back. If you need help, ask for it. You have a school to clean starting Monday, too. Remember?"

Mal sighed.

"But I'm proud of you for taking this on. Real proud."

"Thanks."

Trent gave him a pat on the back. "Carry on." And he headed to the porch.

Ignoring his sore arm and screaming back, Mal went back to work.

At noon, he called it a day. His shoulder was so sore just turning the key in his truck's ignition made him wince with pain. He knew his muscles would adjust as time went on, but when he got home, all he could do was lie on his bed and moan.

Sunday morning, he skipped church and drove to Marie's. Raising his arm was difficult but he was determined to push past the discomfort and put in at least a few hours. The first forty-five minutes were a killer, so much so that discouragement set in.

"Hey you. Came to check on my patient."

He looked up to see Reg getting out of his truck.

"Hey," Mal said.

"How's the head and nose?"

Mal shrugged and winced.

"Why is a shrug making you wince?"

"Arm's sore."

Reg studied him. "Raise it above your head."

"I'm fine, Reg."

"Raise your arm."

Mal blew out a breath and slowly complied. He tried to

mask how much it hurt but apparently didn't manage to do it well enough.

Reg ordered, "Go home. Get in a hot shower. Take a couple of ibuprofen every four to six hours and don't come back out here until Tuesday."

"Reg?" Mal cried.

"That's my name. Don't wear it out."

Mal rolled his eyes.

Reg said, "We're all proud of you for doing this, but it's a big job and you need to pace yourself, especially the first few days. Zoey had a real hard time when she started, so I know this is wearing you out."

He was right, but it only added to Mal's sense of frustration and discouragement.

Reg said, "The fence will still be here on Tuesday."

Mal nodded and said, "Okay."

"I'll give you a call this evening to see how you are."

Mal appreciated Reg looking out for him. "Going home, doc."

"Good." Reg left him at the fence and drove off.

Mal put the paint cans and the other supplies in Marie's garage and went home.

CHAPTER
16

On Monday morning, Gary dragged himself out of bed and got ready for work. He and Nori had been on the phone together until 2:00 a.m., and he was sure their late-night calls were going to be the death of him. Since the reunion, they'd talked regularly about everything and nothing, from politics, to how the girls were doing, to Nori's ongoing campaign to keep her dog, T'Challa, from eating her couches. And each call strengthened their connection. In spite of his complaints tied to his lack of sleep, he'd probably be on the phone again with her that evening, but for now he had to stay awake long enough make it through the day.

He'd just finished his first cup of coffee when Leah entered the kitchen. She took one look at his bleary eyes and said, "Either she's going to have to move to Henry Adams, or we're going to have to move to Boston. You look whipped."

"I'll be okay once I eat something and drink a gallon of coffee."

She laughed. "How late were you up?"

"I think it might have been two or two thirty."

"Young love," she said, placing her hand dramatically over her heart. "Be careful you don't fall asleep in one of the meat coolers. You'll wake up singing like Elsa in *Frozen*."

"Who's going to be singing like Elsa?" Tiffany asked, coming in on the tail end of her sister's comment.

"Dad," Leah replied. "He's tired from being on the phone all night. I told him not to fall asleep in the store's meat cooler."

Tiffany viewed him. "You do look sleepy, Daddy. Really sleepy. You and Nori need a phone curfew."

"That might not be a bad idea. I feel like the walking dead." He needed to wake up, though. Gemma had a dental appointment, so all the store's morning duties were on him. Fixing himself a bowl of instant oatmeal, he grabbed his toast from the toaster and sat down to eat while the girls did the same. He had something to share with them, though. "I'll be meeting our lawyer today."

They looked up.

"I made the appointment Friday, but I kept it to myself because I didn't want you to spend the weekend worrying about when we'll go to court, what the outcome might be, and all that."

Leah said, "I guess it's okay we didn't know because we probably would've worried."

Tiffany nodded in agreement. "I know I would've. I talked to Amari the other day because I needed to figure some things out."

Amari? Gary found that surprising.

Apparently, Leah did as well. "You talked to Amari? About what?"

"Just some stuff. It was personal, Lee."

"And?" Leah asked.

"Do I need to spell the word *personal* for you?"

"Are you crushing on him, Tiff?"

"None of your business."

Gary realized his mouth was hanging open. Tiffany and Amari?

"I'm not hating on him," Leah said gently. "He's kind, a good person, a great friend, and he's always had Brain's back and mine, but—"

Tiff interrupted her. "Can we talk about something else, please? When are we going to court, Dad?"

Gary forced his brain back into gear. "I'm hoping we can get on the docket as quickly as possible. I want this settled once and for all."

"You don't think the court will give us to her, do you?" Tiffany asked.

Leah answered: "Not a chance, Tiff. Don't worry."

But Gary could see that she was worried. He heard it in her voice too, and that sent him back to wondering what she'd discussed with Amari. He also wondered if Leah was right about Tiff having a crush on Trent's son. Not that he had anything against Amari. As Leah said, he was a great kid with a great future. Gary just never imagined his youngest hooking up with someone as street-smart as Amari was.

Gary finished his breakfast and put his dishes in the dishwasher. "I'll let you know what the lawyer had to say when I get home. Have a great day, ladies." He gave them each a quick kiss and made his exit.

Of course, his first customer interaction of the day involved

Mrs. Beadle. She wanted to exchange a sweater, which Gary would've had no problem taking care of had the sweater been one she'd purchased from the store.

The employee at the desk, a young college student named Art, had a plastered-on smile when Gary arrived. Gary insisted that the employees always deal with the old lady politely no matter how much of a pain or how crotchety she might be, and Art's fake smile was a testament to that.

"Good morning, Mrs. Beadle. How are you?"

"I'm doing well, Mr. Clark, but Art here won't let me exchange this sweater, and I don't see why not." Gary picked up the white sweater from where it lay on the counter and made a show of looking it over, patently ignoring the small hole in one of the sleeves. "Mrs. Beadle, the reason is that you didn't buy the sweater here."

"How can you tell?"

"By the name of the manufacturer on the label."

"Oh."

She looked disappointed, but he wasn't fooled. "I think you already knew that, though."

She smiled. "I did. Artie's new here, so I wanted to see if he'd fall for the old okeydoke."

Hearing her use the term made Gary smile inwardly.

Art did a tiny eye roll.

Mrs. Beadle gave Gary a grin. "But he passed with flying colors. He was also very polite."

"That's good to hear," Gary said. "I want the staff to be polite no matter what."

"You're doing a good job."

"Can we help you with anything else?" Gary asked, hoping to get her out of their hair.

"No. I'm done here for the day. You can keep the sweater."

"Thanks, Mrs. Beadle."

"I'll see you tomorrow."

"Okay. Just don't bring Lorenzo with you."

"I think you should have a Shop With Your Pet Day. Lorenzo was a bit rambunctious the last time, but he enjoyed himself."

"The health department would never allow it."

"Probably not, but a girl can dream. Have a good day, Mr. Clark. Bye, Artie." She waggled her fingers and walked to the exit.

"I think I deserve a pay raise," Art cracked.

"Don't we all."

Gemma returned from the dentist just before noon, which freed Gary to welcome the lawyer into his office without having to worry about the goings-on in the store. Her name was Daphne Summers. She was brown-skinned, bald as a member of mythical Wakanda's Dora Milaje, and at least three inches taller than he. "Pleased to meet you, Ms. Summers," he said as they shook hands.

"Same here," she replied with a southern accent.

He gestured to one of the chairs. "How was your flight?"

She sat. "Just fine. It's not often you get to fly in on a private jet, so no complaints at all."

"Thanks for taking our case."

"You're welcome. So now, tell me what's going on with you and your ex-wife."

While Gary explained the situation, she took notes on her tablet. She asked questions about his marriage and he told her the truth.

She stopped and eyed him with surprise. "Her father blackmailed you to stay in the marriage?"

"Yes."

"Wow." She resumed typing while saying, "I grew up in a small town in Mississippi, and small-town power brokers can be terrifying if you're the one they're leaning on. Did she say why she wants to change the agreement?"

"She's about to be divorced again and doesn't want to be lonely."

Daphne cocked her head. "Not because she misses her daughters, or because you're a questionable parent?"

"No."

"Interesting."

Then they talked about what he should do when he received the paperwork from her partners, how long the process might take, and what to expect from the judge and the court. She then asked about the girls. "How do they feel about the change in the order?"

"I'd like them to speak for themselves if that's possible."

She paused and studied him. "Suggesting I talk to your daughters first gives me some insight into you as a parent."

"I hope that's a good thing."

"It is. When can I meet them?"

"They're in school right now."

"Is there someplace I can treat you all to dinner once they're out?"

"We have a local diner, but it's pretty loud there. Would you mind if we ate at home?"

"No, of course not. I'll drive back to Ms. Brown's office and meet you at your place. I just need your address."

Gary gave her the information and asked, "So what are the chances of the girls having to move to Atlanta?"

"Based on what you've shared, I'd be surprised if the judge

entertains a change. Unless there's something you aren't telling me, the court isn't going to uproot your daughters just because Mom's lonely, especially when she didn't want custody
after the divorce."

Gary was relieved to hear that.

Daphne stood, and her height filled his office. "I'll let you
get back to work. Looking forward to meeting your daughters."

He walked her out and noted the stares her stunning presence caused among the shoppers. She didn't comment, so he
didn't, either.

When he returned to his office, Gemma was there. "How'd
it go?" she asked.

"I think we're in good hands."

As promised, Ms. Summers came by after school. Once
the introductions were made, Gary went up to his room so
the ladies could talk alone. While there, he ordered pizza so
no one would have to cook, then got dressed and went for
a quick run. He found running after work to be the perfect
stress reliever and decided he preferred the nearly traffic-free
roads near his house to the town's boring oval track. His legs
were in better shape than they were that first morning and
he could now do a mile without having to crawl home afterward.

When he returned, the girls and Ms. Summers were enjoying the pizza, so he went upstairs to take a shower. He had
no idea what they'd discussed, but they were laughing and
talking, which made him think their meet was going well.

"Your daughters are a delight," Ms. Summers said to him
as he came into the dining room.

He smiled. "I think they're pretty special."

The girls grinned. He placed two slices of the pizza on a

paper plate and sat down to join them. "Did you get all the information you needed?"

"I did. They were very honest and helpful."

That the girls looked pleased was all he needed to see.

Tiff said, "Ms. Summers doesn't think we have to worry about moving."

Leah said, "Which is awesome."

Gary agreed with Leah's take. He wasn't sure how he'd handle things were Colleen allowed to take them away. Now that he finally had some happiness in his life, he wanted to hold on to it with both hands.

The lawyer left a short while later, but not before reminding them to contact her as soon as they heard from Colleen's lawyer. Once she was gone, he asked, "Who feels better after meeting Ms. Summers?"

Everyone, including Gary, shot up a hand. They laughed.

That night, Gary called Nori and told her about Ms. Summers allaying most of their fears.

"Great to hear, Gary. I feel better, too."

She was on her way to Peru tomorrow to hike the famous Inca Trail, a twenty-six-mile trek through the Andes Mountains, cloud forests, and Inca ruins. It was a multiday hike, and Nori had added a few other places to her itinerary, so she'd be gone for ten days. "I'm already missing our nightly calls," he told her.

"Ditto," she replied. "But when I get back, my next trip will be to see you and the girls."

That made him smile. They talked for a short while longer, but he knew she had a plane to catch in the morning and needed her sleep. "I'll let you go so you can get your rest."

"But I want to talk some more," she protested with a mock whine.

He laughed. "Go to bed, Ms. Adventure, and make sure you bring yourself home in one piece."

"Oh, okay," she said with a pout in her voice. "I love you, son of Jor-El."

"Love you, too, Nori. Bye, baby."

She whispered. "Bye."

Gary turned off his nightstand's lamp and settled in to sleep.

BERNADINE SPENT TUESDAY morning on the phone talking with everyone from FBI agent Kyle Dalton about the ongoing search for Janet Roxbury, to her lawyers handling the ownership paperwork for the Three Spinsters restaurant, to Tina, in Nigeria signing contracts for the Bottom Women's investment in an oil company there. The Bureau had finally been able to put a name to Roxbury's driver, a man known simply as Romanov. He had ties to the Russian mob, which meant Roxbury probably did too, a deduction she found alarming. The colonel's surveillance cameras remained on high alert and people in town had been warned about the potential for trouble, but Bernadine wanted the bad guys found and neutralized so everyone could relax.

In the meantime, she'd been pleased by Zoey's gift to Mal, not just because it erased his debt but because it epitomized what Bernadine loved most about her little town: the way people took care of each other. When Zoey first came to live in Henry Adams, Mal had gone out of his way to help her combat her nightmares, and now Ms. Miami had paid it forward.

Bernadine was aware of Mal's ongoing Apology Tour and, like everyone else, was proud he'd stepped up and taken ownership of his crime. Jack said from the raucous way the kids cheered after his apology to them, one would've thought Rhianna had suddenly paid a visit. Luis was at the Dog this morning telling anyone who'd listen how moved he and Anna had been by Mal's talk with Alfonso and Maria. Her former love was mending fences all over the place and was painting a fence, too. That gesture grabbed the attention of the citizenry more than all the rest of the apologies combined. In two more days, he'd be able to invoke the Zoey Rule, and Bernadine guessed more than a few people would show up to help. Although she'd never painted anything in her life, she was considering joining in because she approved of Mal being focused on reclaiming his place in the community and she wanted everyone to know it. The jury was still out on their becoming a full-fledged couple again, however, but she was closer to at least considering it. The agreement they'd made at Tamar's about his texting her had been a first step, even if she had ignored his texts initially. Now she was at least reading them, but so far hadn't responded. She'd considered sending him a thank-you for the coins, then decided he wasn't owed anything for repaying a debt he had no business incurring in the first place. He'd stolen the money; he didn't deserve a pat on the back.

But on Wednesday afternoon, she left work early. Once at home, she changed into her jeans and an old sweatshirt, tied up her hair beneath a scarf, and started out to the Jefferson place. She was on July Road and almost there when she spotted the black van in her rearview mirror. She sped up and hit the phone sync on her dashboard. "Barrett! That black van! It's following me!"

"Where are you!"

"On July Road!"

The van rammed her from behind, and she screamed. Baby spun and almost went out of control. Determined not to do a replay of her near-fatal encounter with Odessa Stillwell, Bernadine clamped down on the steering wheel and kept her eyes on the road.

"You okay?" Barrett yelled.

She didn't answer. She was too busy trying to stay in front of the van. Bullets blew out her back window.

"Bernadine!"

"They're shooting at me!"

"We're at Marie's! Keep coming! We're on the way!"

What was usually a quick trip seemed to take forever. The van sped up beside her. She saw a man pointing a gun at her through an open window. "Pull over!" he shouted. She immediately swung Baby hard to the left to do some ramming of her own instead. The force of the Ford's high-strength steel sent the van reeling and the driver fighting to keep it from flipping.

Rolling now at eighty miles an hour, she screamed, "Take that!"

Up ahead she saw a small convoy of trucks spread across the two-lane road coming her way at full speed. The cavalry! And she laughed through her tears. Trent. Bing. Tamar. Mal. Rocky. The van, now back on her tail, was apparently so focused on her that its occupants didn't see her rescuers until the last minute. They immediately tried a sharp turnaround. The convoy flew by her and that's when she saw the colonel and the big oversized automatic rifle he called the Terminator in the bed of Trent's truck. When the weapon's power hit the target, the van jumped three feet in the air before coming down on its blown-out tires. The van's occupants began shooting back but the Terminator along with the rifles of Henry Adams showed no mercy. The colonel's rapid fire blew out the windows, pierced the trunk, and with each hit the van rocked from the force. Bernadine had pulled over to the side of the road to watch and cheer. The people inside the van decided to abandon ship and took off running across the field beside the road, but the three men and Janet Roxbury didn't get very far, courtesy of Tamar's shotgun. She picked them off one by one and soon all of them were rolling in the grass clutching their lead-filled legs.

Bernadine got out. Weak from fear and adrenaline, she leaned against Baby and tried to pull herself together. While the colonel and Tamar kept an eye on the bad guys, the rest of the cavalry ran back to check on her.

"Are you okay?" Rocky asked.

Bernadine nodded.

Mal's eyes were filled with concern, so she repeated, "I'm okay. Thanks for being my own personal Tenth Cavalry."

Trent did a tour of her truck. "You may need another vehicle, Bernadine. You're leaking fluids and the back is pretty shot up."

"Not again!" She'd replaced Baby three maybe four times already because of Henry Adams adventures.

Mal asked, "You sure you're okay?"

"I am, Mal. Really."

Bing said, "In the movies this is where the guy and his girl make up, so Rock, Trent, let's go."

Bernadine laughed. Mal chuckled. Bing and the others left.

Overhead, the sound of chopper rotors filled the air. She looked up, saw "FBI" decaled on the side and the belly.

Mal said, "We told Marie to call them when we rolled out. They got here quick."

County law enforcement had arrived on the scene as well. Davida Ransom and two other deputies were cuffing the suspects while Will stood talking to the colonel and Tamar beside the decimated van.

Mal said, "I've been out of the loop. Who are these folks and why were they after you?"

Bernadine explained and finished with, "Why they wanted me is anyone's guess. Trying to kill me makes no sense. Maybe they were just trying to snatch me and take me someplace to see if I really knew anything about the Millers' location."

"Well, when Barrett told us you were on the phone and I could hear him screaming your name, it scared me to death."

"Imagine how I felt in the starring role."

Their eyes met and held. In spite of all the police activity swirling around them, she lost touch with everything but the powerful aura Mal exuded. He checked out her attire. "Interesting outfit. Were you cleaning the house?"

She hesitated before answering. She wanted to lie, but confessed, "No. I was on my way here to help with the painting."

"Really?"

She told herself she wasn't affected by his veiled approval. "Yes, and don't read anything into it other than that you needed the help."

"I see." His tone and what she read in his eyes were making it difficult for her to breathe evenly.

He told her, "Like Bing said, this is the part in the movie where the guy kisses the girl, but if I kiss you, you'll probably sock me."

"Repeatedly."

He grinned. "Okay. I'll save it for another time."

Fighting to ignore the way her knees weakened at his words, she was glad when Kyle Dalton walked up and asked, "Ms. Brown, can I talk to you for a few moments?"

She nodded, took one last look back at the much too compelling Malachi July, and let Kyle lead her away.

Although Roxbury and her crew refused to talk when they were taken away, Kyle agreed with Bernadine that they probably intended to grab her and take her to an undisclosed location to make her tell them what she knew about the Millers. Barrett reviewed the camera footage later that evening, and it showed their van sitting in the Dog's parking lot. When Bernadine drove by the building on her way to Marie's, they waited a few seconds and pulled out behind her. Kyle's people also found a small tracking device on Baby's underbody, but there was no way to determine how long it had been there.

"So, is this over now?" Bernadine asked Kyle the next day as they all sat in her office.

"We're pretty sure it is. The three Russians were in the country illegally and will be deported as soon as they recover from being shot. Roxbury is Canadian. She's here legally, but the Mounties have multiple warrants with her real name on them. They'll be flying down to pick her up as soon as she recovers, too."

"Yay!" Bernadine cheered. "No more Russians, hit women, or shootings at movie night."

Lily cracked, "We lead such boring lives here on the Kansas plains."

CHAPTER 17

Gary, his daughters, and their lawyer, Ms. Summers, were seated in the book-lined chambers of Judge Steven Phillips waiting for Colleen and her legal representative. It was now thirty minutes past the hearing's start time and he wondered if their flight had been delayed.

Judge Phillips, a portly middle-aged man with brown eyes and thinning blond hair, took a quick look at his watch. "We'll give them another ten minutes and talk about rescheduling. I have other items on my docket that need my attention this morning."

Gary understood, but he wasn't going to be happy if the hearing had to be rescheduled. He wanted the issue settled today, once and for all.

Five minutes later, the bailiff entered and ushered in Colleen, then left. "I'm so sorry, Your Honor," she said. "We flew in last night but got a really late start this morning, and then there was an accident."

"Is your lawyer here?"

"Yes, he's parking the car. He should be right in."

She nodded at Gary and then cooed, "How are my girls this morning? I can't wait for us to go shopping for the new furniture for your bedrooms. You're going to love the new school I've settled on."

Ms. Summers stood, and Colleen looked up with wide eyes and took a step back. Smiling coolly, Daphne extended her hand. "I'm Daphne Summers, counsel for Mr. Clark and your daughters."

"Oh," was all Colleen seemed able to say as she continued to stare. "Did you play basketball?"

"Volleyball."

"Oh," she said and took a seat.

The bailiff returned. "Her counsel is here, Your Honor."

"Good. Send him in."

And to Gary's surprise, Howie Pratt entered. His too-small brown corduroy suit was paired with a white shirt and a brown bow tie accented with green polka dots.

He stuck out his hand to Gary. "So, Clark. We meet again. Have you spoken to Eleanor lately?"

The judge cleared his throat.

Pratt turned and inclined his head in apology. "Sorry, Your Honor. I'm Howard Pratt. Stanford Law School. Just inquiring about a mutual friend." And then he saw Ms. Summers. "My, aren't you a gorgeous tall drink of water."

Her eyes flashed icily.

The judge snapped, "Mr. Pratt, show some respect. Take a seat."

Howard did, but not before shooting Daphne a smile.

Gary saw Leah give Tiffany a look of disbelief and he was

right there with her. He had a feeling this was going to be an interesting hearing.

The judge looked over the paperwork. "Ms. Ewing, you're petitioning the court to alter the custodial agreement on what grounds?"

"I think Gary is a bad parent."

"And your evidence?"

"Well," she said, sitting up straight, "he just is."

Judge Phillips glanced over at Gary, who kept his face calm.

The judge said, "I'm going to need concrete evidence. Are your daughters neglected? Does Mr. Clark do drugs? Does he not provide ample food or clothing?"

"He's turned them against me."

"Your evidence?"

Howie said, "Your Honor, my client had a perfect relationship with her daughters until the divorce proceedings, and now the relationship is frayed."

Daphne interjected, "Ms. Ewing chose not to ask for custody during the divorce proceedings, Your Honor."

Howie stared at Colleen. "You didn't tell me that."

Gary figured there was a lot she didn't share with Howie, but he kept that to himself.

Judge Phillips asked, "Why did you not want custody?"

"I thought they'd keep me from finding another husband."

"I see, but now you want full custody? Why?"

Leah said, "She's getting divorced again and doesn't want to be lonely."

Howard snapped, "You don't get to speak."

Leah drawled, "Whatever."

The judge said, "Is this true, Ms. Ewing?"

"Yes. I don't want to be alone."

Tiff said, "We told her to get a pet."

The judge was almost able to hide his smile—almost. "Do you girls want to live with your mom full-time?"

"No," Leah said adamantly.

"Tiffany?" the judge asked.

"No, Your Honor. I don't like the way she treats my sister, or me."

"What do you mean?"

Leah explained: "Your Honor, I love science. I'm still in high school, but KU is letting me take college physics classes."

"That's outstanding."

"Mom doesn't think so."

He appeared confused. "Explain, please."

Colleen interrupted: "This is what I meant about him turning them against me. I'm very proud of my daughter's accomplishments, but my ex-husband has her convinced otherwise."

Leah said, "Your Honor. She's not telling the truth. Dad has always had my back. When I was younger and wanted to go to Space Camp, he had to argue with her for days before she finally gave in. And to prove she's not telling the truth? My receipt." Leah pulled out her phone, scrolled a few seconds, and set the device on the desk in front of the judge. "Tap the arrow on the video, Your Honor."

Daphne got up and moved closer so she could see the screen. Howard did the same.

Judge Phillips hit the arrow, and there was Colleen in full rage mode screaming at Leah, calling her ugly and stupid, and telling her she'd never get a husband.

Colleen jumped up and slapped the phone off the desk. She then turned on Leah. "You deceitful little heifer!"

She raised her hand to slap her, but Gary stepped between them just as Howie grabbed Colleen's arm. "Stop it!" Howie yelled. "What's the matter with you!" He threw her back into her chair.

"That never happened!" Colleen screamed.

Tiffany cried, "Liar! I have a video of you yelling at me, too!"

"Fine!" Colleen snarled. "Stay with your boring-ass father. I don't ever want to see you ungrateful little bitches ever again. You hear me?" She snatched up her coat and stormed out of the courtroom.

The judge looked shaken. Leah simply sat, tears in her eyes. Gary put his arm around her and placed a kiss on her forehead. "It's going to be okay," he whispered. Tiff was crying too, so he consoled her as well. He glanced at Howard. "Thank you, man."

"Not a problem. Your Honor, I'm withdrawing from this case."

"Understood."

Howard left the chambers, but the judge's concern for Leah and Tiff was so plain that Gary wasn't sure he even noticed the departure.

Daphne said, "Your Honor, in the face of what just transpired—"

The judge cut her off. "I got this, Counselor. Leah? Tiffany?"

They looked his way.

"I'm sorry this happened. I'm going to make it a condition that before either of you visit your mom again, she takes twelve weeks of anger management classes, six months of parenting classes, and provides me with weekly progress reports."

Leah said, "She isn't going to do all that."

"I know."

Leah studied him for a long minute and then she smiled. "You're good."

He smiled back.

Leah said, "Thank you."

Judge Phillips turned to Tiffany. "Are those conditions agreeable with you, Tiffany?"

She nodded and replied, "Yes, Your Honor."

"Mr. Clark?"

"Yes."

"Ms. Summers?"

"Yes."

"Then this hearing is over. You girls have a great life."

On the drive home, the girls were quiet. Tiffany, riding shotgun, gazed out the window. Leah was in the backseat texting, he assumed, Brain. He wasn't sure either of them wanted to talk, but he needed to know they were okay. "How are you ladies doing?"

He looked in the mirror and met Leah's sad eyes. Tiff glanced his way for a moment, then returned to gazing at the countryside. "Dad's concerned," he said. "Can you humor me, at least for a few minutes?"

He saw a small smile play over Leah's lips. "Just nothing to say, Dad. Mom is who she is. Maybe she'll change one day, but I'm glad Judge Phillips put up that roadblock."

Tiff said, "So am I. I hope she changes, too. Otherwise she's going to be really lonely when she gets old and that'll be sad."

Once again he found his girls impressive. Colleen had acted like a monster and yet her daughters were hoping she and her life turned out okay. He wondered if she'd ever realize how blessed she was.

"Okay, the dad grilling is over. You may now return to your regularly scheduled programming."

He met their smiles and concentrated on his driving.

AT SIZ'S GOING-AWAY party, Bernadine glanced around at the wall-to-wall people in attendance and was pleased at the turn-out and the smiles everyone wore. After the awful night Sam Miller was shot and her own foiled kidnapping by the Russian mob, a celebration was in order. She was saddened by the reality of losing Siz, though. As Rocky mentioned earlier, his moving to Miami was like saying good-bye to one of the town's children, and he and his colorful hair would be dearly missed. Even though the party was in his honor, he'd insisted on cooking, and the buffet table groaned with a bevy of tasty appetizers destined to make everyone miss him and his skills all the more. There were the spinach-stuffed filo-dough squares she loved so much, along with barbecued drummies, fish tacos, meatballs, tiny pizzas, fruit, and a variety of desserts.

During the course of the evening, Bernadine had met Siz's parents and siblings for the first time, and their pride in him was evident in the way they spoke to her about how much he meant to them and how special they considered him to be. His band members, both current and former, were also in attendance, and would be playing a set for them later. The band, Bloody Kansas, had become a weekend staple at the Dog, and their jazz-infused playing would be missed as well. Later, she'd be presenting a few gifts to Siz on behalf of the town, but for now she just wanted to go through the buffet line and get a couple more of the spinach-stuffed pastries and try to find herself a seat. Once she had taken what she wanted from the buffet, she looked around for a seat, but in the noisy crush saw nothing. People were stuffed into the booths around the walls like the spinach stuffed into the pastries on her plate.

"Is the lady in need of a seat?"

She turned to Mal and smiled. "Yes."

"I have an extra, if you don't mind sitting with me."

How could she resist? "Lead the way."

On the far side of the room, Amari watched the OG walking Ms. Bernadine to a booth he was sharing with Ms. Marie, Ms. Gen, and Uncle TC, and hoped the two were going to fix the problems that had split them apart. Now that the money Mal had taken had been paid back, it seemed like a real possibility. The OG and Ms. Bernadine made each other happy, so he wanted them to work things out. He was sitting with Brain, Leah, Tiffany, Mr. Clark, and his lady friend from Boston. They'd been checking out the fascinating pictures on her phone that Nori had taken while hiking in Peru. He hoped she stayed in town long enough for him to talk to her because he had a bunch of questions about her trip and it was too loud in the Dog to hold any kind of serious conversation. Tiffany had been casually taking sneak peeks at him since they arrived, and truthfully, he'd been doing the same. He was still trying to process what his feelings toward her really meant, while continuing to hope they'd disappear. He kept his mom's advice in mind, however, and didn't ignore her when she spoke to him. He just pretended the kiss never happened.

"Is Zoey's band really playing tonight?" Tiffany asked him.

He nodded. "They're covering Janet Jackson's old song 'Miss You Much' in Siz's honor."

Amari thought the Exodusters, as the band was called, was getting better, and both Zoey and his brother had a ton of talent, but their group was still louder than they were good.

The practices kept Devon out of his hair, though, so he didn't mind having to listen to them play occasionally.

A few minutes later, Amari's dad, the OG, and some of the other men began moving tables so Zoey and Devon's band could start the entertainment portion of the party. That meant that the people seated at them would have to stand, but no one seemed to mind.

Tiffany said to her dad, "I need to talk to Amari for a minute. Is it okay if we go outside so we don't have to shout to be heard?"

Amari froze. What in the world did she want to talk about now?

Her dad looked his way, and Amari prayed he'd say no. Instead, he said, "Sure, just don't elope."

Heat burned Amari's cheeks.

Tiffany gave her dad an eye roll. "Thanks, Daddy."

Amari said, "I—I need to let my mom know we'll be outside. I'll meet you out there." He got to his feet, and although he played with the idea of disappearing and going home, he knew he wouldn't. His mom was helping the band set up.

"Hey, Mom."

"Hey, babe. Did you come to help?"

"Um, no. Tiffany wants to talk to me for a minute outside. I just wanted to let you know I was leaving for a few minutes."

She paused before asking, "Does her dad know?"

"Yes. He just told us not to elope."

"You didn't appreciate that, did you?"

"No."

"Okay. Go see what she wants and come right back."

He nodded and made his way through the madness to the door.

It was a late-September night on the plains and it was cold. Amari was glad because that meant they wouldn't be outside very long. "What do you want to talk about?"

"Just wanted to tell you thanks for letting me talk to you about the custody hearing."

"I heard from Brain that your mom kinda lost it." Brain hadn't shared all the particulars and Amari hadn't asked because it was really none of his business.

"Mom was a hot mess, but we won't have to go to Atlanta unless she takes a lot of anger-management and parenting classes."

"So it worked out in the end."

"Yeah."

"Good, I'm going back in, it's cold out here."

"I'm sorry for kissing you."

He blinked. "Um. Let's not talk about that, okay?"

"Okay," she said softly.

Then he felt bad. "Look. When we first met you and I didn't get along at all. Do you remember what you called me?"

"Ghetto boy," she said.

"Right."

She came to her own defense. "I was a brat back then. I'm older now, and—I like you, Amari, and I think you like me."

He didn't reply. He heard the band start up.

"Do you?" she asked.

"Tiff, I don't know whether I do or not, but it's cold out here. I'm going in and I can't leave you out here by yourself, so come on."

"Okay."

But he didn't move. Instead he just stood there looking at her, with the moon overhead and the faint sound of Devon and Zoey's band playing inside. A part of him wanted to kiss her, but for all his Detroit swagger, he didn't know how to ask. So he pulled the door open and let her enter ahead of him.

Seeing Amari and Tiffany come in from outside, Bernadine shot a quick look over at Lily. She was watching them too, and the quiet amusement on her face piqued Bernadine's curiosity. Was something going on between the two teens? With the party still going on, it was a question that would have to wait for another time, so she settled back and watched and listened to the band finish up the Janet Jackson song.

Once they were done and the applause died down, Bernadine walked to the mic to make her presentation. She didn't see Siz, though. "Where's Siz?"

His dad called, "Check the kitchen."

Everyone laughed. Rocky hustled into the kitchen and returned with him a second later. Bernadine said to him, "You already know how much we're going to miss you, so I won't go there. But I do want you to take what's in this envelope as a token of how much we appreciate and love you."

His hair today was navy blue with red highlights. While everyone watched, he opened the envelope and withdrew a check. When he saw the amount, his jaw dropped. He looked to Bernadine and then to Rocky with eyes wide as dinner plates. "Are you kidding me?"

Rocky said, "No, nephew. More than likely you'll be at the bottom of the food chain on your new job, and they'll probably pay you in onions and aprons. We don't want you to starve or be homeless."

"But, Rock, this says fifty grand!"

"And . . . ?"

Tears filled his eyes. "I can't accept this."

His mother said, "Yes. You can!"

Laughter followed. Siz gave Rocky and Bernadine big hugs and wiped his eyes.

Bernadine said, "Now, to make sure you get to work, I had a friend hook me up with a car dealership in Miami, and they have a brand-new SUV waiting for you to pick up after you arrive. The car is paid for, and here's what it looks like." She passed him a picture.

His jaw dropped again. More tears flowed, and he hugged them both once more.

When he recovered he stepped to the mic and said, "I've been blessed with a great biological family and a great Henry Adams family. I'm going to miss both so much. Thanks for my gifts. I promise to make you proud. And when I open my own place, everybody here eats for free! Now let's party!"

His band members took to the area vacated by Zoey and her crew and blew the roof off with "Busting Out" by Rick James.

Watching the people of her town getting their dance on filled Bernadine with joy. Lily and Trent were on the floor along with Gary and Nori, Siz's parents, folks with rhythm and folks with none. Bloody Kansas wasn't playing Rhianna or Cardi B, but the teens were doing their thing, too. Out of the corner or her eye, she spied Crystal shaking it up with a tall, brown-skinned millennial with an Old Testament beard that may or may not have belonged to Moses.

Behind her she heard Mal's humor-filled voice say, "Ain't no party like a Henry Adams party, 'cause a Henry Adams party don't stop." She turned. He smiled. She did the same.

He asked over the music, "May I have this dance?"

She had no idea what to do about him, but tonight she

wasn't going to worry about it. "You sure you can keep up with a sister from Detroit?"

He chuckled. "Watch me."

"Then let's go."

At midnight, the band was still jamming, and so was Bernadine Brown, Mal July, and the people of Henry Adams.

AUTHOR'S NOTE

Second Time Sweeter is our ninth visit to Henry Adams, Kansas. I hope you enjoyed looking in on our favorite small town. As always, questions remain. Has Mal finally seen the light? Is Bernadine willing to let that light into her heart? Can a new chef with meat and veggie tattoos replace our beloved Siz? Is Amari crushing on Tiffany Adele, or does he really have the flu? And Lord help us—is Riley really going to run for mayor?

Stay tuned.

See you next time.

B

ABOUT THE AUTHOR

Beverly Jenkins is the recipient of the 2017 Romance Writers of America Nora Roberts Lifetime Achievement Award, as well as the 2016 Romantic Times Reviewers' Choice Award for historical romance. She has been nominated for the NAACP Image Award in Literature and was featured in the documentary *Love Between the Covers* and on *CBS Sunday Morning*. Since the publication of *Night Song* in 1994, she has been leading the charge for multicultural romance, and has been a constant darling of reviewers, fans, and peers alike, garnering accolades for her work from the likes of *The Wall Street Journal*, *People Magazine*, and NPR.

ALSO BY
BEVERLY JENKINS

BRING ON THE BLESSINGS
Blessings 1

"[A] heartwarming story of love, community, and family.... *Bring on the Blessings* is a tasty reading confection that you'll savor long after the story ends."

—Angela Benson, author of *The Amen Sisters*

A SECOND HELPING
Blessings 2

"A story like none other, and done in a way that only Beverly Jenkins can do. Simply superb!"

—Brenda Jackson,
New York Times bestselling author

SOMETHING OLD, SOMETHING NEW
Blessings 3

"There is beauty in Jenkins' storytelling that should be the standard by which to judge fiction writing...Brava, Ms. Jenkins, you have done it again and left us wanting more."

—*Romantic Times* (Top Pick)

A WISH AND A PRAYER
Blessings 4

"Returning to Henry Adams, Kansas, is akin to attending a family reunion. The characters are rich, and the kids all have a story to be told."

—*Romantic Times*

HEART OF GOLD
Blessings 5

"Her stories are delicious and always leave behind both feelings of satisfaction and want...for her next novel."

—*Fresh Fiction*

ALSO BY
BEVERLY JENKINS

FOR YOUR LOVE
Blessings 6

"A wonderful read that combines comedy, drama, historical facts, and where the blessings keep on coming!"

—*Romance in Color*

STEPPING TO A NEW DAY
Blessings 7

"It's easy to lose hours at a time caught up in this book. An achingly sweet feel-good story of love and redemption of all kinds."

—*Kirkus Reviews*

CHASING DOWN A DREAM
Blessings 8

"Every visit to Henry Adams, Kansas, is like a warm hug... All is not perfect because humans make mistakes, but the knowledge that the people of this town will rise to the challenge, together, is a blessing."

—*RT Book Reviews* (Top Pick)

SECOND TIME SWEETER
Blessings 9

"If you haven't yet gotten your hands on [this] *USA Today* bestselling author's work, you should do so immediately."

—Shondaland